No woman can resist him . . .

Lord Martin Langdon takes pride in his scandalous reputation as a scoundrel, and he considers the art of seduction a most rewarding pastime. So when this dashing rakehell learns of a particularly beautiful woman who is "impossible to flirt with," Martin is determined to prove that not even the prim and proper Evelyn Wheaton can resist his charms.

Except one.

Evelyn knows all about the reckless rogue's shocking reputation and she wants nothing to do with him. She may be looking for a husband, but Martin is certainly not a candidate. The smoldering looks he sends her way, however, are a different matter entirely. She suspects there is great passion to be had if she'd throw caution to the wind and surrender to this scoundrel . . . but dare she risk her heart?

And will Martin, who hides a most tormented past, find true love at last?

By Julianne MacLean

SURRENDER TO A SCOUNDREL
PORTRAIT OF A LOVER
LOVE ACCORDING TO LILY
MY OWN PRIVATE HERO
AN AFFAIR MOST WICKED
TO MARRY THE DUKE

If You've Enjoyed This Book,
Be Sure to Read These Other
AVON ROMANTIC TREASURES

AUTUMN IN SCOTLAND *by Karen Ranney*
A DUKE OF HER OWN *by Lorraine Heath*
HIS MISTRESS BY MORNING *by Elizabeth Boyle*
HOW TO SEDUCE A DUKE *by Kathryn Caskie*
TEMPTING THE WOLF *by Lois Greiman*

Coming Soon

TWO WEEKS WITH A STRANGER *by Debra Mullins*

Julianne MacLean

Surrender to a Scoundrel

An Avon Romantic Treasure

AVON BOOKS
An Imprint of HarperCollinsPublishers

This is a work of fiction. Names, characters, places, and incidents are products of the author's imagination or are used fictitiously and are not to be construed as real. Any resemblance to actual events, locales, organizations, or persons, living or dead, is entirely coincidental.

AVON BOOKS
An Imprint of HarperCollins*Publishers*
10 East 53rd Street
New York, New York 10022-5299

Copyright © 2007 by Julianne MacLean
ISBN: 978-0-06-081936-1
ISBN-10: 0-06-081936-7
www.avonromance.com

First Avon Books paperback printing: January 2007

Avon Trademark Reg. U.S. Pat. Off. and in Other Countries, Marca Registrada, Hecho en U.S.A.
HarperCollins® is a registered trademark of HarperCollins Publishers.

Printed in the U.S.A.

10 9 8 7 6 5 4 3 2 1

Acknowledgments

M any thanks to my great friends, Lorraine and Stewart Creaser, for taking me sailing, sharing your passion for the sea, and for reading this manuscript in its earliest stages. Thank you also to the Romance Writers of Atlantic Canada for all your support, especially the gals on the goals loop. Kelly Boyce and Pam Callow—you both came through for me at the last minute to read the manuscript. You are wonderful friends. As always, thank you Paige Wheeler, my agent who I love more and more with each passing year. Erika Tsang, my new editor at Avon, for your wise editing, and to the entire staff at Avon—thank you for everything you do. Finally, thank you to my cousin and best friend, Michelle Phillips, for the skillful critiques and moral support. To my husband, Stephen, who is the best man a woman could ever dream of marrying, and my daughter, Laura, who keeps me happily entertained with basketball and tickling by the minute. Go set the timer, sweetie ☺.

Twenty years from now, you will be more disappointed by the things you didn't do than by the ones you did do. So throw off the bowlines. Sail away from the safe harbor. Catch the trade winds in your sails. Explore. Dream. Discover.

—MARK TWAIN (1835–1910)

Chapter 1

April 1881

For the first time in Evelyn Foster's very proper and correct sixteen years of life, she was about to do something horrendously, unspeakably naughty. And contrary to what one might think—that she was young and impulsive, and therefore experiencing a thrill from the wickedness—she was not the slightest bit *thrilled*. In fact, she would even go so far as to say she was vexed, irritated, and most decidedly angry, for she would never have entertained such a notion herself—that it might be "amusing" for her and her best friend Penelope to sneak into the boys' dormitory at Eton while everyone was at supper.

Perhaps the most distressing part of it all was that they were sneaking in because of *him*. Lord Martin Langdon, the Duke of Wentworth's younger brother, the mischievous boy who was always getting into trouble for various wild antics—like engineering a teetering bucket of water over his precept's door, or sending a raft down the Thames fashioned with exploding fireworks, directly below Windsor Castle when the Queen herself was in residence.

On top of all that, Lord Martin was, at seventeen, already known to be a self-proclaimed womanizer. He was an objectionable, disreputable young man, and Evelyn knew it in the clearest realms of her intellect.

So why was she having any part of this? she asked herself for the hundredth time, shaking her head as she crossed a moonlit field with Penelope.

She was here tonight because her beautiful blond friend fancied herself in love with the rascal and could not be talked out of it. And Evelyn could hardly sit home wondering what would transpire—because, though she hated to admit it, she had her own strange and confusing fascination with him.

"Hurry up, Evelyn," Penelope whispered, as they scuttled through the dark side streets toward the campus, dressed in boys' clothing they had borrowed from Penelope's younger brother. "We don't have much time, and I don't want to get caught on the way out."

"I'm coming."

And I must be insane, Evelyn thought, feeling the chilly night air on her cheeks as she quickened her pace to keep up.

At that moment, Penelope began to jog, and they hurried across the street, keeping their heads down beneath the brims of their tweed caps.

At long last, they reached the iron gate outside the chapel, and Penelope pushed it open. Evelyn winced at the piercing screech of the hinges. "Doesn't anyone own an oil can?"

"Don't worry yourself," Penelope said. "Follow me."

They crossed the tiny cemetery but stopped suddenly when a beagle barked at them from the other side of the fence.

Evelyn jumped with fright. "Good Lord, what next?"

Penelope grabbed her arm and pulled her toward the back of the chapel. "Ignore him. We're almost there. I know a place where we can squeeze through the fence and get into the courtyard."

Evelyn was breathing hard now, not enjoying this at all. "I think we should turn around. We're going to get caught. And if my father finds out . . ."

Penelope didn't stop to discuss it. She merely

spoke over her shoulder. "I've come all this way, I'm not turning back now. I want to see where he sleeps."

Evelyn halted on the gravel path. "Where he *sleeps*? Heaven help us, Penny. I thought you were just going to slip the note under his door."

"Yes, unless I can get it open with one of my hairpins."

Unable to believe what she was hearing, Evelyn huffed in frustration. "You've gone mad."

Penelope stopped and turned, and though Evelyn couldn't see her expression in the moonlight, she could hear the bright, beaming smile in her voice. "Yes, I have gone mad. Mad with *love*."

Evelyn felt a jolt of irritation.

Or was it jealousy?

No, no. *No*. Not that. She could not let herself entertain such foolishness.

She shook her head and stepped forward to make one more plea. "You know the stories about him, Penelope. He's not worth it. He'll break your heart. If only you would listen to reason."

Penelope reached the back corner of the cemetery near the chapel wall and wrapped her hands around the bars. "That's your problem, Evelyn. You're always logical, when sometimes you just have to trust your heart. Defy reason if you must."

Evelyn continued to stand on the path, watching Penelope squeeze through the fence. Defy reason? For what purpose? To have her heart crushed into pieces and trod upon like her mother's had been for as long as she could remember?

Penelope grunted as she continued. "And I don't understand why you can't see that he's wonderful, especially after what he did for you. You should think of him as your hero, Evelyn. He saved your life! How can you think badly of him?"

Evelyn recalled that day on the lake six years ago, when she had fallen through the ice, and he had pulled her to safety.

"We were children," she said with a shiver. "Of course I will always be grateful for what he did. He was my hero that day. But I cannot overlook the fact that he is no longer that boy. He has grown into a scoundrel, and everyone knows it. I do not see him with starry eyes like you do."

What would be the point? She was an awkward, unattractive girl with spectacles who was too brainy for her own good and possessed an unconventional passion for science and physics. She was skinny as a stick, had dull brown hair and a nose that was simply too long. Never in a thousand years could she attract the attention of a boy like Martin, and the few times she had encountered him in town whenever she and her mother were visiting Penelope's family, he didn't even seem to know who she was or remember that he had once saved her life—even after Penelope introduced them and told him her name. He'd been too distracted by his flirtations with Penelope. Playful, blond, pretty, bouncy Penelope.

Evelyn doubted he even remembered that harrowing day on the lake. He had never, ever mentioned it or revealed the smallest hint of recognition.

Penelope sounded irritable all of a sudden. "He's *not* a scoundrel, and I wish you would stop saying that, because I love him." She turned, preparing to climb down into the courtyard. "Look, you don't have to come if you don't want to. You can wait here. I'll be faster on my own anyway."

Evelyn paused a moment, considering it. She *could* wait here, couldn't she? She could avoid watching her beautiful friend wallow in the bliss of her first romantic love affair, sighing and boasting about how much her handsome prince loved her in return and how happy they were.

Blast it, why did Penelope have to choose *him* to chase after? Couldn't she have picked someone else? Why Martin?

Evelyn watched her friend climb down the wall and disappear from view, then heard her shoes hit the ground on the courtyard below.

"Are you coming or not?" she whispered heatedly.

Evelyn felt the knot in her belly tighten and knew she could not possibly stay behind. She had to go because Martin was in a strange way *hers*, even if she knew she could never have him.

"All right, I'm coming," she said grudgingly, marching to the fence.

A few minutes later, Evelyn and Penelope were standing on the grass outside Martin's dormitory, under Penelope's cousin's open window on the ground floor.

"Hoist me up," she said, raising a booted foot.

Evelyn let out a frustrated sigh and bent forward to form a stirrup with her hands, a maneuver they were adept at, as they'd been climbing the same rocky outcropping behind Penelope's house for years as a shortcut to town.

An instant later, Penelope was climbing into Gregory's room, then turning and offering her hands out the window. "There's no one here. Take hold."

Evelyn locked wrists with Penelope and climbed the wall. It was another maneuver they knew well, and it was unimaginably easier without corsets. Though climbing through the window itself held some challenges.

As soon as she was safely inside, Evelyn, who was an only child, wiped her hands on her breeches and glanced around. The room was very plain, with dark blue bed linens and a single framed picture on the wall. "I've never seen a boy's room before."

Penelope, who had four brothers, merely shrugged. "Let's go. Martin's room is only three doors down, but we need to hurry. I doubt we'll have much more than fifteen minutes before a few of them start coming back."

"Do you have the note?" Evelyn asked, focusing on the practicalities in order to distract herself from the sheer panic she was feeling, having snuck into a boy's dormitory. Not to mention that it was Martin's.

Penelope tapped her jacket pocket. "Right here."

Evelyn had read the note earlier. It was full of flowery, romantic outpourings of love. With Martin's reputation with the girls, he would probably read it and head for the highlands. Evelyn had tried to warn Penelope about that, but she just wouldn't listen. She wouldn't listen to anything Evelyn said.

They opened the door a crack and peered into the quiet corridor. Ascertaining there was no one about, they tiptoed down the hall to Martin's door.

"This is it," Penelope whispered, her eyes bright. "This is where he lays his beautiful head each night. What do you think he dreams about? Me? Could I dare to hope? He did tell me I was the prettiest girl in Windsor. Remember?"

Evelyn stared speechless at Penelope, wondering if this could possibly get any worse. "All right, we're here. Put the note under the door, and let's go before we get caught."

Penelope nodded and reached into her pocket,

but paused before she bent to slip it under. Her eyes shifted to the doorknob.

No, Penelope, don't . . .

But Evelyn didn't say those words because she knew it would make no difference. Penelope was desperate for Martin in every way, and she was not going to leave without attempting to see his bed, and God help them, sniff his pillow.

"I just want one little glimpse," Penelope whispered, wrapping her hand around the knob.

"*Please*, make it quick." Evelyn glanced over her shoulder to ensure no one was coming, then struggled with her confusing mix of emotions—the anger toward Penelope for dragging her into this and the strange exhilaration flooding her veins for what they were about to see. Martin Langdon's bed. She supposed she should admit it to herself. She *wanted* to see it, quite shamefully in fact. So she prepared herself to follow her friend inside.

Penelope lifted a finger to say "shh," then slowly turned the knob. Thankfully, the door didn't creak, and they were very quiet as they tiptoed into the dark room. But when the light from the corridor spilled across the floor, there was a sudden movement to the left. The bed linens flipped over, the mattress squeaked and bounced, and Evelyn and Penelope found themselves gaping with open mouths at a young man's naked chest— Martin's chest!—as he sat upright and squinted into the light.

"What the bloody hell?" he said, holding up a hand to shade his eyes.

Neither Evelyn nor Penelope could speak. Nor could Evelyn tear her gaze away from that bare, muscled chest and his tousled black hair as he ran a hand through it in exasperation. She was stunned, *paralyzed* by the shocking display of skin before her eyes.

God in heaven, he was so handsome, she couldn't breathe.

Her mental prowess returned however, when someone else's head popped up from under the covers—a young woman's head. Her frizzy red hair was matted and tangled, and she was clutching the covers up to her neck.

Evelyn could see her naked arms and shoulders, however, and knew enough about sin and wickedness to understand what monkey business they'd been up to.

She felt suddenly nauseous.

"*Blimey, don't you know how to knock?*" the girl in the bed shouted, then she reached behind her head and biffed a pillow, knocking over a half-empty bottle of rum, which smashed on the floor. The pillow hit Penelope square in the face, knocking her cap off. "*Get out, ya' bloomin' idiots!*"

Penelope's wavy hair came loose from the pins and fell down upon her shoulders.

Martin sat up straighter. "Jesus, you're girls."

He looked carefully at Penelope. "I know you. What's your name again?"

She let out a sob and fled from the room. Evelyn quickly followed, shutting the door behind her. She did not allow herself time to think about what she'd just witnessed.

Another door opened around the corner, down the hall, and fast footsteps approached. She bolted in the other direction, following Penelope into her cousin's room. Penelope was already scrambling out the window, sobbing uncontrollably.

Evelyn darted to the window. "Be quiet, Penny! Someone heard us! We have to get out of here!"

She tossed herself out and hit the ground beside Penelope, then took off in a sprint, grabbing her friend's arm to drag her faster across the dark field, but Penelope was crying so hard, she could barely keep up.

"Don't think!" Evelyn said, without looking back. "Just run as fast as you can!"

They scrambled down a drainage ditch at the edge of the field, then back up the other side to reach the shelter of some buildings. Evelyn looked back at the dormitory and saw lights illuminating the windows. There seemed to be frantic activity in the building.

No doubt, Martin had been caught with the girl in his bed and probably wouldn't be flirting with Penelope anytime in the near future. Not after this. He'd be furious with her, to say the least.

A few minutes later, they were free of the campus lights and making their way home to Penelope's house, walking quickly along the river.

Stopping to catch her breath, Evelyn checked over her shoulder and was panting when she spoke. "I think we're safe now. Let's just hope Martin doesn't tell anyone it was us."

Penelope stopped and sank to her knees on the grass. "Oh, Evelyn! Did you see her? How *could* he?"

Evelyn swallowed hard over her own shock and disbelief, and the strange, intense twinge of possessiveness she was feeling. Who was that girl and what precisely had she been doing to him under the covers? Evelyn didn't want to know. It made her sick just to think about it. Sick.

She knelt beside her friend. "I'm so sorry, Penny."

Penelope continued to weep inconsolably, while Evelyn fought to bury her own distress and pat the dirt down hard on top of it. She would *not* let herself give in to the idea that she was hurt by any of this. She would *not*. What just happened was no surprise. She knew what kind of boy he was and had warned Penelope about it beforehand. Martin was wild and dangerous. He was not worthy of anyone's adulation.

She laid a comforting hand on Penelope's shoulder.

"You tried to tell me," Penelope sobbed, "but I

wouldn't listen. I just wouldn't hear it, but you were right all along. He *is* a scoundrel. A despicable, vile, loathsome cad! I hate him!"

She broke into another fit of sobs.

"You'll be all right," Evelyn said gently. "You'll get over this."

"Will I? How? I loved him, Evelyn! Loved him! He was the only man in the world for me, and now I'll be brokenhearted for the rest of my life! Oh, I don't want to live! I should drown myself in the river tonight! Then maybe he'll regret what he did to me."

"You're not going to drown yourself," Evelyn said firmly. "He's not worth it."

Penelope hiccuped. "You've said that before, but you don't understand, Evelyn. You don't know what it feels like to be madly in love! You're far too sensible. You have no idea what I'm going through!"

Evelyn gazed intently into her friend's weepy eyes for a moment, saw the unabashed despair in them, and wanted to shout back at her with fury and inform her that yes, she did understand. More than Penelope could ever know.

But she did not shout those words because she knew that Penelope was right on one level. Evelyn was indeed sensible. Too sensible to ignore her firm prudence and allow herself to surrender completely to her emotions. And thank God for that. After tonight, she would work even harder to be prudent, because she could never again put herself in the path of such peril. She did not want to end up like Penelope, weeping her heart out over a rake like Martin who didn't deserve her tears.

"No one could possibly know how devastated I am," Penelope sobbed. "He doesn't love me! Oh, why didn't he love me? What's wrong with me?"

Evelyn shook her head. "Nothing's wrong with you. You're a beautiful girl, and someone else is going to sweep you off your feet again before you know it."

"No, I'll never love again. I'll enter a convent."

Evelyn sighed and stood up, helping Penelope to her feet. "Come on, let's get you home. You'll feel better after a good night's sleep."

"I'll never feel better. My life is over."

But Evelyn knew her friend. She *would* get over this, and she would fall in love again, too, probably with the very next young man who flattered her. That was Penelope. She was openly passionate, she enjoyed attention, and the young men certainly enjoyed giving it to her.

Thankfully, Penelope found the strength to stand and walk, and Evelyn put an arm around her to lead her home.

Chapter 2

◯◯◯

During the week that followed, Evelyn and Penelope waited anxiously for a shrill whistle to blow in their direction or for some official representative of the school to demand an appointment with their parents. But no such whistle blew, nor did they hear a word about a bedroom scandal at Eton. Though they supposed such scandalous happenings were quietly swept under the school carpets, especially when they involved the younger brother of a duke.

Hence, they spent the week doing nothing out of the ordinary—wandering in and out of local shops with their mothers, who had been friends since childhood. They sipped tea and ate scones in Penelope's garden, reading and going for leisurely walks along the riverbank before dinner.

Thankfully Penelope's tears flowed less and less as the week pressed on, and by the end of it, she was regarding Lord Martin Langdon as the most despicable boy in Windsor, claiming she had no idea how *any* girl could consider him handsome, for his hair was always in disarray, and he was a rake of the worst order, destined for failure in every regard, not to mention that he had a most unattractive smile.

Evelyn knew very well that his smile was by far his best feature, nothing short of disarming to any female within a ten-yard radius, but naturally she did not argue the point with Penelope. She instead agreed wholeheartedly and assured her that she was quite right on every front. It seemed as if the whole scandalous affair had indeed blown over.

At the end of the week, however, when it came time for Evelyn and her mother to go home, she discovered with some alarm that the storm had not passed at all—for there she was, standing on the platform at the train station, barely five feet from Lord Martin Langdon himself.

Ten days had passed since she'd seen him in his bed, bare-chested and cursing at her, having just sat up beside a naked girl. Evelyn bit down on her lower lip and swallowed with difficulty.

"The train is late as usual," her mother said,

checking her timepiece and taking a step forward to peer down the tracks. "Perhaps we should have had your father send the coach."

Evelyn could not reply. She was too unnerved by the presence of Lord Martin beside her. Did he even know she was one of the intruders that night? And good Lord, was he staring at her? Or was she imagining it because she was completely obsessed with being caught?

She continued to stand on the platform, looking straight ahead while her heart hammered noisily in her chest, until she couldn't take the stress of it any longer. She had to know if he was looking at her, so she discreetly turned her gaze in his direction.

To her utter horror, he *was* staring at her, squinting irritably with pure venom in his eyes.

Evelyn sucked in a quick breath and looked the other way. Good God, he *did* know.

"This is becoming ridiculous," her mother said, checking her timepiece again and tapping her booted toe on the ground. "Stay here with the bags, dear. I'm going to ask the guard how much longer it will be."

Before Evelyn could voice a protest, her mother was heading back into the station, leaving her completely alone on the platform.

Well, not completely alone. She was standing next to Lord Martin.

Evelyn wet her lips. Her heart raced madly as

she struggled to act casual. Could he see her chest heaving?

Then he did the unthinkable. He spoke.

"Well, well, well," he slowly said, rocking back on his heels. "If it isn't Miss Evelyn Foster."

She felt her eyebrows fly up in shock. She hadn't thought he'd known her name—because he never seemed to remember it—and he'd certainly never addressed her before or acknowledged an acquaintance, much less given her the slightest notion that he even knew she existed.

"Do you have any idea what havoc you caused?" he asked, glancing over his shoulder toward the station door, watching for her mother.

Evelyn fought to hide her unease and somehow managed to return his dry but heated gaze. "Havoc *I* caused? It's *my* fault, is it, that you had a woman in your bed? Pardon me, but I beg to differ."

She could hardly believe she was engaging in such an improper conversation. And with Lord Martin, no less.

His blue eyes—with their impossibly long, black lashes—narrowed. "It's your fault I was *caught*, Miss Foster."

All at once, the anxiety she was feeling turned to anger, because she hadn't even wanted to be sneaking into his dormitory in the first place, and everything was *his* fault for being such a habitual flirt and leading Penelope Steeves to believe he was in love with her!

Evelyn couldn't contain herself. With all her many frustrations boiling up to the surface, she faced Lord Martin and narrowed her own gaze from under her thick spectacles. "I do beg your pardon, sir, but when a gentleman like you behaves inappropriately—leading an impressionable young lady to believe there is some genuine affection between you—that gentleman must accept the consequences of his actions."

Martin gazed at her for a long, heated moment, then appeared almost amused, but not quite, for there was a perceptible bitterness about him when he scoffed.

"I beg *your* pardon, Miss Foster, but your friend has a head on her shoulders that is in working order, does she not? You and she both should have known it was unwise to sneak into a male dormitory, where women are strictly prohibited."

Evelyn glared at him. "And what of the woman in your bed, sir? Where was *her* head?"

His mouth curled up in a patronizing grin. "*I don't think you'd want to know.*"

Evelyn sucked in a breath. She didn't know what he was implying exactly, but was quite sure it was beyond scandalous.

But heaven forbid he should think her frazzled by the remark, so she raised her chin, squared her shoulders, and pretended she was unruffled. Though she had no idea what to say.

Martin clenched his jaw and faced forward again, evidently also at a loss for words.

They stood in silence for a few seconds, while Evelyn wallowed in her anger, for what right did he have to blame her for *his* indiscretion? He'd had a woman and a bottle of rum in his room during supper hour, for pity's sake!

Evelyn checked over her shoulder to see if her mother would soon be returning, but she was still inside the station, chatting leisurely with a woman in a large hat.

As the seconds ticked by, the tension on the platform seemed to grow heavier than lead. She could feel it throbbing all around her, and before she knew what she was about, she was breaking the silence again and asking a question rather hesitantly. "What havoc was there, exactly, after you were caught?"

She shouldn't have asked it, but she wanted to know if he had revealed her and Penelope's involvement.

Because God forbid her father should get wind of it. She was enough of a nuisance to him as it was.

He looked at her and spoke with scorn. "I had to explain myself to the headmaster, who was unimpressed with me, to say the least, but that is nothing new. Today I am officially suspended from school and will be forced to go and stay with my aunt in Exeter, and every day she will remind me that I am doomed to a life of complete and utter failure." He squinted contemptuously down the tracks. "I'll be counting the days until the school will take me back. *If* they take me back."

"You're not going home?" Evelyn asked. "To your brother? The duke?"

Lord Martin gave her a snide look and shook his head. "My brother prefers to let other people put me on the straight and narrow."

Evelyn felt a stab of pity for him suddenly, for he appeared without support of any kind, and she had heard some rumors about his home, Wentworth Castle, being a rather dark and dismal place. But then she reminded herself that he had brought all this on himself. He made his own decisions to misbehave.

"Maybe you need to put *yourself* there," she told him flatly.

Lord Martin grimaced, as if he couldn't believe his ears. "You are very self-righteous, aren't you, Miss Foster?"

"And you, sir, are very rude." She had never been so outspoken in her life.

He looked in the other direction, shaking his head dismissively, as if Evelyn were a complete dunderhead who knew nothing about the ways of the world.

She squeezed her reticule. It always hurt to feel

completely unappealing to young men, to say nothing of how it felt when the young man in question was Lord Martin. There were moments when she remembered how grateful she had been to him six years ago when he pulled her out of the freezing water and onto the ice. He had been only eleven years old, and she had thought him the greatest hero in the world. But now . . .

He was hardly a hero today. He was bitter and rebellious and didn't seem to care about anything but his own selfish and irresponsible pleasures. He had sunk very low, and it was, in a word, heartbreaking, to see the hero of her childhood dreams waste the courage and gallantry she had seen in him that day on the lake.

He turned to her for one final word. "Don't worry, Miss Foster, I didn't expose you or your friend. I told the headmaster I had no idea who you were, and he seemed to believe me. He thinks he's looking for a couple of boys."

Evelyn squeezed her reticule in her hands again and felt rather sheepish all of a sudden. "Well, I suppose I should thank you for that, at least."

He did not meet her gaze, and spoke with a cool reserve. "No need."

Just then, Evelyn heard her mother's heels clicking across the platform. "We shouldn't have to wait too much longer," she said, then pointed down the tracks. "Oh look, here it comes now."

Evelyn leaned forward to see the steam train

approaching from a distance. Martin did not look her way again. He bent and picked up his bag, then strolled in the other direction.

A short time later, they were boarding the first-class carriages, of which there were two, thankfully. Evelyn was not surprised when Martin chose the one behind hers.

As soon as they were seated, her mother leaned close and said, "Wasn't that Lord Martin Langdon, the Duke of Wentworth's brother?"

Evelyn gazed out the window and tried to sound blasé. "Was it? I didn't notice."

"You didn't notice, Evelyn?" her mother replied. "Surely you recognized him. He saved your life once, darling."

Evelyn suspected her mother could see straight through her mask of indifference, but she retained it nonetheless. "Well, if it was him, he didn't recognize me. It was a long time ago. I doubt he even remembers it."

"Honestly, Evelyn. How could anyone forget pulling a little girl out of a frozen lake?"

Evelyn shrugged. "Well, maybe he does remember it. He just doesn't know it was *me*."

And something about that made her feel strangely lonesome.

Meanwhile, in the first-class carriage directly behind Evelyn's, Martin was closing his eyes and tipping his head back on the upholstered seat, wondering if that fall through the ice years ago was the reason Miss Foster had ice water in her veins.

Honestly, she was the most uptight, frosty, prudish girl he had ever met, always acting as if she didn't know him, when she must remember that he had saved her life. How could she forget? Bloody hell, he hated the way she always looked down her nose at him, if she even bothered to meet his gaze at all. It didn't matter what he said or did, she never said hello to him or gave him the slightest smile.

Not that it mattered, he told himself. Miss Foster could go strolling on a dozen more frozen lakes with thin ice if she was so inclined. He certainly wouldn't try to stop her, because thanks to her and her foolish friend—what was her name? Penelope something?—he was going to have to spend the rest of the month bored out of his skull in Exeter, with an aunt who would constantly remind him that he was doomed to a life of failure.

Chapter 3

July 1891
Ten years later

With the bright, summer sunshine at his back and a fresh wind in his face, Martin Langdon stood at the helm on the sloping deck of his champion racing yacht, *Orpheus.* He glanced up at the grand sweep of the mainsail and felt the incomparable exhilaration of the wheel tugging in his hands. A salty spray flew upward from the windward rails, and *Orpheus's* bow plunged forward with a thunderous roar into the waves.

"Ready to tack!" he called out to his crew, feeling grateful for this welcome sense of purpose at

the helm and the rare satisfaction that came from knowing he was in absolute control. He felt confident, at ease, and his blood was racing with anticipation for the coming week.

The crew moved into position, and he turned the wheel hard over to leeward and ducked as the boom swung across. *"Coming about! Release the jib!"*

He kept the wheel hard over until they were sailing on the edge of the wind again, then glanced up to check the trim of the sails on the new tack. He settled in on a close-hauled course, smiling at the speed of the maneuver.

"Well done!" he shouted with a smile. "The trophy will be ours again by the end of the week." The men cheered. "Oh, but wait," he added with a warning tone. "Do not be too pleased with yourselves just yet, gentlemen. Our greatest challenge is still ahead of us—and that is to navigate safely through the unfathomable sea of champagne corks that will be before us by nightfall."

His crew—four of the best yachtsmen in England—laughed and shoved each other around.

Though he himself did not share in their laughter, Martin relished the sound of theirs, then closed his eyes for a moment, basking in all the tremendous power of the *Orpheus's* streamlined hull and the overwhelming might of the canvas straining aloft. She was superior to all the other English racing yachts in form and workmanship, and she had set the fashion for the new decade. And because of her, Martin, who had contributed to the genius behind her design, had become the famed racing champion of Britain for two years running.

This week, he would make it three. He was determined.

"There's the *Britannia!*" his first mate shouted, as they sliced through the choppy waters, heading for Cowes on the Isle of Wight.

Martin had come early to study the winds and currents and commit everything to memory. Apparently the Prince of Wales had come early as well, most likely to show off his impressive new cutter, which he'd commissioned just this year.

"She's a beauty," he replied.

Martin's first mate and closest friend, Lord Spencer Fleming, stepped past the windward shrouds and came to stand at Martin's side. He pointed toward the royal mansion on the hill.

"How much shall we wager Her Majesty is sitting on the terrace of Osborne House this very minute with a telescope and a frown, watching all the attractive young ladies stepping on and off her son's yacht?"

Martin glanced up at the house. "I'll wager you wish *you* had a telescope to watch them, too."

"Must you rub salt in the wound?" Spence asked.

"What in the blazes do you mean?"

"I mean that as soon as you set foot on the

Squadron landing stage, every young lady in Cowes will be flocking to your side, and I might as well be a codfish."

Martin chuckled, hoping that would indeed be the case, because he'd been feeling on edge lately and desired the particular distractions that only a week in Cowes could provide. The kinds of distractions that made him laugh and smile and forget certain less agreeable aspects of his life. Thank God the time had finally come.

"And I'll be greeting them with open arms," he assured his first mate, feeling more than certain that a few pretty ladies would cure everything. For the duration of the week anyway, which was all he could ask for.

He turned his head slightly to feel a shift in the wind, noted the closing distance to the Squadron, and knew it was time to decrease speed. Anticipation coursed through him for all the pleasures and amusements about to come his way at last, and for the great sense of accomplishment he would feel when he crossed the finish line on race day. God knew he sorely needed it.

"Let's drop the jib," he said.

"Right then." Spence relayed the message to the crew, and Martin kept the boat steady while the men lowered the sail.

He held their course, sailing toward Cowes, where the waters were calmer and dotted with a colorful fleet of yachts, all here not only for the race, but for the garden parties and balls and champagne, and the delicious gossip exchanged on the exclusive back lawn of the Royal Yacht Squadron. For Cowes week was, without question, one of the most fashionable social occasions of the year, and he was more than ready to settle in and have a devil of a good time.

Moments before the *Orpheus* changed tacks near the *Britannia*, Evelyn Wheaton—the wealthiest widow in England after inheriting her father's millions—stood on the public parade just below the Royal Yacht Squadron, gazing across the Solent and enjoying the salty fragrance of the sea. Her skirts whipped noisily in the brisk wind, and she had to hold on to her hat to keep it from flying off.

Beside her stood Henry Kipper, Lord Radley, a baron who had been a social mentor to her father— God rest his soul. Lord Radley was one of the oldest members of the exclusive yacht club and took great pleasure in that fact. Today, he wore a white sailor's hat, white flannel trousers, the traditional blue jacket of the yachting fraternity, and carried a shiny black walking stick.

"I believe that might be the *Orpheus* on her way in," he said, raising an out-of-fashion quizzing glass to his eyes and squinting into the distance.

Evelyn gazed across the water and spotted the

champion sloop skimming toward the royal
Britannia at an alarming speed.

Of course, she was not surprised. She knew
the identity of the skipper. Who didn't? He was
the country's most celebrated sportsman. He
was charming in public, a hero to the children,
and he set the standard for excellence among
sailors and shipwrights all over the world.

Not to mention the fact that the more voracious
gossips in London enjoyed the delicious tittle-
tattle about him behind closed doors: that the
only thing their champion racer liked better than
a fast boat was a fast woman.

Evelyn knew that better than anyone, didn't
she? She'd seen it firsthand ten years ago. She'd
witnessed the evidence in the flesh, and knew
that he was not *always* the smiling charmer he
pretended to be.

All at once, a flock of butterflies invaded her
belly. She hadn't seen Lord Martin in a very long
time, and it was unsettling, to say the least, to think
that she might actually speak to him this week.

Would he remember her? she wondered uneasily, feeling those bothersome butterflies swarm.
Probably not, thank goodness. She didn't want
him to. She wouldn't know what to say. It would
be very awkward, and she would feel so foolish
for harboring that strange infatuation all those
years ago. She did not even want to remember
their acquaintance, if one could call it that.

Still, she hadn't felt butterflies like these in years, and the sensation was most unnerving. She wished they would stop.

"Does he not worry he might cause a mishap?" she asked with concern as the *Orpheus* heeled over at an impossible angle. "There are hundreds of boats in his path."

Lord Radley lowered his quizzing glass and smirked. "I don't suppose that young man worries about much of anything. That's his third racing yacht after all."

Two young children in white sailor suits and hats went dashing by, their mother following quickly behind, pushing a baby in a pram. Evelyn gazed longingly at the pram for a few seconds, then forced herself to return her attention to the exploits on the water.

"What happened to the first two?" she asked, locating the *Orpheus*. Her heart skipped a beat as the keelboat changed direction again, narrowly missing another yacht.

Oh, he had not changed. Not one bit.

Lord Radley raised his quizzing glass again. "Wrecked them both, I daresay. Ran the first one aground after a month and the next a year later. Quite a shame, really. They were magnificent boats, though perhaps a little too slow for his tastes. But at least he seems to have learned something. He exercises more caution now that he's got a champion yacht."

Evelyn pursed her lips and shook her head. Caution, indeed.

"Some say he's been spoiled by his wealthy brother," Lord Radley said. "The duke replaced both yachts without blinking, almost immediately after Lord Martin wrecked them."

By the looks of things, he'll have to replace this one before long, too, she thought.

"Shall we walk up to the lawn?" Lord Radley suggested, offering his arm. "We shall indulge ourselves in the puff pastries and ask which ladies are having tea on Bertie's yacht today, and speculate about their manners and morals like a couple of carrion crows."

Evelyn laughed, thankful that the butterflies in her belly had finally stopped fluttering. "Lord Radley, you are positively wicked," she said, knowing, of course, that he was jesting.

"And perhaps we shall see if my nephew has arrived yet," he added. "I shall be most pleased to introduce you."

It was the second time that afternoon her escort had mentioned his nephew George, who had just inherited his title as Earl Breckinridge. He was here to sail his yacht in the race as well, and from what she heard, the earl had a spotless reputation and was known to be a gracious and courteous gentleman—quite the opposite of Lord Martin Langdon.

Evelyn suspected Lord Radley would be pleased to see a match between her and his nephew. He did, after all, consider himself her unofficial guardian, and had acted as such ever since her father passed away a year ago, six years after she lost her mother. Lord Radley wished to see her safely and happily married with children, because she was now completely alone in the world.

She had indeed been very lonely since her mother's passing. She'd even been lonely during her brief marriage to the vicar. *Especially* then, she supposed, for she had married him only to remove herself from her father's home, so as not to burden him with her undesirable presence any longer. She still remembered the day he told her the vicar had asked for her hand in marriage . . .

"You had better accept," he said in his cool, stern voice, without even bothering to lift his gaze from the papers on his desk, "because you won't get another offer. Not with your looks. Now get out of here. I'm busy."

Of course when it came to Lord Radley and his nephew, the proposed alliance had little to do with her looks. There was the more important matter of her inheritance, which made her an attractive prize for any man, and she was not blind to the fact that Lord Radley would derive great pleasure from seeing it settled upon his nephew. She was not offended by this, mind you. Quite to the contrary, she was thankful for it, for at twenty-six, she was not as young as the other ladies who were here seeking husbands. And she was completely aware of the fact that she had never been pretty.

She realized with rather perverse amusement that no one could ever accuse her of not being a realist. How could she be anything but? She had always gotten the cold, hard truth from her father, who would have preferred she'd never been born.

Filling her lungs with the fresh, salty sea air, she decided to dispense with those memories and anything that resembled a complaint. She was thrilled to be here for this exciting week in Cowes. Absolutely thrilled. She wanted to marry again because she desired the life she never knew—one filled with children and the laughter they would bring into a home of her own. She'd been in mourning for the past two years, starting with her husband's death and followed immediately thereafter by her father's, and before that, she had already been living without laughter in her life, simply keeping quiet. It was well past time for a change.

In that regard, she was glad she had her wealth to attract a husband. At least she had *something*, and she would not be reluctant to use it to find a husband she could love and respect.

Thus she linked her arm through Lord Radley's and accompanied him up the drive to the back lawn of the yacht club, where there was sure to be much laughter and conversation, and perhaps even a potential fiancé among the crowd.

Chapter 4

~~~~~~~∞∞~~~~~~~

After finding a spot to drop anchor among the hundred or so other yachts in the Solent, Martin and Spence changed into the proper attire for the Royal Yacht Squadron, donning navy, crested jackets and clean white shirts. They rowed to shore with their belongings, for they had rooms booked at the Royal Marine Hotel.

A crowd of onlookers was gathered on the parade, and as soon as Martin stepped onto the private Squadron dock, he was met with flattering cheers and applause, just as Spence had predicted. He stopped to face them; then, to their utmost delight, he smiled and took a great sweeping bow. Someone whistled in appreciation, and a group of young ladies giggled and twirled their lacy parasols in the sunshine.

"Good afternoon!" he called out, directing his gaze to the ladies, of course, and spreading his hands wide. "You'll all be here for the firing of the starting cannons, I hope?"

The ladies continued to giggle, while the rest of the crowd hummed with excitement and anticipation for the race.

Martin and Spence sent their bags to the hotel, then headed for the Squadron, walking past the young guard at the gatehouse, who couldn't have been more than sixteen.

The boy touched the tip of his hat. "Good afternoon, Lord Martin. It's an honor to have you back."

"It's good to be back, Ethan."

The boy's face lit up, obviously pleased that Martin remembered his name since the previous summer.

As soon as they were out of hearing range, Spence leaned close. "It's astounding," he said, "how they all adore you. Quite sickening, really. If only they knew the real you."

Martin acknowledged the teasing insult by nudging him in the ribs.

They entered the clubhouse through the main door and were greeted by other members on their way to the dining room. Choosing a table by the windows, they sat down, and Martin leaned back in a lazy sprawl with one arm draped over the back of his chair.

"Ahh, smell that," he said, exhaling deeply. "There is nothing in the world that can rival the aroma of hot chowder after a fast sail into the Solent."

"Unless it's the smell of French perfume," Spence said.

Martin glanced over his shoulder at two of the old-time members of the club, who still refused to let the ladies inside the building. "Unfortunately, we won't encounter anything quite so mouth-watering in here."

"There's always the back lawn," Spence replied.

Just then, Sir Lyndon Wadsworth, a portly baronet in his fifties and commodore of the club, entered the room and cut a path straight to Martin's table.

"Well, if it isn't the reigning champion," he said, greeting Martin, who stood and shook his hand.

"Good to see you, Sir Lyndon. You've got your hands full with preparations, I gather?"

"Indeed, it never ends."

They exchanged light pleasantries, then Martin invited Lyndon to join him and Spence for lunch.

A half hour later, after they'd all enjoyed steaming bowls of creamy chowder and crusty bread, Sir Lyndon leaned back, folded his hands over his round belly, and eyed Martin intently. "I'm surprised you haven't mentioned a word about the *Endeavor,*" he said with a sly grin.

Martin regarded him with equal scrutiny. "Isn't that Lord Breckinridge's new sloop?"

"Indeed it is." Lyndon leaned closer and spoke in a hushed tone, spurring Martin and Spence to lean forward as well. "Rumor has it, he took every farthing out of the family coffers to commission her. She's quite an extraordinary vessel, they say."

"Extraordinary." Martin inclined his head. "How so?"

After considering the question for a moment, Sir Lyndon shrugged. "She has a unique, inspired design. A number of people seem to think she's going to take the trophy this year."

Martin sat back and tapped a finger on the table. *Take the trophy?* How had he not heard of this? He prided himself in having a keen ear to the ground for everything nautical, yet he knew nothing of this *Endeavor.*

"Is the earl here yet?" he asked.

"As a matter of fact," Lyndon replied, "he just arrived this morning, and it appears he's in pursuit of *two* shiny gold trophies this week."

"There's a second trophy?" Martin asked, leaning forward with interest, because he could rarely resist a challenge.

"Yes, in the form of a wealthy widow staying at

the Royal Marine, and she arrived just yesterday with Breckinridge's aunt and uncle. She's just out of mourning for her father, who died and left her everything last year, and she's outside on the lawn right now—evidently looking for a new husband."

Martin leaned back in his chair again because he was most definitely not looking to become one of those. "Who is she?" he asked.

"Evelyn Wheaton," Lyndon told them. "Unfailingly moralistic and virtuous, they say, and utterly impossible to flirt with."

Now there was a challenge if he ever heard one.

"Who was her husband?" Spence asked.

"A devout country vicar. The sorry chap dropped dead in the middle of a sermon, after only three months of wedded bliss. Apparently, the woman has been in mourning since '89."

Martin expressed appropriate commiserations, of course, but very quickly redirected his thoughts to the *Endeavor*. *What were the dimensions of her sail area*, he wondered. *And what of*—

"Is she a beauty?" Spence asked.

Martin turned his gaze to his first mate. "Are you referring to the boat or the widow?"

"The widow of course," Spence replied, and Martin looked toward the door, suspecting that she might have extra lead in her keel.

The *Endeavor*, not the widow.

"Mrs. Wheaton doesn't turn one's head upon first glance," Sir Lyndon explained. "In fact it is generally agreed upon that she lacks that particular 'spark' that makes a woman exciting. But she does become rather more attractive once you engage her in conversation, and when you hear tell of her bank account, well, most gentlemen agree, she takes on an astonishingly pretty glow."

"I imagine she does," Spence replied with a chuckle.

Martin cut the conversation short, however, by rising from the table. "I imagine she does, too, gentlemen, and I'm looking forward to seeing that pretty glow for myself, but if you will excuse me, Sir Lyndon. At the present moment, I am in need of some information."

Lyndon regarded him knowingly. "Let me guess. You're going to see the *Endeavor*."

"Is she moored nearby?" he asked.

"Very close. You can see her clearly from the Esplanade. She has a black hull with a blue stripe."

Martin gave a polite bow. "Please stay and enjoy your desserts, gentlemen, but I believe I'll forgo the pie today."

He turned to leave, but Spence stood, too. "I'll pass on the pie, too, Martin, because something tells me you won't be examining the *Endeavor* from the beach."

Sure enough, Spence was correct on that point,

because not twenty minutes later, Martin was stripping off his shirt and diving out of the launch into the cold waters of the Solent, determined to inspect for himself the submerged hull that belonged to his competition.

"Bugger all, why didn't we hear anything about her?" Martin asked Spence as they entered the Fountain Hotel and went straight to the bar for a couple of tankards of ale. "She's a bloody racing machine, and when the wind hits those sails, she's going to fly right past us."

"She's a champion, to be sure."

"Did you see the cutaway forefoot?"

"Yes."

"And the spoon bow?"

"Yes."

"Bugger, bugger."

The barkeep filled two tankards with frothy ale and set them down on the bar. Martin and Spence picked them up and retired to the table in the corner where they could talk in private.

Martin rubbed a hand over his face. "Breckinridge is going to take that trophy."

"Not without a fight," Spence replied. "We'll give him a good run."

"I don't want to give him a good run. I want my name on that cup again."

Spence pointed a finger. "You are the most competitive man I know."

Draping an arm over the back of the chair, Martin let out a sigh. "I can't help it. It's in my nature."

Spence's eyes darkened. "*Is* it? I recall a time in school when you were quite content to be dead last at everything, just as long as you had a pretty little tavern wench in your bed to keep you entertained. You were far less . . ." He paused. "*Intense.*"

Martin's smile faded. He didn't like where Spence was heading with this. "I recall that, too, but sometimes life changes. Or people change."

"Or sometimes life changes people? And not always for the better?" Spence eyed him with notable defiance as he raised his tankard and took a deep swig.

Rubbing the tension from the back of his neck, Martin resolved to end this conversation before it ruined any chance he had to enjoy himself this week, because he really needed to enjoy himself. He'd been far too pensive lately, thinking about the past, and they both knew where those thoughts could take him. So he slapped his hand on the table and changed the subject. "We're not going to lose that cup, Spence. We'll beat Breckinridge with skill and daring."

Thankfully, Spence did not resist. Perhaps he recognized Martin's desire for distraction, or maybe he simply wasn't up to fighting Martin's formidable resolve. "If anyone is a genius on the water, Martin, it's you," he said.

Martin downed the rest of his ale, then swiped a hand over his mouth. "And while we're planning our triumph, maybe we'll take a look at that other trophy as well. See what all the fuss is about."

"What other trophy?" Spence asked.

"The wealthy widow, of course." Martin stood.

"But I thought it was your guiding principle to steer clear of the ones looking for husbands, and Sir Lyndon said that's exactly why she's here."

While he waited for Spence to guzzle his ale, Martin considered that. It was true. He did not wish to marry. It was the last thing he would ever do. But in his defense, everyone knew that, including the widow, surely, and if she didn't know it before, she would learn it very quickly when tongues began to wag.

"I don't want to marry her or anything remotely close," he explained. "I just want to flirt with her for a few minutes to prove it can be done, because if you recall, Sir Lyndon said it was impossible, and you know how I feel about the word *impossible*."

Spence stood, too, his amiable nature returning with the promise of flirtations with pretty ladies. He let out a quiet burp. "Well, you'll prove him wrong in record time. She'll likely fall over herself in mindless infatuation as soon as she lays eyes on you. Shall we head over there now?"

"Definitely."

"You're not going to rip your shirt off to examine *her* hull, are you?" Spence asked.

Martin laughed. "No, my friend, at least not this early in the race." Then he smiled and headed for the door.

Chapter 5

Martin was well aware that the back lawn of the Royal Yacht Squadron had become the heart and soul of Cowes the week of the race, and sitting in the wicker chairs were likely to be princes, ambassadors, dukes and duchesses, and many of the most beautiful, fashionable women from both sides of the Atlantic. He could not deny that he'd enjoyed the little garden's "splendors" on many occasions in the past, and today would be no different. He would talk about sailing, and he would charm a widow—two of the things he did best.

With the sun shining brightly overhead, he and Spence meandered through the crowd, attracting considerable attention, handshakes and votes of confidence, which was nothing new. But for the first time, he could sense whispers of another nature from specific cliques. People were leaning their heads together. He heard the *Endeavor* mentioned a number of times, and someone said the *Orpheus* would lose. A hushed debate ensued over by the back fence.

"It appears," Spence quietly said, "there's some difference of opinion over who will take the trophy. But it's good to see we still have some supporters."

"Yes," Martin replied. "Is our opponent here?"

"Over there." Spence gestured toward the other side of the lawn. "Standing in the shade of the tree."

Martin stopped and evaluated the *Endeavor*'s skipper. He wore the usual yachting attire—crested navy blazer and white trousers. He was holding a cup of tea on a saucer and leading the conversation with what appeared to be a lengthy anecdote. Tall and fair-haired, he looked to be in his midthirties, was fit and unfashionably tanned by the sun, which suggested he'd spent a significant amount of time on the water recently. This was not a good sign.

There were three others with him—an older couple and a young woman, most likely the widow. She had her back to Martin and was nodding. He couldn't tell much about her except that she wore a conservative gown of chocolate brown serge with broad puff shoulders and box pleats to the hem. On her head she wore a small straw hat with quills, and her brown hair was tightly knotted.

She could do with some color, he thought, and fewer sharp quills . . .

"Introduce me to Breckinridge if you will," he said.

"I had every intention of it." Spence led the way through the crowd. "Breckinridge, good to see you old fellow."

The earl acknowledged Spence with a slightly disdainful smile, but turned to allow them to join his group. "Greetings, Lord Spencer." Breckinridge pumped his hand. "And Lord Martin, it is a pleasure indeed. How is it possible we have not crossed paths before now?"

Despite his polite words, the earl's tone was condescending at best. He was looking at Martin as if Martin hadn't a hope in hell of winning the race and would soon be on a very long list of nobodies.

Refusing to accept defeat just yet, Martin gave the earl a courteous nod and shook his hand. "It is indeed a wonder, since I've been hearing great things about that yacht of yours. Well done, sir."

"I gather no introduction is necessary," Spence interjected pleasantly.

"None at all," Breckinridge replied. "Lord Martin's reputation precedes him."

Martin detected a hint of sarcasm in the man's voice. He was undoubtedly referring to Martin's other reputation—the one that gained him entry into some of the most prestigious boudoirs in London.

"But I do suppose further introductions are in order," Breckinridge said, instantly casting aside his smugness as he turned his attention toward the others. "Lord and Lady Radley, may I present Lord Martin Langdon and Lord Spencer Fleming?"

Lady Radley, a small, round woman who appeared to be in her late fifties, smiled up at him. "Lord Martin, it is wonderful to meet you at last. We've heard so much about you, and a very good friend of mine—Mrs. John Tremont?—well, she met you at a ball in London. A few weeks ago, to be precise. She had the most wonderful things to say about you. Truly, she is a great admirer. As we all are."

She giggled nervously, and everyone fell silent for an awkward moment.

Breckinridge pinched the bridge of his nose.

Martin, however, smiled down at her and placed a hand over his heart. "Lady Radley, you are most kind. And I do remember your friend, Mrs. Tremont. She was a delightful woman. Do tell her I enjoyed our conversation immensely that evening."

Of course he had no idea who he was talking about.

Breckinridge immediately resumed the introductions. "And this, gentlemen, is Mrs. Wheaton."

Directing his smile to the widow, Martin bowed slightly, and it was not until his gaze lifted and he actually met her deep green eyes behind thick gold spectacles that he sensed a familiarity.

No, it was more than that. For some strange reason, those green eyes were like a punch to his gut. But why? Who was she? A former conquest he'd carelessly cast aside? No, that wasn't it.

Then suddenly, he remembered.

But no, it couldn't be. Could it?

Good God, it was. The wealthy prize widow was, of all people, Miss Evelyn Foster from his wildest days at Eton!

His first impulse was to laugh out loud at the absurdity of the coincidence, but naturally, he preserved his composure. He was having a hard time speaking, however, because he had not expected to meet a woman he had known once before, and certainly not the prudish young girl who had constantly ignored him. The same girl who had snuck into his dormitory and caused him to be suspended, then had the sanctimonious nerve to tell him that *he* needed to put himself on the straight and narrow.

He'd never forgotten that day at the train station, or the way she persistently looked down her nose at him, as if he were a fly in her salad. She was the only girl in Windsor who had looked at him that way, and it had always, quite frankly, driven him around the bend, especially considering how he had once saved her life.

Nor had he forgotten the hellish month he'd spent with his aunt in Exeter straight afterward, when he'd been confined to his bedchamber for seven days straight, forced to write letters of apology to all his instructors, then copy them over and over until his fingers were callused and bleeding. He'd heard the word *failure* far too many times that week.

And here she was—Miss Foster—being touted as the second shiny gold trophy of the race.

Jesus. He'd planned to flirt with her, hadn't he?

Quickly recovering, he studied her face and noted how she kept her eyes on anything but him. Some things never changed, it seemed.

"Mrs. Wheaton," he said with an immeasurable degree of charm. "What a pleasure. It is an honor indeed."

He bowed to her again, wondering if she even recognized him. But of course she must. How could she forget?

She nodded and regarded him in typical

fashion—with a cool, condescending air before looking away.

All of a sudden, he remembered what Spence had said, that the widow would fall over herself in mindless infatuation when she saw him. He, too, had taken it for granted that she would adore him instantly, and as a result, he'd come here precisely to gain the mental advantage over his sailing rival. Charming the widow was supposed to be the easy part.

Ah, how the winds can shift, he thought, with a sudden burst of determination, feeling far more intrigued by this second trophy than he had expected to be. Donning an inquiring gaze, he decided to prod her a bit. "Have we not met before, Mrs. Wheaton?"

Perhaps she'd recognize him if he took his shirt off and showed her his chest. Unfailingly moralistic indeed.

A muscle in her delicate jaw tensed, and she took another sip of tea, dismissing him entirely in that same haughty manner he remembered all too well. "I don't believe so."

"Are you certain? You look familiar."

Her gaze shot up at last, and her eyes were sharp and assessing, brilliantly intelligent. He suddenly remembered she'd had a gift for science when they were younger, which was considered by some to be odd and inappropriate for a young lady of her station. *He'd* always found it rather intriguing.

Well, she still had brains. She seemed to know exactly what he was up to and was warning him to stop.

He smiled inwardly. She had spirit, too, he'd give her that. And by God, she'd grown lovely. He could not deny it. Those enormous green eyes were as disarming as ever. Even more so in fact. And her fuller figure . . . This was getting more and more interesting by the second.

"Perhaps we have," she said, "but I do not recall."

Spencer was probably thinking this race had just begun at a disadvantage, but Martin thought otherwise. He'd navigated waters far more treacherous than these before. This was quite a pleasant little puff of wind, in fact. And a very pretty one.

Feeling quite rejuvenated, he accepted a glass of lemonade from a passing footman carrying a tray.

"This is *just* the sort of thing," he said, "that keeps one awake at night, tossing and turning while struggling to put the puzzle pieces together."

"I know exactly what you mean," Lady Radley replied. She nudged Mrs. Wheaton in the arm and caused her to spill a few drops of her tea. "Try to think, dear. Perhaps you met at a ball or an assembly?"

"I haven't been to a ball in quite some time,"

Mrs. Wheaton said, sounding quite decidedly vexed by her companion's unintentional duplicity.

"Oh, that's right," Lady Radley replied with an uncomfortable grimace, obviously regretting the pushy question, for they all knew the widow had been in mourning for the past two years, and before that, she'd been married to a devout country vicar, however briefly.

"Wait just a minute!" Martin said. "I think I have it. It was years ago at Eton."

The widow boldly raised her chin and glared at him, as if she were daring him to pull the proverbial trigger and be done with it.

He had no intention of publicly embarrassing her, of course, but he couldn't resist the opportunity to inspire more of that spirit no one else seemed to recognize. *Lacking a spark,* someone had said? He thought not. All she needed was a little heat to get her started.

"But in what circumstance?" he asked, tapping a hand on his thigh. "Did I dance with you once at an outdoor picnic?"

"No," she said.

"You're right, that's not it. *Wait . . .* " They all waited on tenterhooks while he paused and pretended to search his mind, then he shook his head. "No, that's not it either. But don't worry, I'll think of it. Trust me."

He smiled devilishly at her, and when she

glared back at him with tight lips, he was quite utterly certain it was the most fun he'd had all day. All year, for that matter.

The discussion then turned to the race, and Breckinridge asked Martin's opinion on the wind velocity over the past few days, and if he thought the fine weather would continue.

Martin answered the question, then posed one of his own. "Now that the races are about to begin, Breckinridge, would you be willing to reveal the name of the *Endeavor*'s designer? I've seen her keel, and I'm guessing it was an American."

The earl grinned at him, as if their entire conversation were part of a game with clever strategies and hidden agendas. "I'd been keeping it secret before now," he replied, "but since you've already seen what's below her waterline, I suppose there's nothing left to hide. You're correct. It was indeed an American—a man by the name of Joshua Benjamin."

Joshua Benjamin. Martin knew of him. The man was gaining notoriety for designing boats with speed in mind and little else. "Ah yes. Mr. Benjamin," Martin said. "What's he like to work with? Does he listen to your ideas?"

Lady Radley slid her arm around Evelyn's corseted waist and interjected. "He's very handsome," she said. "Even our Evelyn thinks so. As well she should. He proposed to her in London a week ago."

Martin was momentarily staggered. "Proposed? You don't say."

Mrs. Wheaton cleared her throat uneasily, as if she didn't appreciate others sharing the details of her personal life. "Yes, but *naturally*, I turned him down."

He detected a hint of that self-important superiority again. "Why *naturally*?" he asked. "Do you have something against sailors, Mrs. Wheaton? Or perhaps Americans?"

She responded matter-of-factly. "No, Lord Martin, not at all. In fact, I seriously entertained his proposal for about two-and-a-half seconds, until I recalled that he already had a wife back home in Schenectady."

Everyone fell silent.

"Evidently," Mrs. Wheaton added just before taking one last sip of tea, "she was unaware of her husband's propensity to enter his vessel in more than once race at a time."

The others stared dumbfounded, as did Martin for a brief moment before he laughed out loud and nearly spit out his lemonade.

Breckinridge scrambled to change the subject. He turned to Spencer and asked about his parents.

Martin was more than happy to let Spencer take over the conversation, for it finally granted him an opportunity to observe Mrs. Wheaton— who had just achieved the impossible. She had made him laugh. Truly, she was one of a kind. She always had been, he supposed, recalling again that day at the train station.

While the polite conversation continued all around him, he allowed his gaze to meander downward and was pleased to admire the alluring feminine curves "Miss Foster" had developed over the past decade, including a lush, generous bosom, which would fare quite nicely in a lighter gown with a lower neckline, he thought. Dressed as she was at present, she reminded him of a pleasure yacht with her sails trimmed too tight, rendering her incapable of moving freely at the speed she was built for.

He wondered suddenly how this aloof young widow would respond to a little wind in her sails and a skillful skipper like himself at her helm. Would he be able to bring the best out of her, like he did with the *Orpheus*?

Yes, he thought with absolute confidence while he admired the grace of her gloved hand as she touched one finger to the corner of her mouth to dab at an errant drop of tea. He certainly could bring the best out of her, and also bring out that spark she kept hidden from the world. A marvelous, masculine satisfaction flowed through him at the thought of it.

The earl made an amusing remark just then about the currents in the Solent, and Martin smiled and laughed, but was aware that his laugh was artificial, for he was distracted by the wonderful challenge of the woman standing across from him.

Breckinridge turned to her. "And will you attend the ball this evening, Mrs. Wheaton? The one on board the *Ulysses*?"

The *Ulysses* was a 290-foot steamship owned by a wealthy American businessman who had commissioned one of the yachts in the race but preferred the champagne at Cowes to the actual sailing.

"Yes, I'm looking forward to it," she replied.

Lord Radley placed a hand on his nephew's shoulder. "Would you like to reserve a spot on her dance card, George? I suggest you reserve it now, because it will doubtless be full as soon as Mrs. Wheaton is announced."

Martin watched the exchange with interest.

"Indeed I would," Breckinridge replied. "If you would be so kind, Mrs. Wheaton?"

"I would be delighted," she replied.

Martin casually jingled the ice chips in his glass before he downed the rest of his lemonade. "I'll be there as well," he said. "And I would be remiss if I did not also request a spot on *both* your cards—Mrs. Wheaton and Lady Radley?"

Lady Radley blushed ardently.

Martin smiled at her. She was a delight.

"And my dear aunt, you'll save a dance for me as well?" Breckinridge added.

But it was too late. Martin had already taken *that* splendid point in the race.

"Yes, dear," Lady Radley replied, sounding preoccupied because she was still gazing in a state of bemusement at Martin.

He gave her another congenial smile. "I'll look forward to our dance, madam." Then he turned his gaze toward the widow. "And Mrs. Wheaton, I will look forward to seeing you tonight as well."

Her reply was conspicuously cool. "Likewise."

Then he and Spencer bid them all adieu and made their way off the Squadron property to go and prepare for the night ahead and the most excellent diversions on board the *Ulysses*.

Chapter 6

～∞～

Evelyn stood on the back lawn of the Squadron with the hot sun beating down on her head, and watched Martin exit the gate.

She could not believe what had just occurred. He had teased her and toyed with her, yet despite all of that and despite her best efforts to remember that she was no longer a childish young girl infatuated with a charming but reckless young man, she was gazing after him in a numb stupor. His teasing had been so fantastically thrilling and electrifying, her heart was still pounding wildly in response.

She was also remembering the hero of her childhood dreams—the dark-haired, blue-eyed boy who had dragged her from freezing-cold water and forced her to crawl across the ice to safety. She hadn't spoken a word to him that day years ago. She hadn't even known his name. She had been in shock, determined only to survive and reach her mother. But *he* had spoken. He had said one thing. He had told her to kick. She would never forget the sheer force of that command—compelling her to obey, no matter how impossible it seemed.

She felt the same urge to kick right now—to break free from the pressures of finding a husband in this opportunistic marriage mart even though she had convinced herself it was what she wanted and what was best for her. But seeing Martin again—feeling the excitement he aroused in her—made her doubt everything. She suddenly wished she hadn't come.

Lord Breckinridge spoke then—quietly to his uncle—and Evelyn turned her eyes toward them.

"Lord Martin is worried," he said. "Could you see it?"

"Absolutely," Lord Radley replied, also in a hushed tone. "But how could he not be? The *Endeavor* is a force to be reckoned with. I'm afraid Langdon's reign as Cowes champion is over."

Evelyn merely listened while a footman refilled her cup with hot tea. She did not wish to join the discussion because she was afraid she might reveal how frazzled she was.

"You know I adore you, George," Lady Radley said, also still in a bit of a besotted daze, "which is why I must warn you not to become overconfident even if you do have the fastest boat in the world. Lord Martin is reputed to be a great helmsman."

The two gentlemen chuckled at her opinion.

"My dear wife," Lord Radley said, "you've let that man's notoriety deprive you of your common sense."

"That's right," Lord Breckinridge added. "My first mate, Mr. Sheldon Hatfield, was acquainted with Lord Martin at Eton and knows the truth about him. He was a useless chump then—reckless and irresponsible—and nothing has changed. He has merely been lucky in the races the past two years because he has not had a worthy opponent."

But after seeing Martin again today and knowing what she knew of him, Evelyn had to agree with Lady Radley. It was difficult to imagine anyone besting him on the water, or anywhere else for that matter. He was powerful and unstoppable, and from her vantage point, *he* was the force to be reckoned with. Especially when it came to that infuriatingly stubborn spark of desire in her heart, which simply would not die, no matter how hard or how long she tried to snuff it out.

That evening, Evelyn spent far too much time and thought on her gown for the ball. She restyled her hair three times, changed her shoes twice, deciding quite positively that she looked hideous in blue.

In the end, she had no choice but to wear the blue disaster because the only other choice was the pink disaster, and there was absolutely no chance on earth she would be caught dead in such a frilly costume tonight, for she did not wish to attract such attention to herself.

Oh, she really did not enjoy balls, and tonight was worse because she was going to dance with Martin. Martin! Perhaps it wouldn't even come to that. He might forget or change his mind. She should expect it, for he had always forgotten her in the past. She considered how she would feel if he did. She would *not* be disappointed. No. If she had any sense left in her head, she would be relieved.

Finally, when it was time to go, she left her room in the Royal Marine Hotel and ventured out into the corridor. She had just turned to lock her door behind her when she heard another door click open across the hall.

A notable few seconds of silence ensued before she heard a man speak. "What a delightful co-incidence."

Startled by the familiar voice, she turned around to find herself gazing upon Martin, of all people, standing in his own open doorway, his hand still upon the knob. He wore formal evening attire—a black suit with a white waistcoat and bow tie made of the finest silk money could buy. His hair was thick and shiny black like wicked midnight, falling in attractive waves to his broad shoulders. His blue eyes were heavy-lidded and openly sensual.

Evelyn strove to maintain at least an appearance of calm by tilting her head slightly and letting out a cool, dejected sigh. "Delightful coincidence indeed."

She hoped he caught the sarcasm in her tone.

He slowly closed the door to his room, locked it, then faced her elegantly. "Are you following me, Mrs. Wheaton?"

She squared her shoulders. "I was about to ask you the same question, right after I boxed your ears for what you did to me today."

He chuckled, and his blue eyes sparkled like starlight. "You *should* have boxed them. Lord knows I deserved it. I was an absolute scoundrel."

They regarded each other for a moment, then Martin pushed away from his door and approached. He sauntered toward her, then stopped mere inches away, forcing her to back up against her own door.

He leaned closer and rested an arm against the lintel over her head, while she struggled to subdue the fiery sensation heating her blood. She was not accustomed to this. Men did not do this sort of thing with her. And it was Martin. *Martin!*

"I admit," he said, "that for a moment this afternoon, I thought you might have forgotten our acquaintance, but then I realized I was wrong. You *do* remember. Some of it, at least."

She wet her lips and fought hard to slow her breathing. "How could I forget? You flirted with my best friend and led her to believe there was something between you, then you broke her heart. And you had the audacity to blame *me* when you were suspended from school."

He grinned. Her eyes fixed upon his full, soft-looking lips, only inches away, and the strong line of his jaw. He was clean-shaven, but she could still see the dark shadow of manly stubble. She wondered how rough it would be under her fingertips after a day's growth. Then she closed her eyes briefly to steer her mind away from such a thought. She did not need to know that.

"Water under the bridge, Mrs. Wheaton," he said with a warm, silky voice.

She quickly shook her head at him in a defensive measure. "After all these years you still take no responsibility for it."

"And neither do you apparently. And to think the world believes you to be unshakably virtuous. If they only knew the whole truth about the famous vicar's widow."

Evelyn reeled at his impudence. "I beg your pardon, sir."

He smiled again, and she wondered where the bitter young man had gone. He was not like he had been at the train station years ago. Tonight

he was exuding more charm than any man had
a right to exude—teasing her again, toying with
her in a scandalously wicked manner.

This was the young man Penelope had fallen in
love with. The man all of England had fallen in
love with, in fact. The carefree rake. The champion. The charmer.

But why was he suddenly charming Evelyn
when he never had before? He'd always ignored
her, looked straight through her, because she was
not pretty.

Oh, what was she thinking? Of course she
knew why he was paying attention to her now.
It was the same reason other gentlemen were.
Because of her inheritance. She was fresh out of
mourning and brought new money to the marriage mart. She could not let herself be truly flattered by this.

*Or maybe he just wants to triumph over his rival,
Lord Breckinridge*, she thought, keeping her head
out of the clouds and firmly upon her shoulders.
She had seen the competition between them earlier.

Either way, his motives did not matter. Whatever they were—charm was charm, seduction
was seduction—and she had to wet her lips again
because her mouth had gone dry.

"So it seems we both have reputations," he
said, "which means that we are similar creatures.
Except that you are famous for being virtuous,

and I am famous for . . . Well, quite the opposite."

Evelyn tensed. "And I thought you were famous because of all your sailing trophies," she replied. "Foolish me."

He smiled again, and it reached his eyes. "You? Foolish? I don't think so."

But she felt very foolish at this moment, responding with lavish desire to the sensation of his hot breath on her face and the intoxicating nearness of his strong, attractive, virile body.

Heart pounding, she drew in a slow, deep breath, and remembered to whom she was speaking. Martin Langdon. Charmer. Thrill seeker. Heartbreaker.

And she was Evelyn Wheaton. Pious churchgoer. Shy mouse. Ugly duckling.

All at once her pessimism took hold. She raised a forefinger and pushed her heavy spectacles up the bridge of her nose, then placed her hand on his solid chest and slowly pushed him back. "You are correct on one point, Lord Martin. I have never been a foolish woman, so you would do well to remember that."

She recognized the sudden look of defeat in his eyes, as if she had just thrown a glass of cold water in his face.

But then he smiled again, and it surprised her, for there was respect in his eyes, as if he thought she was very astute—a formidable opponent, so to speak, which she most definitely was not. She was melting like hot butter right in front of him.

"How do you mean, Mrs. Wheaton?" he asked, feigning innocence.

She shook her head at him and was very aware of the cheeky tone in her voice when she spoke, which was completely out of character for her. She was not the cheeky type. At least she hadn't been before this moment.

"I mean," she replied, "I know *why* you are flirting with me—because like you, I am not famous for just one thing. Yes, I may be reputedly virtuous, but everyone also knows I am presently the wealthiest widow in England. You're not the only man who has made overtures, you know."

She was not about to tell him he was the only man who had made overtures like *this*. Sexual ones. Most gentlemen knew her reputation for being virtuous and used very different tactics. They talked about their flower gardens or how often they went to church. They occasionally quoted from the Bible with a faraway look in their eyes. It had become rather predictable.

Martin's discourse, on the other hand, was a far cry from predictable or biblical. Fire and brimstone was coming to mind. It was a different approach, to be sure.

He raised a finger and wagged it at her, as if he

were conceding this match to her—that yes, she was right and had won the point.

"You're going to be a challenge, aren't you?" he said.

A challenge? So there it was.

She eyed him shrewdly. "It's at least nice to know what I am to you." Then she pushed him farther back still and headed for the stairs.

He followed. "I won't insult you, then, by acting the part of a suitor genuinely in love. I can see you're too clever for that."

Evelyn kept walking as she pulled on her gloves. "It has nothing to do with cleverness, Lord Martin. I simply know you too well."

But she did not really know him. They'd barely had two full conversations. She just felt as if she did, because she had been watching him from afar for so many years.

"And you know I am a flirt," he said.

"I'm pleased to hear you're not denying it."

He slid his hands into his trouser pockets and walked with a casual, self-assured gait. "Denying it would be pointless, I believe, where you are concerned."

"Indeed it would." She started down the stairs.

This time, he did not follow. He remained at the top, watching her descend. She knew he was watching because she could feel his gaze burning at her back.

When she reached the bottom, she stopped and looked up at him. She didn't know what had compelled her to do so. She should have just kept walking.

She raised an eyebrow. "I am going to the ball now, Lord Martin. Doubtless my dance card will be full. Do you still wish to reserve a spot?"

So much for not being foolish. She should have just let him forget, which he surely would have done as soon as he saw all the other women in the ballroom.

He crossed his wrists over the newel post at the top and leaned upon it. "Yes, I would like to reserve a spot. If I may have first choice, I'll take the last dance please."

"Well, you had best hope I don't grow tired and leave early."

He replied with smooth confidence. "You won't."

She pursed her lips. "Don't be so sure."

"How can I not be?" he replied. "Because I think you enjoy a good party, Mrs. Wheaton. More than you let on. Or maybe you don't even know it yet. Maybe you've never experienced a night that was truly exhilarating."

He was gazing down at her with presumptuous assurance, as if he knew exactly what she was about, and it shook her inwardly, because curse him, he was right. She had experienced very little excitement in her life because she had witnessed the consequences of women who loved exciting men. She'd seen her mother's broken heart over her father's many disgraces with other women, and Penelope's heartbreak over Martin and others after him.

Most importantly, she knew about rejection. She had been living with it all her life, since as early as she could remember, beginning with the most painful rejection of all—her father's. And later, her husband's. She knew how much it hurt and had learned to avoid it by never seeking attention. Instead, she was deliberately unapproachable. Her mask of contempt was her shield.

Yet here stood Martin, the first man courageous enough—or perhaps simply intuitive enough—to push that shield aside with the blunt truth.

"I'm not a prize to compete for," she told him, raising her shield again with a willful aloofness, because she did not wish to end up like Penelope or all the other heartbroken women littered in his path. "You can dance with me if you like, but there is no point wasting your time. It won't get you anywhere."

He straightened. "You think my dancing with you would be a waste of my time? Have you never lived for the moment, Mrs. Wheaton?"

Evelyn swallowed uncomfortably, then felt the color leave her cheeks. "No, I have not," she said, and turned to leave. She did not like the question.

"You *should*," he called after her, "because that's

what life is. A series of moments. Nothing more. We must endeavor to enjoy every single one. Forget about the past and future. They have no place in the present."

But Evelyn did not turn back, nor did she respond, because in her opinion, life was much more than a series of moments—for all moments had consequences, and consequences could bring pain.

And pain could not simply be "forgotten."

She supposed he didn't know that. He had probably never cared deeply enough about anything to be hurt by it.

He said one last thing, however, before she reached the door. "I would think that *you*, Mrs. Wheaton—of all people—would understand the significance of that."

She stopped suddenly, and felt a strange heaviness settle in her chest. "Why?"

"Because if I recall, you once had a very harrowing moment—the kind that makes a person think twice about life. Do you remember?"

Her mouth fell open as she contemplated what he was speaking of. Was it possible? Did he actually remember?

She turned to face him. "What are you talking about?"

"That winter day on the lake years ago." When she made no reply, he added, "Do you not recall how thin the ice was?"

She stared at him in stunned silence.

"I . . . didn't think *you* remembered that," she said at last, squeezing her beaded reticule. *Did* he? Had he *always* remembered?

Something in his eyes changed. His head drew back a little. "I do."

The clock on the wall seemed to be ticking very loudly—a testimony to the length of time neither of them spoke.

"Did you always know it was me?" she asked, striving to keep her voice steady.

"Yes. But I was under the impression *you* did not know it was *me*, because you certainly never thanked me."

Had she not?

But her mother had, and others, too. She herself had been too shaken that day, and in the years following, too shy and withdrawn.

Good God, had he resented her all this time for that? Then she recalled the way she had treated him that day at the train station—as if he were no better than a bug under her shoe—and she colored fiercely with regret.

Swallowing hard, she pushed her spectacles up her nose while searching for the proper thing to say. "I was grateful to have your assistance that day, Lord Martin. *Very* grateful. Thank you."

He acknowledged her gratitude with a nod. "Well, it's about time."

She felt her stomach whirl with butterflies

again. "I must go now," she said at last, raising her chin and awkwardly pointing toward the door. "Lord and Lady Radley are waiting for me outside. Good evening."

"Good evening," he replied in a quietly seductive voice.

She turned and headed outside, feeling as if the earth had just shifted upon its axis, because Martin remembered and had probably thought her an ungrateful shrew all these years. If he did, she certainly deserved it because she had never once exhibited any kindness toward him. If anything, she had treated him with disdain.

Then she stopped on the street outside the door as she realized something else. With her famously cool reserve, she had grown into an exact replica of another person whom she had always resented for that very aspect of his character. Her father, God help her. Her cold, unfeeling father, who had rejected her all her life at every opportunity.

It was not a welcome realization, but it was an accurate one, and she wondered with some distress if it was not too late to change the woman she had become.

Chapter 7

The 290-foot steamer, *Ulysses*, was the height of opulence, boasting dark, walnut-paneled walls, shiny chandeliers, and velvet upholstery, all laid out in the Renaissance Revival style. The room smelled of new varnish, Havana cigars, perfume, and champagne, and was alive with laughter and conversation.

Belowdecks in the main ballroom, Evelyn spent the whole of the evening dancing with a number of different gentlemen. They were all polite and respectful, though she could sense which ones were seeking to impress her because they had designs on her inheritance. They had a certain aura about them.

She wondered in turn about her own aura—the chilly disposition she was most known for. Had she hurt and rejected many young men over the years because she slighted them or ignored them completely? For all she knew, she probably had, though she'd never intentionally meant to hurt anyone. She'd only ever meant to avoid being hurt herself. She certainly hadn't imagined for a moment that her affability—or lack of it—would even *matter* to any of those gentlemen. But perhaps it had. It had mattered to Martin, because he remembered.

Another set ended, and her dance partner—a congenial baron from Norfolk—returned her to Lord and Lady Radley, who were enjoying the strawberries and chocolate.

"My dear, you have been danced off your feet this evening," Lady Radley said, extending a hand.

"Yes, it seems I have," Evelyn replied. Feeling warm, she clicked open her fan and cooled her cheeks.

Lord Breckinridge joined them and handed her a glass of champagne. "I see you have been dancing every set," he said. "I do hope you've at least allowed yourself time to catch your breath."

She was breathing rather quickly in fact. "It's been a wonderful evening so far," she said, resolving to sound cheerful and open and approachable.

"The baron told me that his family has just discovered a—"

Breckinridge interrupted. "I *myself* have been conversing with Jack Seaforth, the owner of this steamer. Did you know she has a forty-five-hundred-horsepower steam plant, and can do eighteen knots and cross the Atlantic in seven days?"

"No, I didn't," Evelyn politely replied, trying not to reveal her frustration at being cut off mid-sentence.

"Indeed. You are dancing on twenty-four-hundred tons of pure luxury. Every man's dream." He raised his glass.

Lord Radley raised his glass as well, and Evelyn took a sip of the expensive champagne. Breckinridge then spoke more about the dimensions of the ship, so she gave up on her story about the baron, who had found some ancient Viking tools in the ground on his estate.

Meanwhile, Lady Radley seemed distracted, gazing across the dance floor, swaying in time with the music.

"Have you danced yet this evening?" Evelyn asked her.

"Not yet. I've just been watching all the young people." Her eyes shifted back to the dancers.

Evelyn followed Lady Radley's gaze and saw the object of her interest—Lord Martin, moving around the floor with a pretty blond woman in a yellow gown. Lady Radley's eyes were damp and dreamy, and she was tapping her foot to the music.

Evelyn, too, felt strangely dreamy, watching the two of them swirl smoothly around the room, chatting and smiling at one another, looking completely absorbed in their conversation.

He really was a charmer, she thought. He was handsome and sociable and charismatic. She and Martin were complete opposites in fact. He loved women and enjoyed making them feel sensual and desirable, while she made men feel daunted and unworthy of her attention. She could no doubt learn a great deal from him.

Watching him over the rim of her glass, she took another sip of the deliciously effervescent champagne. Just then, he and his partner waltzed around to the corner where she and Lady Radley stood, and their eyes met. His partner was giggling about something, but he found an opportunity to smirk at Evelyn as if *they* were partners in some secret scheme.

Lady Radley placed a hand on her arm. "Did you see that smile? He looked at you, darling. Did you not notice? Oh, surely you did. What I wouldn't give . . ."

Evelyn leaned closer to Lady Radley and spoke in a hushed tone. "You think he's very handsome, don't you?"

Lady Radley sighed. "Oh, yes, he is, but it's so much more than that. There's something dark and mysterious about him boiling underneath all that charm. Have you ever noticed that? But I suppose it runs in his family. Do you not remember the stories about his brother, the duke, before he married that rich American heiress?"

"What stories?" Evelyn asked.

"I suppose you're too young to remember." She glanced around and lowered her voice to a whisper. "People used to say their castle in Yorkshire was haunted, and that all the Wentworth dukes had black hearts. Martin's own father was a beastly man who drank himself to death, and his grandfather did himself in as well, quite violently they say. They were a very unhappy lot."

"I had heard their castle was rather dismal," Evelyn said, "but I never heard any of this."

Lady Radley touched her arm and continued to whisper. "A few years ago, no one saw or heard from Lord Martin for a long time, then he suddenly reappeared crashing boats. Most people insist he had merely been traveling abroad, but some who remember the history of his family wondered if he had gone mad and spent time in an asylum or something of that nature. Which I am *convinced* is not true. That was all utter nonsense. Either way, the rumors have been laid to rest now. The present duke is a most charismatic gentleman and from what I hear, has a happy home with a beautiful wife and darling children, and the ghosts, evidently, have stopped howling."

Watching Martin dance, Evelyn twirled a loose tendril of hair around her finger.

"All that unhappiness must be in the past," Lady Radley continued, "for young Lord Martin has a *wonderful* heart, don't you agree? He makes a woman feel beautiful. Even a woman like me."

That much was true at least, because for a brief time in the hotel corridor earlier, Evelyn had felt beautiful, too—though not just physically. She'd also felt vibrant and adventurous and had become aware of a vitality she didn't know she possessed. She'd been coy and playful, and it had been a rare and welcome feeling, so unlike how she usually felt. She wanted to feel that way again. "Did he not ask for a spot on your card when we spoke on the lawn this afternoon?" Evelyn asked.

"Yes, and he did not forget. We'll be dancing next." She straightened and laughed self-consciously. "Oh, but at my age . . . What a foolish woman I am."

She quickly sipped her champagne and glanced up at her husband, who was deep in conversation, completely oblivious to the thoughts and dreams of his wife.

The orchestra finished the piece, and the dancers stepped apart and engaged themselves in conversation. Lady Radley squeezed her arm. "Here he comes," she said.

Martin approached and delivered his greetings. "And I believe I have the honor, Lady Radley? I've been looking forward to it all evening."

He held out a gloved hand, and Lady Radley giggled, swept away by the flattery. "Oh, Lord Martin, you are such a charming young man. The honor is all mine."

Leading her onto the floor, he inclined his head at Evelyn, meeting her gaze briefly as if to say it was her turn next, and there was no escape. Her palms became instantly clammy inside her gloves.

For the next few minutes, she watched Martin lead Lady Radley around the floor and speak words that made Lady Radley's cheeks flush with color and her eyes sparkle with delight. Lord Radley seemed unaware of his wife's pleasures, while Breckinridge went on continuously about the races he had won over the summer.

The dance soon came to an end, and it was Evelyn turn to be flattered and treated like a beauty. As she watched Martin approach with that alluring, masculine swagger, she became aware of her pulse quickening.

He escorted Lady Radley back to her husband, then turned to Evelyn. "The last dance of the evening, Mrs. Wheaton. I believe I have the honor. Unless, of course, you have danced your fill."

Evelyn's lips parted in surprise. Was he giving her the opportunity to refuse him? Did he *want* her to?

She began a reply, but Lord Breckinridge interrupted again. "Indeed, Mrs. Wheaton has barely caught her breath, Lord Martin. It's been far too warm in the ballroom, as I'm sure you've noticed."

Martin turned to him and spoke firmly. "Has it? Then I shall escort her onto the deck for some much-needed fresh air."

The two men stared fixedly at each other for a few seconds, and the dynamic was not lost on Evelyn. Again this was not about her. It was about the competition. She would do well to remember that.

She would also do well to decide for herself what she wanted and not permit Lord Breckinridge to speak for her by interrupting.

She turned to Martin. "That is very considerate of you, Lord Martin. I am certain fresh air is just what I require."

Martin's charm did not falter as he offered his arm. "Shall we take the companionway then?"

His eyes glimmered with pleasure when he met her gaze, as if he believed she was the most fascinating woman in the room—the *only* woman, in fact. She linked her arm through his, and when he covered her gloved hand with his own, she felt its warmth all the way down to her toes and became caught up in the raw magic of his appeal. She felt lost in a fiery rush of physical awareness.

Her pulse quickened again, and she looked

away as she always did, across the room as if there might be something or someone more interesting to behold there.

There was not, of course. Nothing was more interesting than Martin at her side, leading her to the passageway that would take them to the companionway and up to the promenade deck to a perfect view of the stars. She was merely trying to hide the pleasure she experienced from his flattery. She did not want him to know how deeply she was affected by it because she feared that if he sensed her desires, he would eventually refuse them, as gentlemen always did, and she would be humiliated and hurt.

She thought of her father suddenly and her many appeals for his affection or approval, answered only by his blatant demonstrations of aversion.

She *hated* that he could still affect her life in this way, even from beyond the grave. She could not let him continue to do this to her. Nor did she want to be the person *he* had been.

So she gathered her skirts in a fist to climb the steps and gave Martin the most dazzling smile she had ever given any man in her life.

It was a proud moment—her first noble rebellion against the inhibited person she had become. And she was most pleased when he returned her smile with a dazzling one of his own.

Chapter 8

⟨◦◦⟩

"**F**resh air at last," Martin said, leading Evelyn to the rail, where they could admire the yachts moored in the Solent. Hundreds of lantern lights twinkled in the velvety darkness, and distant bells rang. The air was cool with only a gentle whisper of a breeze, and Evelyn marveled at the reflection of the moon on the dark water, sparkling upon the waves.

"Thank goodness," she replied with a deep, appreciative sigh. "It was rather warm below, wasn't it?"

Leaning an elbow on the rail, he crinkled his nose. "Stuffy, I'd say."

"I hope you are referring to the quality of the air, Lord Martin, and not the company?"

He leaned a little closer and spoke in a hushed tone. "Well *that* wasn't a very proper thing for a proper widow to say."

He was teasing her again as he had in the hotel corridor and trying to get a rise out of her. It was as if he somehow knew that she wished to break out of her shell, and he was poking at her. She wasn't sure if she loved it, or was completely unnerved by it.

"I wasn't the one who said it," she replied with mock effrontery, followed by a slightly flirtatious sidelong glance.

He smiled. "Oh, but you were. I simply said it was stuffy. You implied that your companions were dull."

Evelyn clasped her gloved hands together over the rail and pursed her lips. Honestly, he was like no other gentleman she'd ever encountered, and he made her want to laugh—something few men even attempted to accomplish. It was exactly what she needed right now—complete and utter audaciousness.

After a moment, he faced forward, too, and stretched to look straight down at the water. "We're dreadfully high up, I daresay."

"We are indeed," she replied with a soft chuckle. "It's a tremendous ship. In fact, Lord Breckinridge informed me earlier that I was standing on twenty-four-hundred tons of pure luxury."

Martin's eyebrows lifted, then he stepped back and stomped his foot on the wooden deck. "My God, I believe he might be right."

Evelyn relished the playful sarcasm in his tone. "He said a ship like this was every man's dream," she added.

"Not every man's," he softly said, leaning his forearms on the rail again. "I dream of other things. And when it comes to being out on the water, I prefer the power of the wind."

A breeze lifted his dark hair, and Evelyn admired the classic beauty of his face, bronzed by wind and sun. "Why is that?"

"It's peaceful," he told her as he gazed out over the dark sea, "and a sailboat doesn't smell like an engine room. It smells like fresh air and freedom."

"That can't be the only reason," she said. "Surely there must be a greater allure for you. You like the speed, don't you? The danger and excitement? You enjoy taking risks and winning trophies?" Surely that was the more relevant motivation.

He turned to face her, looking as if he found her opinions surprising. "Have you never been sailing before?"

"I've been on boats," she replied, feeling rather naïve all of a sudden. "But they've all been steamers."

"Well, that's not the same at all," he explained.

"To be on a sailboat is to be as close to heaven as anyone can get."

Close to heaven. She'd never heard anyone speak that way before—with such genuine, open passion.

Nevertheless, she could not quite give up her view on the subject. "I'm sorry, but I simply do not understand the appeal of being on a boat that is tipping so severely that the sails nearly touch the water and the passengers have to rush to one side to keep it from capsizing. That is not my idea of 'peace.'"

He threw his head back and laughed. "You've got it all wrong, my dear. A good skipper has everything under control."

"But where's the 'heaven' you describe?"

He paused a moment, looked up at the stars while he contemplated his answer, and when he spoke there was a hint of melancholy in his voice.

"The simple act of hoisting the sails puts me in a wistful mood," he told her, "and when I feel the wind in my face and I'm focused on the waves and the trim of the sails, my troubles seem to disappear, and sometimes I even forget who I am or where I've been."

The murmur of laughter and music from below seemed to fade away as she listened to Martin speak, wondering why he would ever need to forget who he was, for he was the most celebrated sportsman in England, envied by every man, adored by every woman. But then she remembered those rumors about the men in his family being such an unhappy lot.

"And to be at the helm . . . " he continued. "Well, there is nothing quite like those moments when all hell is breaking loose, and the sea is wild and the spray is stinging your face, yet you know you are proficient enough to keep the boat safe from harm and bring her back in once piece."

For some reason she could not explain, Evelyn felt a painful twinge in her chest. A pang of apprehension for his future perhaps, because he took risks? For no one could control the sea. He of all people should know that, having wrecked two boats in the past.

"Promise me you'll go sailing while you're here," he said, his voice becoming light again, which helped to allay her misgivings. "You're in Cowes. You can't go home without trying it."

"Oh, no, I couldn't," she replied. "I'm just here to watch the race."

He turned to face her, and his gaze swept from her eyes down the length of her gown, then back up again, slowly, as if taking in every inch of her and finding her appearance greatly to his liking.

A nervous fluttering arose in her belly, for men never looked at her that way. She was not accustomed to admiration.

"You can't go through life watching other people have all the fun," he said. Then he leaned closer and whispered in her ear and the moist heat of his breath sent gooseflesh tingling down the entire left side of her body. "Don't you ever want to try new things? To explore and feel truly alive?"

Evelyn breathed in the cool night air, mixed with the musky scent of his shaving soap or cologne or whatever it was, and felt a dizzying thrill run through her, from the top of her head straight down to her toes. It made her want to do everything he was suggesting—and more— because when had she ever done anything new? When had she ever felt as alive as she did at this moment?

She swallowed hard over the shock of her response though she should not be surprised. He was a handsome, mysterious, virile man who sailed boats on stormy seas, looked at her with sexual prowess like he wanted to devour her, and he'd been a hero in her eyes since she was a girl. He was like no other man in the world—charming on the outside, but dark and enigmatic under the surface—and there was something about him that touched her deepest desires. The ones no one knew about. The ones she couldn't even admit to herself because she feared them.

All at once she realized the conversation had become too intimate. Yes, she had wanted to be more amiable and less aloof, but surely she had let things go too far. He was speaking to her deepest thoughts and emotions when she should have kept her guard up and maintained a reasonably safe distance at least. Especially from a man like him, who knew how to seduce and did so on a regular basis.

"I could take you," he said in a low, silken voice, surprising her yet again with his direct manner when he should not be suggesting such a thing, and certainly not like *that*—with such heated persuasion, as if he were insinuating all kinds of other activities that would take place on board his boat after he'd dropped anchor in a secluded cove. "I could even teach you. Show you how thrilling it can be."

There was no point pretending not to recognize what he was proposing—that they could enjoy more than just a cruise on the water. It was shocking to the depths of her soul.

"I'm not looking for *that* kind of thrill," she said, angling her head at him with a warning, and retreating into her customary cool demeanor.

He grinned and stepped back, giving her some space at last. "Ah, yes, the virtuous widow. I forgot with whom I was speaking."

They stood in silence for a moment, leaning on the rail and looking down at the quiet water until Martin nudged her with his elbow.

She could not help herself. Her lips curved into a smile, then she laughed.

"My God," he said, "I think that's the first time I've ever heard you laugh."

"I laugh," she told him. "Just not around you. I've not had the opportunity."

He eyed her carefully. "I would dearly love to change that. Please, come sailing with me." He held his hands up, palms open. "I promise, I'll be a gentleman. No hanky-panky. No flirting. No inappropriate thrills. I'll teach you how to sail, nothing more."

She remembered what he'd said in the hotel, that life was just a series of moments, and though she still did not agree with the idea that consequences played no part, she gave in to the possibility that there might be some wisdom in what he was trying to show her—that one had to enjoy life day by day and seize opportunities when they presented themselves, because one never knew when it could all end.

Just then, a number of guests from below emerged onto the deck, including Lord Breckinridge and Lord and Lady Radley.

Evelyn stepped away from Martin. "Is it over?"

"Yes," Breckinridge replied, glancing with distrust at Martin as he offered his arm to her. "But most of us are heading over to the Esplanade for an evening stroll. You'll join us, Mrs. Wheaton? We can walk to the Umbrella Tree."

The Umbrella Tree was a large weeping ash upon the Green, known to be a favorite place for courting couples. It was presumptuous to make such a remark, and she suspected it was for Martin's benefit, not hers. She also suspected Martin knew it.

Nevertheless, her time with him was at an end, for they had been standing under the stars far too long. It was time for her to leave the ship with the others.

"That would be lovely, thank you." She accepted Breckinridge's arm. "Good night, Lord Martin."

He bowed at the waist. "And to you, Mrs. Wheaton."

He made no more mention of his invitation to go sailing, and Evelyn breathed a sigh of relief, for she did not want the others to know, nor did she wish to continue resisting his plea, because he surely would have pressed until she had said yes, for it was not in his nature to back down from a challenge.

"And do you enjoy croquet, Mrs. Wheaton?" Lord Breckinridge asked as he escorted Evelyn along the waterfront toward the Esplanade.

Lord and Lady Radley were strolling in front of them barely talking, gazing off in opposite directions, while Martin was walking with his first mate, Lord Spencer, and some other ladies at a distance behind them.

"Yes, I do. Very much." She made an effort to sound enthusiastic.

"Well, if you would be willing to join me in a game this week, I have a very fine set of balls."

Good Lord! Did he just say what she thought he said?

"They were a gift from the Queen herself," he added, his cheeks coloring sharply.

Evelyn let a chuckle slip out, then covered her mouth with a hand, but it was no use. She couldn't keep the laughter in.

Lord Breckinridge stopped on the walk and frowned down at her. "Mrs. Wheaton, perhaps I should escort you back to your hotel. I fear there might have been too much champagne at the ball this evening."

"No." She laughed, still trying to fight it. "Truly, I'm fine."

But this was not like her at all! She was usually so very composed.

"I believe you will thank me for it tomorrow, as it will prevent you from further embarrassing yourself." His shoulders were stiff and his voice low with annoyance.

He turned and attempted to lead her in that direction, but she did not follow because his reproachful manner was grating upon her happy mood, especially after her most refreshing encounter with Martin, who always seemed to be looking for a reason to laugh and whose desire to have a good time was surely becoming contagious. He certainly would have laughed if he'd been here to learn about Breckinridge's fine balls.

"If you don't mind," she firmly said, "I would like to continue walking, as it's a lovely evening. But if you would like to retire, I would be more than happy to join your aunt and uncle."

She did not mean to sound rude. She simply did not wish to be escorted away in this manner.

He glanced back at Martin and Spence surrounded by pretty ladies, then pasted on a courteous smile. "That won't be necessary, Mrs. Wheaton. Of course I will continue walking with you."

She, too, pasted on a smile and did her best to be polite while they strolled in silence for a short time, passing in front of the Royal Yacht Squadron until they reached the Umbrella Tree.

Lord Breckinridge stopped. "Would you like to rest a moment?"

"That would be very nice, thank you."

They walked to the benches and sat down. "What a lovely night," he said.

"Indeed it is," she replied.

They sat in awkward silence, watching a constant stream of ladies and gentlemen strolling along the Esplanade, talking and laughing. Evelyn squeezed her hands together and shifted uneasily on the bench, realizing that this was not a new sensation—this stiff discomfort. She had often felt this way with her husband, especially before they were married. During their brief engagement, they had taken many quiet walks just like this one and said very little to each other.

"I heard the most interesting story tonight," she said, attempting to fill the empty silence and perhaps start again with Lord Breckinridge. "It seems that Baron Freemont discovered some old Viking tools on his estate. One of his dogs was digging in the dirt beyond his garden and—"

"I have a dog of my own," Lord Breckinridge said. "He's a filthy beast sometimes, but he belonged to my father, and my mother refuses to part with him. He barks incessantly when it rains."

Lord Breckinridge went on to describe the amount of rain that fell each year on his estate, and how it was the perfect amount for the fields, and he had very little trouble with drainage.

It was not long before Evelyn realized that the earl had very little interest in her as a person. He asked her no questions about herself, and when she offered anything, he interrupted with a piece of information about his own interests or accomplishments. He was here with her because his uncle had encouraged him to be, which was all about her inheritance, of course. It was why he was trying to impress her. There was no other reason. He was tolerating these moments with her at best, just as she was tolerating them with him.

She looked down at the water and saw Lord Martin and his first mate on the beach. Lord Spencer was carrying a young lady over his shoulder like a sack of potatoes to the water's edge, and she was kicking and screaming. They were all laughing, and Evelyn wished with all her heart that she were down there on the beach with them instead of sitting here on the bench under the Umbrella Tree with her back stiff as a board and her gloved hands folded primly on her lap.

Lord Spencer set the screeching lady down and began chasing Martin. Still dressed in his evening formalwear, Martin escaped into the water and dove in headfirst with a resounding splash.

Evelyn gasped and covered her mouth with a hand, as Lord Spencer dove in behind Martin. Within seconds, they were both laughing and splashing each other, while the others on the beach were howling with glee.

"*Disgraceful*," Breckinridge said, standing up and offering Evelyn his arm. "Please allow me to escort you back to your hotel and spare you this embarrassment."

Still watching in disbelief, she feigned the disapproval he expected of her. "Disgraceful indeed."

She allowed Lord Breckinridge to escort her back—not because she was horrified, however, but because she couldn't bear the wistful longing that squeezed at her heart while she was forced to sit with a stiff, overformal earl and pretend to disapprove of the others, who were frolicking without restraint down on the beach.

What would it take to no longer feel like an outsider to joy like that? she wondered with a sigh as she strolled politely across the grass on Lord Breckinridge's arm. Nothing more than an invitation from a scoundrel, she supposed, which she'd already received, hadn't she?

They stepped onto the paved walk and started back to the hotel in silence, while Evelyn reconsidered that invitation and wondered with great impetuosity when the opportunity to accept would arise.

A short time later, Martin stood in the corridor outside his door, digging into his trouser pocket for his key and dripping water everywhere. He had left the beach almost immediately after seeing Evelyn leave the Esplanade with Breckinridge because the thought of her with the earl—when he himself wanted another opportunity to talk and flirt with her—had taken all the joy out of the evening.

He glanced over his shoulder and listened for a sound from inside her room. Was she there? Or was she still with Breckinridge?

Just then, her door creaked open, and Martin exhaled with a smile. He waited a few seconds, then turned around and spread his arms wide,

attempting to explain the palpable smell of sea-
weed in the hall.

"I tripped."

She folded her arms over her delightfully
ample bosom and leaned a shoulder against the
doorjamb, looking disapproving under those
thick spectacles, which he found absolutely adorable. Here was the woman who never failed to
challenge him, and seemed to enjoy it, too.

"You most certainly did not," she replied. "I
was watching you the entire time."

His mood suddenly buoyant, he sauntered
across the hall, closing the distance between them
until he stood only a few inches away from her.
"Were you indeed?"

He removed his bow tie and wrung it out in
front of her. She looked down at the water dripping on the floor, stared at it aghast, then looked
up at him again with the reproachful expression
that he sensed was becoming a recurring joke
between them.

"Are you going to get me in trouble for that?"
he asked with a grin.

"I should," she replied, but with a hint of playful rebellion in her eyes that surprised him in
some ways, but not in others. "I should call the
hotel authorities right this instant," she added.

He took another step closer until his lips almost touched her pretty nose. "But you're not
going to, are you?" He felt her suck in a breath.

"I haven't decided yet."

Her blasé tone was a most commendable effort, he thought. She deserved a prize.

"And what can I do to convince you to let me get away with it?" he asked.

She inclined her head and raised an eyebrow. "It's salt water, you know. It's going to leave a mark."

His voice was low, casual, suggestive. "Maybe we can get down on our hands and knees and scrub it clean together."

Her lips parted slightly with alarm, but then she located her cool, composed façade, and scoffed. "I'm not getting anywhere near the floor with *you*," she said.

Martin wanted to laugh and applaud her recovery, but he resisted the urge because he understood moments like these and knew they required a rather delicate finesse.

"What are we going to do then?" he asked. "Perhaps there's a way I can bribe you to keep quiet?"

With any other woman, he would have touched her cheek at that point and slowly backed her into her room, but she was not any other woman. She was allegedly impossible to flirt with, Sir Lyndon had said.

Martin was quite sure he had already proven that claim grossly inaccurate. And after speaking with her on the ship tonight, he was beginning to see the inaccuracy of many other things as well—

his own previous impressions of her included. She was not a cold fish. She was simply repressed, with her lid on too tight, and in great danger of boiling over.

He wondered why. Did she not *want* joy? Did she think it wrong?

"Perhaps there is something," she replied.

He drew his head back in surprise. "You don't say."

"I do. I've been thinking about our conversation earlier, and I've changed my mind. I would in fact like to try sailing. I would like to see what all the to-do is about."

Martin swallowed, attempting to hide his astonishment. "Well," he said matter-of-factly, "there certainly is a great deal of *to-do*, but let me make sure I understand this correctly. You want *me* to take you?"

She cleared her throat and dropped her hands to her sides, and he could see she was almost afraid to be asking. He knew better than to tease her with it, however, because he had a feeling she might bolt back into her room and change her mind again if he did. Or God forbid, ask Breckinridge to take her. So he waited quietly for an answer, taking it all very seriously.

Finally, she nodded.

He grinned in response. "I think something can be arranged."

"And can I trust you to bring me back safely?" she asked, sounding rather uncertain.

He experienced a momentary rush of guilt, knowing he was going to answer in the affirmative when he knew all too well that contrary to his confidence at the helm of a sailing vessel, sometimes a man was powerless to keep people safe.

He kept that notion to himself, however, and spoke with an outward show of confidence—because he *would* bring her back safely. He would.

"Absolutely."

She wet her lips, still seeming unsure. "I don't wish my reputation to be compromised."

"I understand that," he said, "but rest assured, I can be most discreet. No one will even know we are gone."

She bit her lower lip. "That's not exactly what I had in mind. I was thinking that perhaps you could invite a few others. Lord and Lady Radley for instance?"

She was looking far too hopeful. "That would make it all very proper, wouldn't it?" he asked.

"Yes, it would."

He tapped a finger on his chin, pondering the suggestion. "Let me see. Inviting others on your first sea voyage. Um, *no*."

"No! You expect me to go alone with you?"

"Yes."

"On a yacht? Just the two of us? You've lost your mind."

With that, she backed up and shut the door in his face.

Martin tried not to laugh, and remained where he was standing, because somehow he knew she would be back.

Sure enough, a minute later, she opened her door and peeked out. When she discovered him still standing exactly where she'd left him, she jumped, apparently startled.

"What are you doing, still standing in my doorway?"

"What are you doing peeking out at me?"

Rolling her eyes in frustration, she opened the door all the way and folded her arms again over that gorgeous bosom.

"I thought you'd be gone," she said.

"I'm not."

"I can see that."

They both stood facing each other, until Martin ran a hand over his wet hair. "Look, I'm soaking wet, and I'm getting a chill. I've got to take these clothes off." He shrugged out of his wet jacket and waistcoat, right there in the hall.

Her eyes widened in shock. He had to admit, he did enjoy shocking her prudish sensibilities. Hell, it was time *somebody* shook the apples off her tree.

"So are we going sailing tomorrow or not?" he asked directly.

"Tomorrow?" she replied, sounding as if she might still change her mind.

"Yes. Seven o'clock sharp." He turned to let himself into his own room across the hall and turned the key. "I'll have the launch waiting for you at the pavilion at the far end of the Green. There won't be anyone out that early in the day. Wear something warm and don't be late." He pushed his door open.

"I didn't say yes," she blurted out.

He entered his room, then stuck his head out. "No, but you wanted to, so I said it for you. See you at seven."

Without a second's hesitation, he shut his door and listened.

She remained in her doorway for a moment or two, obviously waiting to see if he would peek out at her as she had done, but he wasn't about to do anything so foolish. He didn't wish to give her another opportunity to say no.

He continued to listen for a few more minutes until at last her door clicked shut. Then he chuckled, stripped off his shirt, and rang for some hot water.

Chapter 9

The next morning at 7:00 A.M. sharp, wearing a navy-and-white-striped yachting dress with a white sailor's hat and a three-quarter coat, Evelyn left the hotel alone and crossed the parade. A cold, wet fog loomed over the Solent, and she felt the mist on her cheeks.

She walked quickly along the waterfront, ignoring the sensible part of her brain, which was telling her to turn around and go back to her room because this was utterly inappropriate. It was something her impulsive friend Penelope would do. But she did not turn around, because she wanted this adventure. For once in her life, she wanted to be carefree like Martin had been on the beach the night before. She wanted to learn to be like those women and laugh out loud, not caring what others thought about it—others like Lord Breckinridge. All night long, she had not been able to get Martin's words out of her head. *Don't you ever want to try new things? To explore and feel truly alive?*

Yes, she did. She was tired of being the proper, reserved, unsmiling widow. She had been alone with her quiet, humorless life for too long. She wanted a home filled with laughter and conversation. It was time she learned to behave that way herself.

Arriving at the pavilion, she slowed her pace. Martin was there as promised, standing on the beach at the water's edge, wearing a foul-weather jacket and looking outward. The fog was thick all around him.

She watched him for a moment. He seemed distracted, or perhaps entranced by the water, then he turned.

Their eyes met, and she sucked in a breath. He looked rugged and dangerous, with his coat open in front and a sheath knife in his belt. He looked nothing like the son of a duke. He looked more like a dangerous gunslinger out of one of those popular American novels.

But then he smiled and waved, and started up the beach to greet her, and he became his charming, aristocratic self again. She stepped off the walk and onto the shifting pebbles to meet him halfway.

"I knew you would come," he said with a smile. "But don't change your mind now."

"What makes you think I would change my mind?" she asked, walking beside him to the small rowboat at the water's edge.

He simply raised an eyebrow and gave her a knowing look, as if he'd heard every word of the noisy debate that had taken place in her mind on the way here. She gave a resigned sigh.

When they reached the boat, he offered his hand. "Madam?"

Evelyn accepted his assistance, and felt the rough calluses on his hand, even through her gloves. They were not the hands of an idle gentleman. These were the hands of a champion yachtsman.

She stepped in and seated herself on the bench near the transom. Martin pushed the boat over the pebbles and hopped in at the last second before it began to float. It rocked precariously for a few seconds until he settled himself on the bench facing her.

"It's not far," he said, picking up the oars and turning them around.

All of this was like a strange dream, she thought, watching him row them into the dense fog. She could barely believe she was here, sitting in a rowboat with Martin Langdon, about to spend the day alone with him. She would never have believed it if someone had described this moment to her ten years ago.

"Here we are," he said, slowing them down and bringing the launch up next to the yacht at the stern. He secured the oars and tied the launch to the mooring, then reached for a sack, which he tossed up onto the boat.

Evelyn was becoming increasingly uneasy, because she had no idea how she was going to get herself out of the launch and onto the bigger boat, as there was no gangplank. "This looks challenging," she said.

"I'll show you what to do." He grabbed hold of a brass rail, raised a foot over the back beam, and hoisted himself up and over. He disappeared for a few seconds, then returned and fastened a rope ladder over the side. "It's a bit of a stretch, but you'll be fine. Take my hand."

Evelyn stood, and the little boat rocked and bobbed up and down. Her instincts told her to keep low.

"That's it," Martin said. "Now put a foot right here and hold on to this, then step up and over." He hauled her up and in a flash she was standing on deck with her gloved hands upon his shoulders, his huge *un*gloved hands wrapped tightly around her waist. "That wasn't so difficult, was it?" His deep blue eyes glimmered.

Unsettled by his nearness and the excitement

she felt at his touch, she took a hasty step back. "No, it was much easier than it looked."

He eyed her intently, then turned. "Allow me to show you around. This is the cockpit, and up front is the foredeck."

Everything was bird's-eye maple, gleaming with new varnish. The tall mast was wood as well. She followed him to a small hatch, which he unlocked and opened, then climbed down a companionway to the cabin below.

Evelyn paused up on the deck, looking down at him. "Perhaps I shouldn't," she said hesitantly, seeing that it was a cozy-looking cabin with a small galley area on one side and a cushioned bench along the other.

He inclined his head at her. "You can't stay up there all day. You're going to need to get out of the wind eventually, and I promised to be a gentleman, remember?"

When she still made no move, he held out his hand again. His expression became serious, as did the tone of his voice. "Don't worry, Evelyn, you can trust me. I won't ravish you. Unless, of course, you want me to."

He should not have made such a wicked remark, nor should he have used her given name, but much to her surprise, she didn't dissolve into pieces from either impropriety. She did as he asked and climbed down the companionway.

"This is where we prepare our meals," he explained, gesturing to the galley. "And we eat over here." He lowered a table that was fastened to the bulkhead. "Two men can sleep here as well, but these are the preferred accommodations—the master's quarters."

He led her to the private V-berth at the front of the boat—a small, enclosed space with a mattress and bedding, large enough for at least two people. She imagined what it would be like to sleep there, so hidden away from the world.

"It looks very comfortable," she said.

"It is, and quiet, too, when you're anchored at night. Would you like some coffee?"

She paused. "Shouldn't we get going?"

"It's too foggy at the moment, and there's no wind. Things should improve in an hour or so, if you don't mind waiting." His blue eyes were friendly and open, and she slowly managed to relax her reservations.

"In that case, coffee would be very nice."

He went to light the stove. While he started the coffee, Evelyn wandered around the cabin and paused to look at a photograph tacked to the bulkhead over the table—of Martin and his crew holding the Cowes Cup.

"Was this taken last year?" she asked.

He turned from the coffeepot. "That was two years ago. We are definitely in need of a more recent photograph."

"Then you'll just have to win the race again at

the end of the week." She studied his exuberant smile in the picture.

Martin left the coffee to brew. "That is my ambition of course, but you must have heard the predictions about Lord Breckinridge's boat, the *Endeavor*."

"I've heard *him* say it's fast," she replied.

He sat down at the table and gestured for her to join him. She took the seat opposite.

"I've seen the boat for myself," he explained. "She is indeed a winner."

"Are you worried? *You*? The famous, unflappable champion?"

He narrowed his gaze at her but maintained a mischievous smirk. There was always playfulness in his eyes, she had discovered.

"Are you making fun of me, Mrs. Wheaton? I'll have you know, sailing is serious business." He leaned forward over the table. "Perhaps you'll change your opinion at the end of the day, after you've experienced it for yourself."

Evelyn had to give in, because what did she know about sailing after all? "Perhaps I will."

He seemed pleased she didn't argue the point, then leaned back again and rested an arm along the back of the cushioned bench. "So tell me," he said with a faintly inquisitive look in his eyes, "what have you been doing since that day I saw you at the train station ten years ago, when you told me I needed to put myself on the straight and narrow?"

She was surprised he could so quickly retrieve the exact number of years since they'd last seen each other, and remember something so specific about what she'd said. "I was married, as you must know."

"Only for a brief time, I understand."

"Three months."

His voice bore genuine compassion. "I'm sorry for your loss."

She wet her lips. "Thank you."

"It must have been especially difficult so early in your marriage when you were barely out of your honeymoon."

She squeezed her reticule on her lap. "The vicar and I didn't take a honeymoon."

"No? Nevertheless, whether you traveled or not, the first few months of marriage are usually . . . How shall I put it? *Exciting,* in some form or another. It's a new life after all."

Evelyn shifted uncomfortably, wondering if he was referring to something more specific than just the "new life" that marriage represented. She suspected he was, and felt an uncomfortable heat rush to her cheeks, for it was not something she wished to speak about. That aspect of her marriage had been very awkward.

"It was a different life," she replied, struggling

to sound at ease when she was the furthest thing from it. "But looking back on it, the marriage was so brief, sometimes it feels as if it never happened. There were no children, and it was just a brief flash of time really, gone forever now. All I can do at this point is move forward and try to start again."

He lowered his gaze, and when he lifted it, his eyes were somber. The expression surprised her. It was different from what she was accustomed to seeing and made her think of what Lady Radley had said about him the night before, about something dark and mysterious boiling beneath his surface. There was so much she did not know about him, she realized.

Suddenly he tapped a finger on the table, seeming anxious to change the subject. "So go ahead," he said, "ask me a question about sailing. It's what we're here for after all."

"All right," she replied, struggling to get her mind around a new topic. "Do you sail the *Orpheus* year-round? Even in the winter?"

The light in his eyes returned. "I take her out of the water for the colder months, and it's always a joy to sail her again for the first time in the spring."

The coffeepot was gurgling, so he rose and set two tin cups on the stove. "How do you like your coffee?" he asked.

"Black, please."

He poured both cups and brought them to the table. "When did you learn to sail?" she asked, after he sat down again.

"I took it up after I returned from America. My brother was—"

"You went to America?"

Her question silenced him. He sat motionless for a moment, then flexed his hand around the cup and continued speaking. "I spent four years there, and upon my return my brother was eager to see me do something that would engage me. He commissioned my first yacht not long after I got back." He sipped the coffee and set down his cup. "Speaking of which, do you feel that?"

She set her cup down as well. "Feel what?"

"Movement. There's a breeze."

Indeed, she felt it, too—a gentle undulation—though it was so faint she was amazed he had noticed.

"Is there enough wind for us to sail?" she asked.

"Let's have a look."

He carried his coffee cup to the companionway, then hoisted himself up onto the third step to look outside. "The fog is moving out. We can at least get started, though we won't set any records." He downed the rest of his coffee in a few gulps and descended with swift, eager steps. "You can wait here if you like, while I get us away from the mooring, but I would prefer to have your assistance."

"Assistance?"

"I'll need you to hold the wheel steady for me once or twice."

That didn't sound too difficult, so Evelyn agreed and finished the last of her coffee. He locked the cups away, then led her up on deck and gestured to the bench near the wheel.

"Take a seat right there," he said.

She did as he asked, and he immediately set to work moving around the boat, rigging the mainsail and jib. She enjoyed watching him work, admiring the swift grace of his hands as he tied knots and fed lines through blocks and cleats.

He moved past or around her a number of times as he went from one end of the boat to the other, and she leaned forward or back to stay out of his way.

"There's a good breeze now," he said, hopping down onto the deck directly in front of her. He bent to pass under the boom and stepped up onto the foredeck on the other side. He set about hoisting the mainsail, doing everything very quickly.

A few minutes later, they were free of the mooring, and he was standing at the wheel, glancing up at the sails and down at the water. As soon as they were under way, he reached for Evelyn's hand and pulled her deftly to her feet.

"I'll need you to take the wheel now," he said.

"Just for a minute while I raise the jib." He slid his hand around her waist and guided her to stand in front of him.

"I don't really know what to do," she told him.

"You don't have to do anything. Just hold it steady right here."

His large, warm hands wrapped around hers and he showed her where to grip the spokes. She could feel his firm chest against her back, and the contact upset her balance. She adjusted her stance while she fought to suppress the feverish excitement in her belly.

His lips brushed against her ear, and she felt the moist heat of his breath when he spoke. "That's it," he said. "You might feel it tugging, but don't let it turn. Keep it in this position."

She held it firmly and tried to keep her breathing under control. When he seemed sure she was comfortable, he let go. "I'll just be a moment."

Though she did not feel altogether confident, she nodded and watched him go to the forward sail. Again, he moved quickly and skillfully, his body straining as he pulled on the ropes to hoist it. Before she knew it, he was hopping down into the cockpit again and sliding up next to her, taking over the wheel. His nearness caused the passionate fluttering in her belly to return.

"Well done," he said.

The boat picked up speed, and she felt the

chilly wind on her cheeks. "There's quite a strong wind now, isn't there?" She reached up to hold onto her hat.

He looked up at the mainsail. "Not exactly. It just feels that way because we're sailing upwind. On our return, we'll have the wind at our backs, and it will seem almost completely calm."

Still holding on to her hat, she looked up at the mast. Both sails were pulled tight. "I've always wondered how it's possible to move forward when you're sailing *into* the wind."

"We never point directly into it," he explained. "If you look at the direction of the waves and feel the wind on your face, you'll see that we are sailing at an angle toward it, and with the sails trimmed just right, we'll get where we want to go."

"And where is that, exactly?" She supposed she should have asked that question before she agreed to sail with him today.

"I plan to take you around The Needles."

"The Needles. What in the world . . . ?"

There was laughter in his eyes. "Be patient. All in good time."

Evelyn tried to relax and not worry about things. She settled in but felt some apprehension when she looked at the boom. "Is there any danger that will swing across and knock us into the water?"

"Not unexpectedly. At least not while *I'm* at the helm."

She continued to watch it, to see if it would move. "But what if you leave me here again to do something to a sail, and I'm the one steering?"

He considered that a moment. "Good God, I hadn't thought of that. In that case, if I yell duck, hit the deck as fast as you can."

"What?"

He started to laugh. "I'm joking, Evelyn. You need to *relax*. That's why we're here, isn't it?"

She raised her chin and faced the wind directly. "We're here because I've never been sailing before, and I wished to try it."

He chuckled softly. "I think there are a lot of things you've never done before and wish to try."

Her eyes widened. "I have no idea what you could possibly be referring to, Lord Martin. In fact, I don't think I *want* to know."

"Oh, but I think you do." He was still chuckling, leaning toward her, gazing at her with a teasing light in his eyes.

More than a little unsettled, she found herself retreating behind her familiar stone wall of dignified reserve, even though she knew he only found it amusing and would take great pleasure in finding a way around it.

"You are a scoundrel, sir, for I have given you no cause to think such a thing, much less speak of it."

He faced forward again, standing tall before the wheel. "But you have, Mrs. Wheaton. Or

Evelyn . . . May I call you that? You see, you've agreed to go sailing alone with a notorious rake— who you once saw with your very own eyes naked in bed with a laundry maid—when Lord Breck-inridge could just as easily have taken you sail-ing today. Unlike me, he would have agreed to bring his aunt and uncle, and it all would have been perfectly respectable."

She didn't know what to say to such scandalous allegations because they were all true.

"But you're not allowed to worry about respect-ability today," he continued. "Not here on the wa-ter, because this is the place where all restrictions disappear, and the only thing worth worrying about is which way the wind is blowing. Those are the rules of my boat, madam. There is no past. The future isn't upon us yet, so we need only concern ourselves with the present. You can say anything you wish to say, or do anything you wish to do. You have my permission to be completely free."

She wondered if he said that to every woman he brought on board.

"I don't need your *permission* to be free," she told him, but she sounded defensive, even to her own ears.

He nodded with an air of respect, although she knew he was just being polite. "Right then—we know what we're about. So let's head out to open water. Take the wheel if you please."

He stepped back and waited for her to take

hold. When she had a good grip, he leaped grace-fully onto the foredeck and made his way past the windward shrouds.

"Brace yourself, Evelyn!" he called out with a smile, holding on to a line while the wind blew his thick hair in all directions. "It's time to gain some speed!"

Chapter 10

Evelyn sat on the bench beside Martin, trusting him to see them safely down the Solent as they left Cowes behind and sailed toward deeper waters. Gulls circled overhead, occasionally diving to catch a fish. The morning sky was still white with low-hanging clouds, though it had brightened, and the fog was blowing out to sea.

"Would you like to hold the wheel again?" Martin asked.

"Do you need me to?"

"No, but I promised to teach you a thing or two, didn't I? So why don't you come here."

She wet her lips, dry from the wind in her face, and stood up. She was learning very quickly how to move on the boat, always in motion, pitching and rolling. She had to take great care in getting from one place to another.

When she reached Martin, he stepped back and let her take hold. Again, he stood behind her and wrapped his hands around hers. She inhaled sharply at the sensation of his rough, stubbled jaw against her cheek.

"Let's turn it slightly," he said, "and see what happens to the sails."

She felt the pull of his strong hands around hers and looked up as the boat shifted direction. The canvas snapped tight and wrinkled slightly.

"Is this better?" she asked, fighting to remain focused on the boat and the sails, when she was completely distracted by the nearness of his hard, lean body behind her.

Again, he dipped his head to speak close to her ear, and she closed her eyes for a moment, reveling in the timbre of his deep, masculine voice. "Not really, but do you see how the sails have to be trimmed to suit the direction of the boat? Watch what happens if we do this."

He turned the wheel farther over still, and the sails flapped noisily for a moment before he turned it back.

Evelyn continued to hold the wheel, recognizing the sensation of being in control of the rudder, while Martin explained how the direction of the wind was key, and how all the elements worked together to affect speed.

"It's physics," she said, becoming fascinated by the complexity of the air and water flow working together, and comprehending how the shape of the hull and sails and the size of the keel all played an important part in the boat's movement.

For the next hour, he taught her about the science of it all, and though he let her steer the boat by herself, he always remained close by at her side, except for when he had to adjust the lines, which he did so quickly and ably when they tacked.

"You certainly know what you're doing," she said to him later that morning, as the boat heeled to starboard.

"I like to think so."

She remembered what Lord Breckinridge had said about Martin the day before, and what she herself had thought when she'd watched him sail into Cowes.

"I believe some people might underestimate your skills," she said. "Lord Breckinridge in particular."

Martin's eyes gleamed with interest, as if this were information that could help him win or lose the race. "What makes you say that?"

"Well . . ." she replied somewhat reluctantly, "his first mate on the *Endeavor* went to school with you at Eton and remembers your reputation for being wild and reckless, and because of that, I believe he assumes you will make rash decisions."

"Who is his first mate?" Martin asked.

"A gentleman by the name of Sheldon Hatfield."

Martin looked out to sea, nodding. "Ah yes, he would certainly think me reckless, among other things."

"Why?" Evelyn had the distinct feeling there was something scandalous behind this. But with Martin, there was *always* something scandalous in the milieu.

"I once took a lady friend of his riding and gave her a spirited horse. She was screaming the entire time."

"And you found that amusing?" Evelyn asked, raising an eyebrow.

He smiled. "Of course. But then she needed to be rescued, and I had to take charge. It was quite a daring rescue, if I do say so myself. Not to put too fine a point on it, but Hatfield dislikes me so much *because* of the rescue. He was rather smitten with the young lady in question, you see."

"And you seduced her," Evelyn said knowingly.

"I wouldn't say 'seduced,' but she did entertain a bit of a crush afterward. I had to avoid her for weeks."

She took in a deep breath and exhaled slowly. "As I'm sure you had to avoid *many* young ladies. I can think of one in particular."

"Your friend. What was her name?"

"Penelope Steeves! I cannot believe you! How can you not even remember?"

There was humor in his eyes as he shrugged. "She was very pretty, wasn't she? Blond hair?"

"Weren't they all pretty and blond?" she replied with mocking derision.

Martin chuckled. "So tell me, why didn't Miss Steeves join you this week? Are you no longer friends?"

"Of course we are still friends," she replied. "But she is Mrs. Richardson now, and her husband passed away this year. She is in mourning, as I have been until recently."

"I'm sorry to hear that."

He faced the wind, and they sailed on. He seemed lost in thought for a long time, until his tone changed and he returned to the topic of their earlier conversation. "Regardless of what Hatfield thinks of me," he said, "let me assure you, Evelyn— a reckless man cannot skipper a boat, at least not effectively. The strictest discipline is required, and one can never let down his guard or take too lightly the power of the sea, except at his own peril. Even at anchor, you are susceptible to the tides and currents."

She pondered that. "So the idea is never to feel completely comfortable? Or too much at ease?"

He squinted into the wind while she waited for

him to answer. He did not look at her when he replied. "That's right."

"Is that what happened when you wrecked your first two boats?" she asked. "You were too confident?"

A flash of surprise crossed his features. "You know about that?"

"Many people do. I heard it from Lord Radley."

His eyes became stony with a hint of contempt. It reminded her of that day at the train station, when she'd seen a side of him that was very different from the persona that made him famous.

"That's no one's business," he said.

"My apologies," she replied, surprised by the sudden change in his mood and not sure what had caused it. "I didn't know."

He shook his head dismissively. "It's fine. Things were different then."

She recalled what he'd told her earlier—that his brother had commissioned those boats just after he'd returned from America. Had something happened to him when he was abroad?

At that moment, he walked to the port side and leaned out to look carefully at the jib. Before she could ask him anything more, he told her to keep the wheel steady and left the cockpit. He walked along the side rail to the bow and checked every block and cleat.

She watched his face, saw how focused he was on what he was doing, and wondered if any of it was necessary. The sails looked fine to her. But she was no expert sailor, she realized.

He lingered up front for a long while, hanging on to the forestay and looking straight ahead over the water. Later, when he returned, she waited a moment before she spoke. "So is that what you love about sailing?" she asked. "It keeps your mind busy and occupied?"

He still seemed distracted as he tipped his head up to inspect the mainsail. "I guess that's part of it. I like to get everything working just so in order to get the most out of the boat, and I can't rest until she's moving as fast as she can."

Evelyn turned the wheel slightly. *"And you tell me I'm the one who needs to relax?"*

His gaze darted to her profile, then he laughed and shook his head. "I did say we were similar creatures, didn't I? We have that in common, I suppose—we both need some slack in our lines."

"Speak for yourself!" she replied, feigning great umbrage. "I like my lines pulled very tight, sir, because with my inconceivable beauty, I have to do *something* to keep the wicked rakes like you at a safe distance."

He stared at her, dumbfounded, then they both gave in to their laughter. She wondered how it was possible they could be having this conversation. Who knew *she* could be amusing?

"You're quite a woman, Evelyn." Then he wagged a warning finger at her. "It's a good thing

I didn't know you better back at Eton, or you would have been in considerable trouble."

Her heart jolted at the compliment, for it was so very gratifying to hear him say such a thing after all those years when she believed he thought her dull and unattractive. Especially when he was not playing the part of the charmer right now. He seemed very genuine. She steered the boat with a smile.

"You know," she said, "I think you were right earlier. There is something about being on a sailboat that makes you feel different. I don't feel like my usual self."

His voice became husky and low, sensual, but not at all presumptuous. "And does it feel good, Evelyn?"

Just the sound of her name on his lips was astoundingly erotic in her ears. "Yes, I believe it does."

"Then maybe you should be this *different* self more often."

Desire burned through her as she recognized the flirtation between them. Meaningless to him, perhaps—a man who seduced women casually and on a regular basis—but not to her. Never to her. Not with him . . .

But with that thought, came an almost stabbing sense of alarm. She turned her face away. She could not let herself imagine that this was something deep or meaningful. She had to remember that in his mind this was simply another day of sailing, and she was just another amusing female conquest. She could not let herself feel anything too deeply, or give in to any improbable hopes, because he was not like her. He was a different sort of person. He lived for the moment and felt nothing too deeply.

Later, she sat on the high side of the boat with her back against the center skylights while the *Orpheus* sang through the choppy waters, leaving a wild, churning wake off the stern. The sky was blue now, and the sun was shining brightly.

"We're almost to the point!" Martin called out. "Turn around! Look port side!"

She swiveled on her bottom and raised a hand to hold on to her hat, seeing for herself the breathtaking vista before them. Chalky white cliffs towered over the sea, and at the northwestern tip of the island, a straight line of jagged outcroppings rose up from the water. A red-and-white lighthouse clung to the farthest rock.

"They look like icebergs, all in a line!" she shouted.

They rounded the lighthouse and cliffs, where foamy surf pounded against the rocks.

"It's spectacular!" Evelyn stood and held on to a line with one hand while she held her hat with the other. Her skirts were whipping wildly around her legs as they came about. She'd never seen a sight like this in all her life.

Martin held the wheel, smiling in accord.

Once they'd rounded the sharp tip of the island, Evelyn made her way back to the cockpit. "What will we do now? Will we turn around?"

She felt a small flickering of disappointment deep in her core suddenly, because she did not want this to end. A part of her wished she could continue sailing with Martin forever.

"Are you hungry?" he asked, his gaze roving from her eyes to her lips, lingering there for a few seconds before darting back up again.

She wished—as she so often did—that she were prettier.

"I'm becoming so," she replied. Then she pushed her spectacles up the bridge of her nose.

He stared at her for a moment, seeming almost captivated by her eyes, and she thought she must be dreaming. He was not captivated. He could not be. Not with her . . .

Then he said, "Hold this."

She took the wheel.

He slowly moved closer, and she thought he was going to take her face in his hands and kiss her. *God in heaven, would he?* Was it possible he could want to? A fiery thrill shot up her spine at the thought of it.

His hands came around to her ears and he grasped her spectacles by the wires and removed them from her face. Without them, she felt open and exposed.

He smiled reassuringly then looked down at them. "I don't know how you can see through these, Evelyn."

He reached into his jacket pocket for a handkerchief, puffed on the lenses, then proceeded to wipe them clean, for they were coated in salt.

Evelyn swallowed uncomfortably, feeling foolish for thinking he might kiss her. Of course he did not want to. What had she been thinking?

He cleaned the lenses with tiny circular motions of his thumb, held them up to the light, then wiped again. As soon as he was satisfied they were clean, he put the spectacles back on her face, carefully hooking the wires around her ears.

"Better?"

She managed a smile. "Yes. I can see you much more clearly now." Though she felt as if her newfound confidence had just plunged over the side, into the sea. He was a handsome, exciting man who loved beautiful, exciting women, and she was certainly not one. She was an interloper here today, pretending to be something she was not.

Moving to take the wheel again, he pointed just ahead. "I know a place we can dock. If you're energetic enough, we can walk to the beach and eat on the sand."

She considered telling him that she was not hungry and was ready to go home because she was suddenly not in the mood for a walk on the beach. Nor did she feel like eating.

But she did not let herself say it because she had come out for an adventure, and she was going to laugh and be cheerful like the other women she had always envied, the ones who knew how to have fun.

"That sounds fine," she replied at last, determined not to retreat into that starchy, introverted prude everyone knew her to be. She might not be capable of beauty, but she could at least pretend to be jovial.

Sheldon Hatfield—a portly man whose cheeks were puffy and bloated—stepped onto the landing stage in front of the Royal Yacht Squadron and paused a moment to breathe in the delectable scent of victory in the offing. He removed his leather gloves and tapped them on his hand, then spotted Lord Breckinridge standing on the street waiting for him with a frown.

While his valet struggled up the steps behind him with the heavy bags, Hatfield huffed at the earl's sour mood on this promising day and started up the slip toward him.

"What took you so long?" Breckinridge asked without offering a proper greeting. "You were supposed to be here yesterday."

Hatfield removed his hat and ran a hand over his balding head. "What the devil is wrong now? Has the damn boat sprung a leak already?"

Breckinridge shifted impatiently. "The *Endeavor*

is still floating. It's Lord Martin who needs to be sunk."

Hatfield's thin lips twisted into a pained grimace, which only reduced what little appeal he possessed, for he was a perpetually sluggish man and boorishly indignant.

"What's he done now?" Hatfield asked.

The valet stumbled past them, carrying the bags to the Globe Hotel, but the two gentlemen remained on the street.

"He's taken an interest in the widow. She's missing today, and so is he."

Hatfield turned and looked out at the water, searching the Solent for the *Orpheus*. "Surely they're not together. You must be mistaken."

"I make no mistake."

He faced Breckinridge again. "But he doesn't need her money. His brother the duke is richer than Croesus, and it certainly can't be her looks."

The earl spoke in a hushed tone. "You're right on that point. She has the wit and charm of a tick, so the only conclusion to be drawn is that he wants her simply because I do, as I am his greatest threat. The man's a competitor through and through. He reminds me of my godforsaken brother. It irks me to no end."

Hatfield was well aware of the earl's feelings toward his younger brother. William had always been the handsome one, the smarter one, the more charming one. Their parents had made no secret of the fact that they found it quite regrettable that George had been born first.

Hatfield and Breckinridge paused and nodded politely at a passing couple. As soon as they had gone by, Breckinridge ground words out through clenched teeth. "Damn him, Hatfield, I spent every last farthing I had on this boat to win this race, and I'm kicking myself for it now because I'm in debt up to my eyeballs and Mother is furious and wants to call William home from Europe."

"Ooh," Hatfield said.

"Precisely. Which is why we can't let Martin win the widow because I need her fortune. I need it to shut Mother up."

"There are a few American heiresses here . . ." Hatfield suggested.

"*No,*" Breckinridge firmly said. "I'll be damned if I'll marry some passionate American girl. I want an Englishwoman, and she must be proper. A mute would be nice, so she wouldn't argue about the money or nag me like you know who, but we can't have everything."

"If it's a mute you want, Mrs. Wheaton is the closest thing."

"Indeed. With that in mind, we must crush Lord Martin in the race."

Hatfield thought about Martin and all his successes, then withdrew a handkerchief from his waistcoat pocket. He wiped the greasy film off his forehead and sneered. "Don't worry, Breckinridge. Now that I'm here, everything is going to change. Rest assured, we'll crush him long before the race even begins."

"I'm listening," the earl slowly said.

Hatfield started off toward the yacht club. "Good, because I have a few ideas. Let us go and have a drink, shall we? The sun was bloody scorching during the crossing, and I'm parched."

Chapter 11

Martin steered the *Orpheus* up alongside the private dock, then hopped down and tied the lines. As soon as that was done, he returned to the boat and lowered the sails.

"You might wish to leave your coat here," he said to Evelyn as he coiled a line around his arm. "It's warmer on dry land."

"Thank you, I will," she replied with a smile.

He'd certainly seen a different side of her today, he realized with pleasure, recalling the sight of her standing on the bow of the *Orpheus*, holding on to the shrouds with the wind in her face and a look of pure delight in her eyes. She'd been a vision with those skirts flapping wildly around her legs, so different from his long-standing perception of her. And when they rounded the point, something had awakened inside him. An emotion he'd not felt in a very long time—a deep, genuine affection that reached beyond the surface thrill of the conquest. It reminded him of the feelings he'd known only once before in his life, when everything was different in America.

Feeling a sudden knot in his stomach at the inadvertent direction of his thoughts, he turned his mind to other things as he always did and hopped down into the cockpit to set back to work. He secured everything on the boat, then went below to fetch the lunch sack, returned to the deck, where Evelyn was waiting, and offered his hand. "Shall we?"

She accepted his assistance, and soon they were away from the dock and venturing along a gravel road. They reached a sandy cove where the waves lapped gently on the shore. Martin stepped over some rocks, then turned back to offer his hand to Evelyn once more. Together, they carefully picked their way down.

He found a good spot on the beach to sit, then pulled a blanket out of the bag and spread it out on the sand. He knelt to withdraw the lunch he had packed, along with a bottle of wine.

"Thank you for all this," Evelyn said, sitting back on her heels.

"It is entirely my pleasure." He uncorked the

bottle and looked straight into her eyes as he handed it to her. She hesitated before she took it.

"Did you want me to pour?" she asked uncertainly.

For a moment he wondered if he should be so bold, then decided that yes he should, because there was little to be done about the situation. "I didn't bring glasses."

Her eyes darted around at the empty bag and everything on the blanket, and there was a hint of confusion in her voice as she slowly took the bottle from him. "But how will we drink it?"

Martin made a drinking motion with his hand, then stretched out on the blanket beside her.

"Are you insane?" she asked.

He smiled. He wasn't sure why he took such pleasure in shocking her whenever the opportunity presented itself, but there it was. He couldn't help himself. "You've never drunk out of the bottle before?"

"I most certainly have not."

Leaning on an elbow, he softened his gaze. "Evelyn, I realize we are not presently on my yacht, but we are still enjoying today's voyage, so the statute still applies."

"What statute?"

"No rules. Remember?"

She stared down at the bottle. "I couldn't possibly."

"Why ever not? There's no one here to see."

She looked back at him and seemed to be turning all of this over in her mind, then at last she placed her soft, alluring lips on the bottle, squeezed her eyes shut, and tipped it up. She guzzled far more than a genteel sip, and after she was done, she wiped her mouth vulgarly.

Martin threw his head back and laughed. "That's my girl!"

She laughed, too, although she appeared to be having some difficulty recovering from what she'd just gulped down. "Lord Martin, you're a very bad influence!"

He sat up and smacked her on the back. "We'll make a drunken sailor out of you yet, Evelyn."

"You beastly man."

He sat back again, still laughing. "Indeed I am beastly, and I make no apologies."

He offered her an egg sandwich and admired the generous curve of her hip as she settled into a comfortable position on the blanket. They ate in silence for a few minutes until he reached for the wine and winked at her while he guzzled, then reclined on his side.

"So tell me, Mrs. Wheaton, is it true you've come to Cowes to find a husband?"

She finished chewing, then swallowed. "Yes, it's true. I wish to have children and a family of my own, and like you, I make no apologies."

He gazed out at the sea. "I applaud your practicality."

"You applaud it, but you would never dream of being so practical yourself."

Her tone was playful and teasing, and he was glad. The same words spoken in a different tone could take the pleasure out of the whole day.

"Indeed you've got me pegged," he said. "I have no intentions of becoming a husband. I'm quite happy with my life as it is."

"And all the women in it," she said quite daringly, surprising him yet again as she reached for a pickle and took a crunchy bite.

He gazed at her face, at her smooth, clear complexion and the adorable dimple on her chin. "Yes," he replied in a casual, relaxed voice. "Though only one woman is holding my interest today."

She narrowed her gaze at him from behind those round spectacles, as if he were a child trying to get away with stealing a cookie before dinner. "You don't really think I'm going to fall for that do you? I'm not so gullible, Lord Martin—or so easily deluded."

He sat up. "What makes you think I'm deluding you?"

"Because I know I am not a beauty, but I make no apologies for that either."

He stared at her, stunned.

"I came sailing with you today," she continued,

"to learn what it is like, not to be a part of your conquest in this race, so you might as well give up using that famous charm on me because it's not going to work."

He scoffed. "Good God, woman! Can you not take a compliment?"

"Perhaps not," she replied, but he detected a note of indecision.

That was all he needed. He leaned closer. "You should learn how to take one, my dear, because I could shower you with them if you would only say the word. And I truly wish you would."

Evelyn swallowed apprehensively, for no one had ever wished to shower her with compliments before, and she was quite frankly unwilling to believe any of it. She had to remain on guard where her passions were concerned, because if she gave in to them, God help her, she'd be done for. "I don't want, or need, your flattery, Lord Martin."

"Oh, but I believe you do. I also think you need to be kissed. Quite *thoroughly* kissed in fact."

Her head drew back in shock. Remaining on guard against her passions was one thing, but resisting his advances was quite another.

"I can assure you I need no such thing, and certainly not from a scoundrel like you."

"A scoundrel like me. Indeed."

He leaned closer and cradled her chin in his hand, and heaven help her, just the heat of his touch melted whatever resolve she had left. It kept her from retreating into that guarded fortress again—the place where she would only try to reject him before he had the chance to reject her.

He leaned closer, still, and the instant their mouths met, she felt with shock the soft, hot texture of his tongue sliding into her mouth. Her breasts rose and fell with the quickening pace of her breathing, and unfamiliar shivers of delight coursed through her body. She had never been kissed like this. Ever. She closed her eyes and could do nothing but surrender to the burning heat of it. *Was this real?* she wondered in a love-struck haze she would surely chastise herself for later. *Was Martin truly kissing her? And was she letting him? Yes, yes she was.*

She reached up to rest her hands on his broad shoulders while passion raced through her veins. She felt a throbbing sensation between her thighs from the chaos of vibrations in her body, and it sent her head spinning.

Slowly he drew back, and she opened her eyes. He was regarding her closely.

"Was that necessary?" she asked with breathless, lingering desire, knowing she wasn't fooling him for a second with that feeble attempt at hauteur. She'd just dissolved into warm putty in his hands, and he knew it.

"I believe so."

He leaned into her again, kissing her deeply a second time. She let out a whimper, a sound she'd never heard herself make before, and reached out to hold his face in her hands, to run her fingers through his beautiful thick hair. A symphony of little sighs poured out of her.

Oh, she had definitely made the right decision to come sailing today, she thought with a rapturous smile. Think of what she was learning. It was all truly sublime.

"You're delicious," he said, kissing down the side of her neck until she could barely breathe inside her tight bodice. His fingers played in the upswept hair at her nape. "You're beautiful, Evelyn. You must know it. Look at me. I want you like a schoolboy."

He wrapped his hand around the back of her head and pressed his mouth firmly to hers again, and she met the kiss eagerly with lips parted, fists gripping his lapels. She could barely comprehend the ferocity of her desires.

He eased her onto her back and rolled onto her. His gaze lifted briefly to ensure they were still alone, then he settled himself between her thighs and slid a hand down her leg. Slowly, he lifted her skirts, and her heart pounded an erratic rhythm as he slid his hand up her thigh, then across to the slit in her split drawers. He found the damp center between her legs.

She let out a gasp of both shock and delight. He stroked her with his open palm, and she became intoxicated by the hot, searing motion of his hand.

She opened her eyes and looked up at his handsome face against the blue sky, and discovered he was intently watching her expression.

"My husband never did anything like this to me," she told him, certain she had surprised him with the confession, which came completely unbidden.

"Then he didn't know how to love you properly."

He kissed her again and twirled his tongue inside her mouth, then kissed down the front of her gown to her quivering stomach.

"Oh, this is wicked," she whispered, knowing she should put a stop to it, but how could she when it was all so new and daring and exciting?

He grinned and slowly slid his finger inside her. She sucked in a breath and writhed with pleasure on the blanket, then groaned on the outstroke and licked her lips voraciously.

"It feels good," she whispered. "*Too* good."

For a moment more, she basked in the erotic splendor of what he was doing to her, but then her heart began to pound with uncertainties. She knew where this was going, but wasn't sure she could manage the emotions. She opened her eyes and stared up at him.

Martin stilled his hand. "What's wrong?"

"I think perhaps we should stop," she said.

He paused a moment, then slid his hand out from under her skirts and discreetly tugged them back down to cover her legs. "You're not enjoying it?"

"Of course I am," she replied. "I just don't want to be toyed with, Martin. I don't want to be hurt."

"I'm not toying with you," he insisted.

"Yes, you are. You do this all the time, and it's nothing to you, but it's not nothing to me. I never do this kind of thing. I'm not like your other women."

"My other women? What could you possibly know about them?"

"I know I'm different from them."

He rested a hand on her hip. "Yes, you are, and I assure you that is a compliment."

She covered her forehead with a hand and shut her eyes. "Maybe I just don't understand why you're here with me when you know that I came to Cowes looking for a husband. If you are not here looking for a wife, then it can't be my inheritance you're after, unless you're trying to trick me into thinking you don't want it."

"Trick you? That's ridiculous, Evelyn. And I'm not after your inheritance."

"Then it must be the fact that Lord Breckinridge is pursuing me. He is your rival, and you wish to triumph over him in one way or another."

"No," he firmly said, but she had seen the competition between them more than once and he seemed to know it. "Well, yes," he amended, "I do want to beat him in the race." She was relieved he was being honest about that at least. "But that has nothing to do with this. I assure you, I was not thinking of Breckinridge just now when I kissed you, and most certainly not when I was sliding my hand up your skirt."

God help her, she found the words tremendously erotic. They caused a pleasurable little quivering in her core.

"But why did you kiss me?" she asked, fighting to stay focused on the subject at hand. "Because I *needed* to be kissed? I'll have you know, I don't need your charity or pity, nor do I want to be a joke among your crew."

He got to his knees and sat back on his heels. "What are you speaking of, Evelyn? What joke?"

She pushed her spectacles up her nose. "Me. I'm the joke."

"How so?"

"You're going to tell all of them how you seduced the unseduceable. How you conquered the virtuous widow, and they'll all slap you on the back and congratulate you."

He collapsed back down and raked a hand through his hair. For a long moment, they kept their eyes locked on each other.

Martin finally spoke. "I hate to be the one to inform you, Evelyn, but you are not what you think you are. You are neither dull nor plain, and you are *completely* seduceable."

She stared at him for a few seconds, then felt the tension in her body unravel slightly. She managed a smile. "I suppose I am, aren't I?"

"Quite," he replied with a chuckle.

She laughed, too. "Perhaps there are some benefits to being a trophy between competitive men."

"Benefits for the gentleman who wins you, Evelyn, because you are a beautiful, fascinating woman, and that is no lie. What happened just now had nothing to do with my desire to win any race. I was simply mad with lust for you and couldn't keep my hands to myself. I had to have you because I found you irresistible." His expression grew curious. "Did your husband never say such things to you?"

"The vicar? Oh no."

Martin leaned forward. "Was he a fool, then? Or blind?"

She tried to explain how it was. "It was an arranged marriage, so we had no courtship. There was certainly no seduction involved. He simply came to my father one day and requested my hand, and naturally, my father agreed."

"Why do you say it like that? Why *naturally*?"

She met his eyes without flinching. "Because we were not wealthy then, and I had only a modest dowry, and my father always told me the chances of my getting married for any other reason were remote at best, because I was not the kind of woman men found desirable. So he leaped at the offer, and so did I. My mother was gone then, you see, so I was more than happy to leave his house."

Martin's eyes softened. "Your father sounds like a very . . ." He paused, as if he were struggling to find the right words. "He sounds like a very *interesting* sort of man."

She gazed out at the water and thought of all the years she had tried to earn her father's love without the slightest return of affection or encouragement. She remembered all the cruel words and the cold expressions of loathing.

"I remember trying to climb up on his lap when I was very little, and he would push me away as if I were something repulsive. Perhaps that's why I've always felt such a need to be perfectly behaved. If I couldn't be charming or beautiful, I could at least refrain from disappointing him in other ways. I could simply stay out of his sight and not draw attention to myself."

"I'm sorry, Evelyn."

"Don't be sorry for me. He was an insufferable wretch." It was not something she ever would have said before, and the words felt strange but liberating on her lips. "I understand it better now that I am older. He was unkind to me, you see, because he never wanted to marry my mother, but he *had* to, because of my accidental arrival in their lives. At least he had the decency to marry her, though he didn't change much about the way he lived after the fact. He broke my mother's heart every day. I never understood why she loved him the way she did. I suppose he was handsome, and he could wield some charm when he wanted to. Though he never wielded it around me. He only wielded malice and spite."

Martin gazed out over the sea. "Suddenly I understand everything about you, Evelyn."

She shot him a quick glare. "I didn't say it to make you understand me," she told him. "Or to seek your pity. It's just the way it was."

He simply nodded. "It might help you to know that I, too, had an insufferable wretch for a father. He came from a very long and distinguished line of peckerheads."

The anxiety she felt, talking about her father, began to fall away, and she managed a smile.

"It's true," he continued, his tone light, despite the rather dark topic of conversation. "Surely you heard the stories, that our castle was haunted and cursed, and we were all doomed to madness?"

She grinned sheepishly and hugged her knees to her chest. "I did hear something of the sort."

"Most of that was a lot of silly invention, except for the way my father was, and his father, too, I suppose. Sadly, my brother James got the worst of them, and by the time I came along, the old man wasn't around much, for which I will be eternally grateful. Though I did see the back of his hand once or twice."

Her smile faded. "I'm sorry to hear that."

He shrugged and met her gaze. "It's all in the past now. I hardly think of it."

Perhaps, she thought pensively, there was something to be said for dispensing with the past.

They continued to sit quietly in the gentle breeze, then turned at the sound of a horse on the road.

Martin got to his feet. "It's a family. They're getting out of their carriage."

Evelyn smoothed out her skirts. "They want to enjoy the beach, I suppose."

"That would by my guess."

He sat down and ran a hand through his hair, while Evelyn craned her neck to try and see them. Just then, two young children came bounding over the rocks—a little boy about three, and a sister who looked a few years older. Behind them came the parents, stepping more carefully, carrying a picnic basket and buckets. The children screeched and laughed and ran straight down to the waves to dip their feet.

Martin watched them for a long time with a melancholy look in his eye, until the boy turned and ran from a fast wave, his little feet taking him straight into his father's arms. Both parents laughed, and the boy squealed as the father lifted him into the air.

Finding the whole scene most entertaining, Evelyn smiled at Martin, but he was not looking at her. He was staring out at the sea again, looking somber and impatient. He said nothing for a long time.

"Is something wrong?" she asked. "Do you wish to go?" She felt deflated all of a sudden, and wondered if perhaps he did not enjoy children.

He turned his gaze to her as if he only just realized she was still beside him, then got to his feet.

"What in the world has come over me?" he asked, flashing his famous charm once again. "I have brought you to this beautiful beach and not shown you any of it. Come, let us take a walk and see if we can spot some swallows and warblers. Then I will sail you back to Cowes by moonlight and show you what sailing is *really* all about."

After their all-too-serious discussion, she was pleased to smile unreservedly again and equally pleased to anticipate their journey back to town. She reached up and took his hand.

A few hours later, the return trip was all he'd promised it would be. By the time they sailed away from the dock, dusk had fallen, and soon they were at sea again, with the wind at their backs and the silvery moon over their heads.

It was a relaxing run, and Martin lounged back on the bench with a wrist draped over a spoke of the wheel, one leg propped up, while Evelyn reclined on the high side of the forward deck, lying on her back with her hands folded over her belly. Stars appeared one by one, like tiny sparkling diamonds, and she watched them contentedly while listening to the creaking, softly moaning blocks and rigging.

She had not expected to feel like this on the way back—so content and at ease. She glanced back at Martin, who quietly stood up from the bench and gazed at the moon. She watched him for a long time and knew that he, too, was enchanted by the night.

Rising carefully, she made her way aft and reached him without uttering a word. He said nothing either. He only smiled at her, and they stood side by side, breathing in the fragrance of the sea and watching the moonlight on the water.

Then Martin spoke. "This afternoon, Evelyn, you told me that your husband had never touched you the way I did today. Is that true?"

She was not accustomed to such forthrightness about taboo subjects, but everything was different today. *She* was different. "Yes, it's true."

He turned toward her. She could see him clearly in the moonlight. "How, then, did he consummate the marriage?"

"He did it very quickly," she replied. "And it only happened twice."

Martin's head dipped closer, as if he weren't quite sure he'd heard her correctly. "*Twice?*"

"Yes." She swallowed uneasily.

He gazed off in the other direction. "Please tell me he at least kissed you."

She had thought about her "deflowering" many times over the past two years, and had always known it was not the experience of most women. "No, he never did. It was very uncomfortable, and he . . . he wept afterward. I heard him in the next room."

"*He* wept?"

"Yes . . ." She felt strange talking about this. "I think he believed he had sinned."

Martin shook his head and took hold of the wheel with both hands. "It shouldn't have been like that, Evelyn. You have not had good men in your life."

She inhaled deeply, breathing in the cool, salty air, not knowing what in the world to say next. Then something spilled out of her mouth before she had a chance to contemplate it. "It was disappointing . . ."

"No doubt."

". . . because I wanted to have children."

Martin looked down at her. "Sex within marriage is not just about making babies," he said. "You know that, don't you?"

Did she? She supposed she did. At least she did now.

But what did *he* really know about sex within marriage, when he made a habit of running as fast as he could from any kind of permanent attachment to a woman?

Something stopped her from questioning him

on that, however, when she recalled the look on his face on the beach earlier, when he had watched that little boy run to his father's arms. And now, because of the way he was absently stroking the wheel with his thumb.

All at once, her stomach lurched with the unexpected shock of a deeper understanding.

"How would you know about that?" she asked, but somehow she already knew the answer.

He paused for a long moment. "Because I was married once, too."

Good Lord. She thought she had known what kind of man he was—that he was not capable of committing himself to one woman—but she had been wrong. He had married someone and spoken vows before God?

"This happened when you were in America?" she asked.

"Yes, and we had a child."

A child. She felt as if she'd been knocked backward by the boom, but she had not been. They were still coasting straight ahead, and the boom had not moved.

"What happened to them?"

Did he leave them? she wondered. No . . . His blue eyes had a faraway look in them, which she recognized as the deepest, darkest kind of suffering.

"Our house burned to the ground," he told her, "while my wife and child were inside."

Evelyn could barely comprehend what she was hearing. He had been married, and he'd lost his wife and child in a fire. They had both died. She could not imagine how horrific and devastating it must have been, and how he must have suffered.

And oh, how she had misjudged him. She had treated him with disdain on so many occasions because she presumed he was reckless and shallow. She had underestimated his depth as a person. She had assumed he'd never known pain or heartbreak, but he had. He'd known the very worst kind.

"You asked about the boats I wrecked, Evelyn . . ."

"Yes?"

"The truth is, when I came back from America, my brother watched me stagger in and out of a constant drunken stupor for a full year, and that was why he commissioned them—to give me something to do, something to excel at. I didn't intend to wreck them. I was not suicidal or anything of that nature. I was just not always sober, nor was I paying complete attention, because I was thinking about my wife, Charlotte, and my son—*Owen*."

She nodded, understanding.

"But I am over that now," he said. "I no longer stagger in and out of taverns, and I won't be wrecking any more boats."

No, he would not, and she knew why—because he had chosen a new life, one where he lived for the present and never the past, where he sought pleasure to drown out pain, and by doing so, he kept himself well distracted. It was an uncomplicated, indulgent life to be sure, but she was not entirely sure it was a full one. And that night, sailing back to Cowes by moonlight, her heart broke for him in more ways she than she could count.

Chapter 12

"Where the hell were you?" Spence asked, when Martin walked into the Fountain Hotel late that night and took a seat at the bar. "I thought we were going to sail around the island today."

Martin signaled the barkeep for a tankard of ale. "I had other business to take care of."

"So you leave us here waiting around, without saying a word? I felt like a bloody idiot asking everyone at the Squadron if they'd seen you. You could have at least told us to take the day for ourselves. I would have enjoyed the sleep."

The barkeep set down a frothy tankard in front of Martin, from which he promptly took a deep swig. "I apologize. I just needed to get away."

Spence leaned closer and spoke in a hushed tone. "You weren't with that widow, were you? Because I damn well didn't see her around either."

It had been an exhausting day. Martin felt emotionally drained after the trip back when he'd confessed things he had never meant to confess, and he did not come here to be harassed. He just wanted to have a drink.

"What if I was?" he testily replied.

"Bloody hell, I can't believe you," Spence said, taking a sip of his ale and swiveling on his stool. He leaned an elbow on the bar. "I could forgive you for sailing off with one of those pretty little blondes with their parasols spinning, but what are you trying to do with Breckinridge's woman? Everyone's going to say you were just trying to steal her away in order to beat him in that *other* race because you're afraid you're going to lose the one that matters."

Martin felt his temper rising. "First of all, she is not Breckinridge's woman, and I'm not afraid of losing, because it's not going to happen."

"How do you know that?" Spence asked. "Do you forget what his boat looks like?"

Martin shook his head dismissively and took another swig of ale. "I haven't forgotten. We're going to beat him, that's all there is to it."

"As simple as that, is it? Just because you say so? Well, it would have helped if you'd been here today to take the *Orpheus* around the island. The crew could have used the practice. We need to study the winds."

"I studied them myself."

He threw his hands up. "Then I guess we're all set! *You're* all we need. *You* can do all the thinking and see everything from every angle. I don't even know why you need a crew in the first place. You're the Cowes champion all on your own."

He downed the rest of his drink and stood. Martin turned on the stool, shocked by his friend's unexpected fit of temper. "Spence, what the hell's gotten into you?"

"It's the same old thing, Martin." He tossed a few coins onto the bar and headed for the door.

Martin slid off his stool and followed his first mate out onto the narrow street. "Spence."

Spence didn't wait.

Martin caught up with him. "Stop, dammit! You have no right to pass judgment on me for taking a day to myself. All you ever do is badger me and tell me I've become obsessed with winning, that I've forgotten what real life is about, but you love the win just as much as I do. It's why you're angry with me now."

Spence finally stopped and faced Martin in the street. "So you enjoyed a taste of 'real life,' did you? You took the widow out, showed her all your impressive skills on the water, and seduced her into your cozy berth. Did you feel like the victor when all was said and done?"

Martin was stunned. He stood blinking at his friend. "It wasn't like that."

"I find that hard to believe," Spence replied, starting off again.

Martin had no choice but to follow. "I said it wasn't like that. She's different."

"Trust me, we all know she's different. You can see it as plain as day. *Plain* being the operative word."

Catching up to his first mate again, Martin grabbed him by the arm. "Honest to God, Spence, say that again, and I'll flatten you."

Spence looked down at Martin's hand on his arm and shot him a warning look. They were both breathing hard and fast. "Can't you see?" he said. "All you know how to do is find new ways to distract yourself from what's really killing you inside—which is the fact that you think you failed the two people you cared for most in the world. You obsess over anything that will make you feel like a winner, and it's changed you." He waved a hand through the air, as if to say he was giving up. "I'm sorry, I won't stand by and congratulate you while you use that woman to make yourself feel heroic, because that's what you're doing, and you know it." He turned and stalked off.

Martin did not follow this time. How could he,

when he felt as if he'd just been kicked in the chest?

The next morning, Evelyn woke up with the uncomfortable realization that all her safe, sensible thoughts and beliefs had been annihilated.

She'd had the most extraordinary time sailing with Martin the day before—the man she'd always believed had no honor even though he had once saved her life. Strangely, he seemed to be saving her still. He'd awakened her to passion, showed her that it was within reach, even for her. On top of all that, she'd discovered that he had once loved very deeply and had done the one thing she believed him incapable of—he had made a commitment to one woman for the rest of his life.

She sat up in bed, turned her eyes toward the sky outside the window, and wondered what she was going to do. She'd always been able to keep her attraction to him at bay because despite her body's desires, in her head she knew he was not worthy of her devotion. But everything was different now. He *was* worthy. He was capable of love, a love deeper than she herself had ever known. *She* was the one who was not worthy. What did she know of life and love after all? Nothing. She had been so arrogant and self-righteous, thinking herself above him.

She rose from bed and contemplated all this

while she had breakfast in her room, then dressed and went to knock on Lady Radley's door, as they had made plans to go walking together.

The door opened almost instantly. "Good morning, my dear," Lady Radley said, inviting Evelyn in. "We missed you yesterday. There was a lawn bowling event at Stanhope House, then we went for tea at the Corinthian, and Bertie was there talking all about his new cutter. It was such a marvelous day. I was disappointed you missed it, but you enjoyed yourself, did you not? I can't imagine you would have wished to be doing anything other than what you were doing."

Evelyn stopped in the center of the room and raised her eyebrows. "What do you mean, Lady Radley? I simply went to the museum in Newport."

That's what she had told them. She'd left a message at the desk early in the morning.

Lady Radley smiled surreptitiously, then sat down on the bed and patted the spot beside her.

Evelyn sat down, too, glancing uneasily at her companion, who was wiggling on the mattress to find a comfortable position.

"You don't have to keep secrets from me, dear," she whispered. "I think I know what you were up to, and you can trust me to be discreet."

"I still don't know what you're referring to," Evelyn insisted.

Lady Radley patted her on the knee. She was

clearly enjoying this. "It can be our little hush-hush secret. All I want are a few details. What was it like? What was *he* like?"

Evelyn took a moment to collect her thoughts. Had it been that obvious to everyone that she and Martin had gone off together?

"How did you know?" she finally asked.

"How could I *not* know? It was so clear to me that he fancied you the other night at the ball, and when he took you up on deck . . . Well, I could have swooned with envy. Which is why I want to know what happened yesterday. Tell me *everything*, Evelyn. I beg of you, and don't spare a single detail."

The old Evelyn would probably have been distressed by such questions, but this morning she cared less about propriety and wanted to laugh again like she had with Martin when she'd sipped wine out of the bottle on the beach. She wanted to confess her scandalous adventures to someone.

"All right, I'll tell you," she said, "but you must promise to keep it secret. You must tell everyone that I was at the museum in Newport, just as I claimed."

"Of course I will. You have my word."

So Evelyn confessed the truth. "Lord Martin took me sailing yesterday."

"Just the two of you?"

She nodded.

Lady Radley touched a hand to her cheek and

stood up. She crossed to the other side of the room, as if taking her time pondering the news, then her eyes lit up. "Oh, you lucky woman. What did he look like at the wheel? No, don't answer that. I already know. I have imagined him so many times, so young and virile."

Evelyn chewed on her lip while Lady Radley seemed to drift away for a moment.

"And you spent the whole day with him," she continued. "Did he hold your hand when you got on and off the boat?"

Evelyn smiled. "He did more than that. He practically had to hoist me up over the rail because we boarded from the launch."

"You don't say." She returned to the bed and sat down again. "You were very late getting back. Were you sailing the entire time, or did you go somewhere on the island?"

Evelyn explained how far they had gone, and described their lunch on the beach and their walk afterward. She recounted the fun they'd had building a sand castle and admitted she drank wine from the bottle.

Naturally, she refrained from mentioning the *other* frolicking that had gone on at the beach, deciding she could only be so bold. Besides—that was private, between her and Martin, as were their more intimate conversations about other things during their return trip by moonlight.

Lady Radley sighed and flopped backward onto

the bed. "You have given me much to dream about, Evelyn. Thank you."

Evelyn regarded her curiously for a moment. "Do you ever dream about your husband?"

Lady Radley lay there, staring up at the ceiling, then smiled wistfully. "There was a time in the early years of our marriage when I didn't need to dream. We were in love when we first married, but then, well . . . It's not quite the same anymore."

"Why not?"

She paused. "I don't know. I suppose you have children and you grow older and don't have the energy you once had. Then you seem to forget about each other. At least, he has seemed to forget about me."

Evelyn spoke gently. "You miss him."

Lady Radley nodded, her wistfulness gone now, replaced by a quiet melancholy. "I miss what we had."

But then she sat up and smiled brightly and patted Evelyn on the knee again. "But that is neither here nor there. Life is wonderful today because you had an adventure and captured the attention of the greatest hero in England."

"I doubt I'll hold it for long," she said.

"Perhaps he's going to compete with the others for your hand."

Evelyn shook her head. "He does not wish to marry."

Lady Radley stood up and went to her dressing table to put on her earrings. "Are you certain?"

"Yes. He has told me so very clearly."

She huffed. "Well. I hope you're not going to dismiss him completely because of that. You might as well enjoy his attentions, whether he is after a betrothal or something altogether different, if you grasp my meaning."

"Lady Radley," Evelyn said, "are you suggesting what I think you are suggesting?"

She fastened her other earring. "Yes, and why not, I ask you? You've been married before. There is nothing to stop you from enjoying yourself this week. Life is too short. Six months from now you might be someone's wife, and I know you well enough to know that you would never be unfaithful, even to a man you did not love. So have your adventures *now*, Evelyn, while you can. You'll regret it if you don't."

Was it true? she wondered, as she followed Lady Radley out into the corridor of the hotel to begin their morning walk. Would she regret what she did *not* do more than what she *did* do? Even if the most lasting souvenir of a wild and wicked affair with the hero of her childhood dreams was to be a broken heart?

After a brief walk to the Medina ferry and back, Evelyn and Lady Radley spent the rest of the afternoon on the back lawn of the yacht club with the other ladies, sitting on the wicker chairs, basking in the sunshine, and watching the sail-boats come and go from the Solent. There was much speculation about the race and who would take the trophy, and most people seemed to believe it would go to the *Endeavor* this year, as she was without a doubt a magnificent boat of revolutionary design.

Evelyn had seen Lord Breckinridge and his crew row out to the *Endeavor* hours ago and hoist the sails. They had sailed westward and had not yet returned.

The *Orpheus,* on the other hand, was already gone when she and Lady Radley had arrived at the clubhouse. Martin had likely taken her out early that morning to sail around the island, as he mentioned he might.

Though she wanted him to be prepared for the race, she could not deny that she was disappointed in one regard, for since her scandalous conversation with Lady Radley that morning, she had begun to entertain some secret hopes that she might see him on the lawn and flirt with him.

And *then* what? Could she—Evelyn Wheaton, proper widow—despite all her cautious reservations, follow the advice of her romantic female friend and actually enter into a wicked, scorching affair with the famously alluring champion of Cowes, Lord Martin Langdon?

Feeling a sudden rush of heat to her cheeks, she quickly clicked open her fan and cooled herself.

Oh, this would not do. It would not do at all. She had come here to find a husband. A husband! She could not be fantasizing about wild antics in her hotel room with a notorious rake, or naughty out-of-wedlock shenanigans in the private forward cabin of a sailboat at night. She had to stop thinking about that rocking sensation under her body, and she most certainly should not be thinking about—

"Look! There's the *Orpheus*!" someone shouted, and Evelyn nearly fell backward out of her chair with her legs in the air.

Quickly collecting herself, she tried to appear blasé and turned her gaze to the west. Indeed there they were. The huge spinnaker was shooting the yacht forward on the final approach.

Others on the lawn clapped and cheered, though there was not much to applaud as it wasn't a race, and for all they knew, the *Orpheus* could have just clocked the worst time on record.

"Shall we go greet the crew at the landing stage?" a beautiful young woman suggested, flapping her hands with excitement like some kind of bird.

Evelyn sat back in her chair and launched her parasol over her head.

"Do you want to go?" Lady Radley asked, leaning close and whispering conspiratorially.

"I don't think so," she replied.

"Why not? Everyone else is going to greet them."

"That is precisely why we shall not."

Lady Radley sighed with frustration and lifted her parasol, too, and they sat in silence while all the other young ladies on the lawn made a mad dash for the back gate.

Then Lady Radley eyed her shrewdly. "Ah, I see."

"What do you mean, '*I see*'?"

"I see what you're doing."

Evelyn studied her for a moment. "And what am I doing, exactly?"

"You're going to be the challenging one."

Feigning indifference, Evelyn squinted out at the water. To be honest, she hadn't actually thought of it that way. It had been her pride that kept her from chasing after him along with all the other silly, screeching girls.

Or perhaps not pride. Perhaps it was that old familiar refusal to even *try* to compete with the ones she knew were prettier than she.

Nevertheless, Lady Radley's idea did have some merit. A challenge. He was a man who thrived on them, wasn't he? "Well you know he *does* like to compete," she said.

Her companion was quiet for a moment under the shade of her parasol, while they watched the *Orpheus* draw in its spinnaker. Then she leaned in and raised a curious eyebrow. "Does this mean you're going to have an adventure this week, Evelyn?"

She did not answer the question right away, because she was still not really sure of the answer. It was so far out of her realm of experience, and she wasn't sure she could be courageous enough to risk her heart. So she chose only to smile and ask a question of her own. "Isn't there an assembly for the competitors at Northwood tonight?"

"Yes, there is, and it promises to be a fantastic crush."

Evelyn continued to watch the boats while she basked in the sun's warmth. "I wonder what I shall wear."

Lady Radley patted her on the knee. "I know exactly what you should wear, dear. Something that shows off your brains."

When Martin stepped onto the landing stage at the Squadron, he was greeted by a horde of giggling young women, all waving frantically at him. None of them looked a day over twenty.

Spence stopped on the slip and rolled his eyes. "Here we go."

Martin was at least glad he and Spence had put last night's quarrel behind them. Earlier that morning, as soon as they'd hoisted the mainsail, the challenges on the water had distracted them both from whatever hostilities remained. They hadn't discussed or resolved anything, but they had at least swept all of it under the carpet so to speak, as they so often did. That particular maneuver over the years had often freed them to continue their friendship and focus on whatever tasks were at hand.

"Lord Martin!" one of the ladies called out to him as he reached the end of the dock. "We were watching your magnificent run. We all think you're going to win again, don't we, ladies?"

She beamed flirtatiously at him. He stopped for a moment, wondering if—and how—he could get out of this, then finally gave up and approached them. The one who had spoken stared up at him with wide, awestruck eyes, and her mouth fell open.

"I appreciate the confidence," he said, giving each of the girls a courteous nod.

"It's our pleasure, Lord Martin," one of the others said, her voice quivering as if she were experiencing some kind of tizzy.

Normally, in a situation such as this, he would know just what to say to make them all giggle and blush anew, but for some reason presently, he was at a loss. To be honest, he didn't really care whether or not he made them giggle. He was very tired from the test run and wasn't feeling like himself today.

In the end, however, he managed a chivalrous response, though he had to dig deep to pull it off.

"Ladies, I am heading up to the Squadron lawn for a cool drink of lemonade. You'll all accompany me, I hope?"

"Oh, yes, yes!"

He smiled graciously and led the way up the drive to the back gate. Spence followed behind, striking up a conversation with one of the young women.

They entered the grounds, and Martin spotted all the mothers over by the fence. Politely, he extricated himself from the young ladies' company, found a footman, and requested a glass of lemonade, then joined Sir Lyndon, who was socializing with a few of the older club members.

"Martin, we watched you come in," Lyndon said. "Well done, my boy, well done."

"Thank you, sir." He turned to look around the crowded yard at all the laughing, gossiping guests, wondering who else was there, and perhaps wondering more specifically about one person in particular.

Then he spotted her.

She was sitting in a wicker chair with a lacy parasol over her head, wearing a dark crimson dress and matching hat that brought out the auburn highlights in her hair. She was listening to her companion, Lady Radley, who was gesturing expressively with her hands as she spoke.

Evelyn glanced in Martin's direction, and their eyes met. She leaned forward slightly and smiled at him. It was not a broad smile, but it was clever and knowing and faintly teasing, as if she found the obvious spectacle of giddy young girls both entertaining and ridiculous.

For a split second, he was immobilized with both relief and adoration. She was not the same woman she had been the other day when he'd first met her on the lawn with Breckinridge and the Radleys. She had been aloof and almost contemptuous that day, but this afternoon she was meeting his gaze directly and nodding with an open, mischievous countenance. She was practically glowing, outshining every other woman in view.

All at once, he felt a stirring of emotion from deep inside himself, as if he were looking at a flower that had just opened to the sun. He regarded her for a moment and forgot all about the race and didn't hear a word Lyndon was saying. Perhaps he should go over there.

But then an unexpected surge of anxiety came out of nowhere and stopped him. He felt a tight knot of tension in his stomach and put a hand to it. It was the same knot he had felt the night before, after his argument with Spence. Disturbed by it, he turned back to face the men.

"What was your time?" Sir Lyndon asked, his eyes gleaming with curiosity.

Martin took a few deep swigs of his lemonade, then raised his glass and spoke with humor. "You know better than to ask me that, Sir Lyndon, you cheeky devil. Only my crew and I are privy to that information."

Sir Lyndon nodded, but with a hint of disappointment he could not hide. "You can't blame a man for trying."

The men started chatting again, but Martin was having a hard time listening. He did not feel himself.

He glanced uneasily over his shoulder and saw the group of young ladies standing under the elm tree, still staring at him, watching his every move, whispering to each other and giggling. They were *always* staring—they and countless other women just like them. Could he never have some privacy and space?

God, what was wrong with him? This was just the sort of thing he had been looking forward to when he'd sailed into Cowes a few days ago. He had longed for this superficial amusement and couldn't wait to throw himself into a wicked good time.

He looked down at his foggy lemonade, then downed the rest of it in one gulp while Spence chatted with the other gentlemen in their group. He waited for a break in the conversation, then spoke up. "I must be off." He set his glass on a tray as a footman walked by.

"But you just got here," Sir Lyndon replied.

"My apologies, but I have a few important

matters to attend to." He didn't in fact, but there it was. "Good day, gentlemen."

With that, he walked out, hoping that by nightfall he would be ready for frivolous revelry again. For frivolous revelry was much easier than this strange, unexpected discontent.

Chapter 13

It was past ten by the time Martin and Spence arrived at Northwood House, a sumptuous Georgian mansion in the grand style, situated upon a grassy hillside overlooking the Solent. The host and hostess welcomed them into the Grand Salon and within seconds, they were holding champagne flutes in their hands and laughing with some of the other competitors in the race.

Martin eyed the buffet table because he'd slept through dinner and was ravenous; but as luck would have it, who was standing next to the tower of cream cakes but Evelyn—looking equally delicious in a stunning, pale yellow gown of light, diaphanous fabric that seemed to flutter around her legs on a nonexistent breeze.

And her bosom . . . Well, she looked delectable with pearls crisscrossing over her lush, alluring breasts. .

He experienced a jolt of uneasiness suddenly, just as he had on the back lawn of the yacht club earlier that day. Tonight, however, he could not help but accept the more compelling reasons why he felt such discomfort—because he was experiencing a desire that went deeper than his usual superficial flirtations, and he had never intended for that to happen.

It was a milestone of enormous proportions, he supposed—that he could admit to himself that his feelings for Evelyn went beyond mere amusement for the sake of distraction. But despite the fact that he acknowledged those feelings now, he did not welcome them. He did not want to worry about where they could lead, because he did not want them to lead anywhere.

Besides, he had a race to win. That was why he had come to Cowes. He had not come to get himself tangled up in a romance that might pull him under.

Thus, he did what he always did. He repressed his troubles and forced himself to return to comfortable habits. He conversed and smiled, he flirted with beautiful women, he laughed and partook of a generous variety of diversions on the buffet table, and even secured some sailing secrets, learning who planned to use what maneuvers on race day. Then someone tapped him on the shoulder, and he turned.

"Lord Martin! How long has it been?"

It was Sheldon Hatfield—Breckinridge's first mate, the man who had despised him at Eton because of the girl on the horse. He had lost most of his hair and grown very round through the middle, Martin could not help but notice. And he was drunk.

Martin bowed slightly at the waist. "Hatfield, how are you?"

The man swayed unsteadily on his feet, sloshing his brandy to and fro. "I swear, if it weren't for the drink in my hand, I'd think the ocean was still under me." He slapped Martin hard on the shoulder. "But I won't bore you with that. You're back to defend your title, I see."

"Wild horses couldn't keep me away."

He pointed a finger. "But you had best brace yourself my friend. We made a good run today and set some records, so we're going to make it very hard on you. You've seen the *Endeavor*?"

"I have. She's a very impressive sloop."

"Indeed. I helped design her, you know." He raised his glass and took a drink.

"*Did* you?"

"Yes," he replied. "I told that Benjamin fellow to paint her black, by golly."

Martin raised his eyebrows. "Well done, Hatfield. She looks very sleek."

"That she does." He swung his glass through the air as he spoke. "I presume you've been cracking the whip with your crew? Getting them ready for the race? You can't let them rest, you know. You've got to keep harping at them and let them know who is boss. You've got to make them work for their supper, so to speak; otherwise, they'll do more harm than good." He lifted his glass to take another drink, and spoke into the snifter. "Lazy bastards."

Hands clasped behind his back, Martin looked over Hatfield's shoulder, and saw Breckinridge approach Evelyn on the other side of the room. "I'll keep that in mind," he said.

"Or maybe you've had enough glory as Cowes champion?" Hatfield continued. "I heard you're more keen on the other trophy this week. Though I can't say I understand it much myself. I'd hardly call her a trophy, and she's certainly not up to *your* usual standards."

Martin's gaze shot back to Hatfield's puffy face and bulbous red nose. "I beg your pardon?"

He swung his glass around again, gesturing toward Evelyn and Breckinridge. "You know . . . the holier-than-thou widow. Richer than the mint, they say. Maybe she'll be your consolation prize when you lose the race, but my guess is you'll tire of her anyway as soon as you cross *her* finish line, if you grasp my meaning."

"Hatfield . . ."

"You really ought to do the poor woman a favor and leave her to Breckinridge. He'll at least put a ring on her finger, and she'll be grateful for that." He stuck his nose into his glass and started to tip it up. "Though *she'll* have to foot the bill for the trinket, I daresay."

Before the brandy even had a chance to drain into Hatfield's open mouth, Martin struck the glass from his hand. Perplexed and appearing disoriented, the man blinked a few times.

"You've had too much to drink, Hatfield," he said. "I suggest you call it a night." He set the glass on a table beside him.

Hatfield glared indignantly at him. "You just want me to leave because you know I'm going to beat you in the race and because of that, I'm spoiling your fun tonight."

Studying Hatfield's hazy eyes, Martin inclined his head to inform him that their conversation was at an end. "We'll see about that," he said.

Then he crossed the room to seek out a much more attractive and intelligent conversationalist— one who was in danger of being wooed by a man who had chosen a drunken fool for a first mate.

*   *   *

"And then he insisted that we pay for the chair," Lord Breckinridge said, "regardless of the fact that we had changed the paint color of our drawing room, and the fabric no longer matched." He gestured toward the back garden. "Shall we get some air?"

Evelyn smiled dutifully, hoping that a fresh breeze might breathe some life into their conversation. It would at least stimulate her brain with some oxygen. "Yes, thank you."

They ventured outside onto the veranda and looked up at the moon. Evelyn could not help but compare it to the moon she had admired the night before, which had been clear and bright, surrounded by stars. Tonight there were no stars, only clouds passing across the sky.

"It's a lovely night," she said.

"Indeed. There is nothing so fine as a cool breeze."

They stood side by side, looking out at the back garden, but Evelyn could see nothing, for it was pitch-black.

"I'm sure it is a beautiful garden in the daylight," she mentioned, struggling to fill the awkward silence.

"Yes, I'm sure," he replied.

They continued to stand on the veranda, not looking at one another. Evelyn chewed on her lower lip. She pushed her spectacles up her nose.

Breckinridge cleared his throat. He clasped his hands behind his back. "It's a lovely evening," he said, repeating her earlier observation.

"Yes, it is," she replied, wondering if it was possible for a person actually to suffocate and die gasping from boredom.

They stood there for another agonizing minute or two, maybe more, then Evelyn glanced over her shoulder. Martin was standing just inside the open doors. His eyes met hers, and he stepped to the side to keep her locked in his gaze.

She smiled and faced the garden, then glanced back at him again. He rolled his eyes at her, as if he were making fun of Breckinridge's bungling conversation. Evelyn fought not to laugh.

"Well, that was refreshing," Breckinridge said. "Shall we go inside?"

Evelyn quickly cleared her throat. "I do beg your indulgence, Lord Breckinridge, but I would like to remain here alone a little longer if you don't mind. It's very peaceful."

He hesitated, as if stumbling over what to say, then bowed slightly. "Of course. Enjoy the night, but I must beg your indulgence as well. Please allow me to take you back to your hotel at the end of the evening, Mrs. Wheaton, as my aunt and uncle have departed, and my uncle has entrusted you to my care."

Evelyn looked inside. They had not told her

they were leaving. How could they have done such a thing? She supposed it was Lord Radley's scheme to put her and his nephew together.

"Thank you," she replied. "I would be most grateful."

He bowed again and left her alone. She faced the garden, then tilted her head back to look up at the clouds. Less than ten seconds later, she heard slow footsteps, then a man's voice.

"Are you wondering, like I am, why all the stars have disappeared?"

Every nerve in her body quivered with excitement. "They haven't exactly disappeared," she said, without lowering her gaze. "They're merely hiding."

Martin came to stand beside her. He looked up, too. "The moon is hiding as well. But look, there it is. Oops, gone again."

She could not help but laugh. "Those shifty stratocumuli." She glanced across at him with laughter in her eyes, but found him looking rather somber and contemplative. "What's wrong?"

His voice remained quiet. "I must apologize to you, Evelyn. I was completely unsociable tonight."

She had indeed been very disappointed that he had flirted with every woman in the room except for her, but did not wish him to know that. "You were hardly unsociable," she said. "You had the whole room at your feet."

"But what good is that," he asked, "when they

are all strangers, and none are as lovely as you?"

The tender compliment, delivered with such sincerity, warmed her blood in the most pleasant way, and any lingering disappointments faded into oblivion, along with her best intentions to be a challenge to him. Suddenly, all she wanted to do was speak from her heart and tell him exactly how she felt. She turned to face him more directly and spoke in a calm voice, without anger. Just truth.

"You say that, Martin, yet you avoided me like the plague tonight. There was no need for it, you know. I'm not one of those young, lovesick admirers who will latch on to your coattails. Is that what you thought?"

His brow furrowed, as if he were baffled by her response. "That's not how I see you."

"No?"

"*No.*"

Wetting her lips, she relaxed slightly. "Well, it seemed a little that way." At least she thought it had.

Someone dropped a glass inside, and the smash drew her attention. There was an abrupt silence in the assembly room, then a general murmur until a footman scurried to clean it up. A few seconds later, everyone turned back to their conversations.

Evelyn looked up at Martin again. He was staring down at her as if he had never looked away.

"I did avoid you tonight," he finally said, "but I also realized that I did so because I've become an expert at avoidance."

She inhaled sharply. "I'm not sure I understand."

"You're different from other women," he said, "and I told you things yesterday—very private things—that I never tell anyone."

"Are you referring to what happened when you were in America?"

He nodded.

She began to reason out theories to explain what he was trying to tell her. "Maybe you've come to a point in your life where you're ready to talk about it."

"No," he replied. "It was because of you. No other reason."

She felt a confusing mixture of excitement and apprehension. "What are you saying, Martin? Why did you come out here?"

He took a moment to articulate his thoughts. "I came out here to tell you I avoided you tonight because you made me want you more than I've wanted any woman in a very long time, and I became spooked."

She could feel her heart beating faster. "I was a little spooked, too," she said, "because I had a wonderful time yesterday. Almost *too* wonderful."

All at once, she wanted to step into his arms, to embrace him and feel the passion she had felt on the beach the day before. To discover what was beyond it. She knew so little about love and desire and the workings of her body. She wanted to learn it all from *him*. From Martin. The only man who had ever truly stirred her passions.

She felt her cheeks burning with anticipation and need, and thought, surely, he must see it as plain as day.

"I wonder," he said, "if perhaps you might consider—"

Just then, a shadow appeared in the doorway, and they both turned.

"Lord Martin, I didn't see you come out here," Breckinridge said, looking at both of them with displeasure.

Martin faced Breckinridge. "Ah, but it's a glorious evening, is it not? I needed some fresh air, and whom did I find strolling on the veranda as well, but the most enchanting woman in the room— Mrs. Wheaton." He bowed to her.

He was shamelessly flaunting his legendary charm. Evelyn recognized it, because it was not how he really was with her.

Breckinridge's jaw clenched visibly. Evelyn suspected he was frustrated because he knew he could not compete. Not when it came to charm, at any rate.

Nevertheless, he bowed to her also. "An enchanting woman indeed. Mrs. Wheaton, my coach awaits."

It was an impressive effort at chivalry, she had to admit, and she would give credit where credit was due. She smiled and inclined her head at him. "Thank you, my lord. I am obliged."

Then she turned to Martin and inclined her head at him as well. "Lord Martin?"

He bowed. "Mrs. Wheaton."

And because it was the proper thing to do, she went to Breckinridge and took his arm. She had agreed to let him escort her back to the hotel, after all, and she could hardly change her mind.

Besides, she had promised herself she would be a challenge to Martin, hadn't she? She could not go begging *him* to escort her home. It was much better that he watch her leave, and perhaps wish that she had stayed.

Sheldon Hatfield leaned a shoulder against the wall in the back corner of the saloon and watched Breckinridge escort the widow out. His blurry gaze then swept to the open French doors and the veranda beyond, where Martin was leaning both hands upon the balustrade, still looking out at the back garden.

Sheldon took another drink. He despised men like Martin, who were blessed with everything— good looks and consistent good luck. Martin was the worst of them. He had more of both those things than anyone deserved.

But perhaps what galled Sheldon most of all

was that *she* had never given him the time of day, not even years ago back in Windsor. The rejections from her then—when her father didn't have a penny to his name and she was the least attractive girl in town—had been a greater insult than any other.

And now Breckinridge wanted her. Well, he could have her as far as Sheldon was concerned, and then she'd get what she deserved, because Breckinridge would toss her into the country and spend all her money on cheap whores in London.

Better *that* than letting Martin enjoy her, Sheldon thought miserably—because Martin already had far too many pleasures on his plate. It was time somebody knocked that plate right out of his hands and watched it smash to pieces on the floor. Yes, it was time Martin Langdon went hungry for a while.

Chapter 14

U pon returning to his room after the assembly, Martin shrugged out of his jacket and tossed it onto a chair. He pulled his bow tie out from under his collar and tossed it onto the chair as well, then went to the dresser and poured himself a brandy.

He turned around and looked at the empty bed. He supposed he should not have come back so early. He should have found another party to attend, or he should have stayed longer at Northwood. But once Evelyn had departed, all the usual allures of society gatherings had disappeared, swallowed up by the unrelenting shadow of her absence.

Damn Breckinridge for his ill-timed interruption. If it weren't for him, Martin would be walking on the beach with her at this very moment.

But did he really want that, he wondered uneasily, knowing where it might lead? She was not the sort of woman a man could toy with. She had made that very clear. He did not *wish* to toy with her.

He glanced toward his door and thought of how divine she had looked in that yellow gown this evening and how she had smiled up at him so brightly on the veranda when they were speaking of honest things. He felt a deep ache of frustrated desire. He wanted to be with her now, there was no point denying it, and nothing seemed important enough to keep him from her, not even his greatest, most willful intentions to avoid what could become a complicated entanglement.

Soundly sweeping away further hesitations—because he wanted her, dammit, his *body* wanted her—he picked up the brandy decanter and another glass, left his room, walked across the hall, and knocked hastily before there was time to change his mind. A few seconds later, her door opened a crack, and he leaned a little closer to discover she had been in bed. He knew this because she was wearing a white nightdress, no spectacles—bloody hell, her eyes were huge—and her hair was spilling over her shoulders in long, wavy locks.

He'd never seen her with her hair down. It was a shock to his system, rousing a very masculine hunger in him. His gaze drifted from her deep green eyes down the front of her gown to her bare toes, then back up again.

"I woke you," he said, with no apology.

"Lord Martin," she whispered, gathering the lacy collar of her gown in a tight fist and peering into the hall to make sure no one was about. "What are you doing here, knocking at my door at this hour? If anyone sees you . . ."

He raised the decanter and glasses. "I thought you might be thirsty."

She raised her eyebrows at him skeptically.

"And we were so rudely interrupted earlier," he explained, "I thought we could continue our conversation."

Still holding her collar closed, she hesitated a moment, then stepped back and opened her door. "I can't believe I'm doing this," she whispered. "I daresay you've corrupted me."

He crossed the threshold and his gaze fell upon the disheveled bed. "Not quite yet."

She shot him a quick, admonishing look, then darted across the room to tidy the covers. When she faced him again, her pink cheeks were flushed, and she pushed a lock of hair behind her ear.

"This is a surprise," she said, making an effort to appear unruffled, which he found utterly adorable because she was completely flustered. She was the virtuous widow after all. She had never invited a man into her room before.

"I thought it might be," he replied, "so I brought brandy to numb the shock."

Her cherry lips curled up in a grin, and she dropped her hands to her sides. "That was good of you."

Martin moved to the table, poured her a drink, and handed it over. He poured another for himself, then lifted his glass and clinked it against hers. "To a good night's sleep."

"Or something else just as good," she replied, and he let out a pleasantly astonished chuckle. Had she been *hoping* he would come?

Regarding her for a brief appreciative moment over the rim of his glass as he sipped the fine brandy, he noted the provocative curve of her bosom beneath her thin nightdress and the wavy softness of her hair. He moved to the tall chest of drawers, leaned back upon it, and spoke in a friendly voice.

"Your room is different from mine." He raised his glass, gesturing toward a painting on the wall. "That's very nice."

She turned and looked at it. "A local artist."

"And a very talented one."

They said nothing for a few seconds. They simply stood across the room from each other, their gazes warm and languorous while they sipped the strong brandy and contemplated what might happen next.

For her part, Evelyn was working hard to hide her frazzled nerves. She could barely comprehend that Martin—handsome, vigorous, exciting Martin—had come to her private hotel room in the middle of the night. And he had said the most wonderful things to her earlier on the veranda at the assembly. He had told her he wanted her more than he'd wanted any woman in a long time. She'd never imagined, after all these years, that she would ever hear him say such things.

He pushed away from the cabinet and strolled to the window. "So tell me," he said, "are you really going to marry Breckinridge? The general impression I'm getting is that people think you are."

She had not expected him to ask that. She supposed she didn't know what she had expected. This was all so far beyond her normal horizon. "He hasn't asked," she replied.

"But he will."

"Do you know this for a fact?"

He casually shrugged. "I would put money on it."

While he waited for her to answer, she looked down at the amber-colored brandy and swirled it around in her glass before she took another sip, then walked to the window to join him there. She parted the drapes with one finger to look out, then decided she was not going to answer his question. She did not want to make any of this too easy for him.

"Let me ask you something else then," he said, leaning a shoulder against the window frame. "If you came to Cowes looking for a husband, Evelyn, and you heard me tell you yesterday that I do not wish to marry, why did you let me in here?"

She let out a sigh, realizing he was not going to make this easy on her either. "You are certainly direct, sir."

"And you are very good at avoiding the answers to my questions." He smiled and raised his glass to her before taking another sip.

Seeing the amusement in his eyes, she set down her glass and stepped closer. The tip of her breast touched the back of his hand where he held his drink in front of him, and her nipple tightened instantly. She felt her breath come short.

"I let you in, Martin, because I am hopelessly attracted to you, I always have been, and I couldn't bring myself to turn you away."

The open declaration came as a surprise even to her—she couldn't believe she had said it—and it arrested *him* on the spot as well. But then he gazed down at her from under his dark lashes and began to lightly stroke her nipple with a knuckle. The potent sensation through the fine linen of her nightgown caused her blood to simmer hotly.

"And I want to learn what it feels like to be with a man like you," she added, still in a state of disbelief that any of this was actually happening. "A man who knows the ropes."

He continued to rub the back of his hand in a light circular motion over her breast until she feared her legs might give out under her.

"May I assume," he asked, "that you are referring to something other than lessons in sailing?"

She smiled. "You already taught me how to steer your yacht. I think we can move on."

His eyes focused on her lips. She wet them with the tip of her tongue, from one corner to the other. For a long moment he watched her mouth as if he were waging a battle in his mind, then he carefully dipped his head and pressed his brandy-flavored lips to hers.

All at once, Evelyn felt roused to a new peak of excitement as shivers of lust ran up and down her spine. It was all so magical and intoxicating, like nothing else in this world.

He set down his glass on the windowsill and slid his arms around her waist, then cupped her bottom in his strong hands and crushed her firmly up against his erection, which she felt through the fabric of their clothing. He thrust his tongue into her mouth, and his hips ground fiercely against hers until she was sure she was going to dissolve into liquid. She would do anything for him right now. Anything.

But then he dragged his lips from hers and whispered against the side of her neck. "Let us be sensible for a moment, Evelyn. You told me on the beach that you do not wish me to toy with you."

"I've changed my mind," she assured him breathlessly. "I've decided that I have been living too long without pleasure or joy. I discovered that on your boat, and I don't want to care about the consequences. I'm tired of being safe."

His chest rose and fell as if he'd just run a mile up hill. "But I don't wish to hurt you, and you know how I feel about marriage and children."

"You won't hurt me."

"How do you know?"

Growing frustrated with talk—because she wanted him desperately, despite the aftermath— she slid her hand down the front of his trousers and rubbed his firm, swollen shaft with her palm. "I'm a woman, Martin, not a child. I can take care of myself. I am asking you . . . please. Don't deny me this pleasure, which I have wanted for so long and have never known."

He silenced her pleadings with a kiss, crushing his mouth to hers again and ravishing her with his tongue. She let her head fall back to offer her neck to him, and he tasted the base of her throat. "I've never been kissed like this," she said, "and I want more."

"You'll get it," he replied, his voice husky with need.

He swept her up into his arms and carried her around the bed, setting her down on the soft mattress. He stood back and unbuttoned his shirt while she lay on her back looking up at him, wondering if this was a dream. She was with Martin, and he was going to make love to her. Finally. *Please, dear God, don't let it be a dream.*

He tossed his shirt to the floor. The smooth contours of his chest paralyzed her with desire as he flexed and relaxed his muscles. He was so inconceivably strong and powerful from all the days and weeks aboard his yacht. She felt a curious pull in her belly and raised a knee and squirmed impatiently on the bed.

At last he came down upon her and pressed open her lips with his tongue. He kissed her passionately while his hand cupped her tingling breasts, then slid down her pulsating belly to caress her thighs.

"You taste like heaven," he whispered, blowing into her ear. He kissed her neck and unbuttoned the top of her nightgown, spreading it apart, planting kisses on each raised nipple. "And I thought I would go mad tonight when I saw you with Breckinridge."

She raked her fingers through his hair and gloried in his possessiveness, then caressed his cheeks while he licked and flicked with his tongue and drove her insane with lust. Lifting her hips off the bed to push against his pelvis, she trembled with need and fought the urge to beg him to do it now—to plunge into her at once and satisfy this impossible yearning. She could barely believe any of this was really happening.

He slid his hand down over her hip and gathered her nightgown in a fist, tugging it up inch by inch until it was bunched around her waist. A fiery heat ignited deep inside her as she felt his feathery touch on her quivering thighs. He took her in his arms, then his lips grazed over the top of her gown, between her breasts and across her navel. He slid down to kiss her knees and inner thighs, then moved up and up until he could bury his face in her hot, pulsating center.

Overcome with both shock and delight, she lifted her hips in response. He slid his hands under her bottom to pull her even nearer to him as he slipped his tongue into her folds and tasted her with his hungry mouth.

It wasn't long before her body began jerking, and she cried out, then pressed her hands at his temples to direct his attack. Heaving violently, she gasped with desire, but before the mounting pleasure exploded within her, she took hold of his shoulders and pulled him up for a deep, wet kiss.

He had worked her up to such a state of arousal that she became obsessed with seeing this through. Impatient, desperate to hurry, she reached down to grab hold of his erection, only to discover he was still partially clothed. Quickly, he peeled off his remaining garments while she sat up and stripped her nightgown off over her head and tossed it aside.

Nude before him, Evelyn burned with need and wanted only to open herself to him completely. "Hurry, Martin. Please."

Stepping out of his shoes, he said, "I don't normally like to hurry at times such as this, but I think the situation demands it."

"Yes, oh yes." She realized suddenly it was not how she'd imagined this would be. She had not expected to feel such urgent need.

"I promise next time," he said, "we'll go slower, but right now, I'm afraid nothing can hold me back."

Bold and unashamed, she pulled him down to her again and drew his lips to hers and shoved her bottom up to meet his charge. At the same time, she turned her head to the side and shut her eyes and braced herself for the pain, because there had always been pain before.

He slid into her, smoothly and with ease, stretching her slick opening to the hilt. There was no pain, only hot, surging desire, for she was damp and soft and unresisting.

Opening her eyes again, she looked up at him in the lamplight. He was braced above her on both arms, looking down at her while he moved with deep, sweeping strokes. It was a moment she would never forget—the beauty of his sun-bronzed face, the classic definition of his features, his blue eyes glimmering with desire. He had awakened her to every possible kind of joy and filled her with a fantastic yearning to know what other pleasures existed outside the normal sphere of her old life.

She spread her legs wider and wrapped them around him, resting her heels on his strong, muscular back. He slid all the way in, then drew out slowly, and the sensations were almost unbearable, agonizing in their intensity. As he plunged deep inside again, she rubbed herself against his pubic bone and threw her head back as he pumped wildly into her.

Her sighs soon grew to moans, and she reached the heights of rapture, her arms wrapped tightly around his neck as she buried her face in the crook of his shoulder and exploded with sizzling triumph. Moments later, he reached his own climax and flooded her with liquid, throbbing heat. She quivered again, pulsing, shuddering, and he thrust hard into her one last time, then collapsed his full weight upon her, heavy and damp with perspiration.

They lay there for a moment, limp and exhausted, until he let out a groan and rolled over onto his back. *"My God."*

Evelyn was aware only of satisfaction. "Now I understand," she said, working hard just to breathe, "what all the fuss is about."

He chuckled softly and gathered her into his arms. "Congratulations, my dear, you are officially corrupted."

"And eternally grateful. I never knew it could be like that."

Martin held her close, then inhaled deeply and kissed the top of her head. "It was rather out of control."

"Definitely," she said, "but in the best possible way."

He paused, rubbing a finger over her shoulder. "Perhaps not in all ways, Evelyn. I wasn't very responsible."

She lifted her chin to look up at him. "What do you mean?"

"I should have withdrawn sooner."

Ah, she thought with a resigned sigh, her intellect finally waking from the eroticism of this wonderful dream. These were the practicalities of casual intercourse. "I'm sorry, I wasn't thinking . . ."

He stared up at the ceiling and shook his head. "It was my responsibility to do the thinking, not yours. But is this a safe time, do you know?"

She hesitated. "I wasn't aware there *were* safe times."

"Shortly before and after your monthly?" He waited for an answer.

"Oh. Then I think yes, it must be a safe time. I expect it soon."

"When?"

She anxiously cleared her throat. "Before the end of the week, I believe."

It was an answer he seemed relieved to hear. He reached for her hand. "Good. But I apologize. I didn't mean to spoil things."

"You didn't."

He chuckled with a strange sort of amused disbelief and leaned up on one elbow. "You know, it is utterly baffling to me, Evelyn, that you could ever think yourself not desirable to men. I just lost my head over you completely. I kept meaning to withdraw at the right time, but I simply could not stop myself."

Her mouth curled up in a smile. It was deeply satisfying to know she had that power over him.

"I promise I will be more careful next time," he said, brushing her hair back off her face. "And if I appear negligent, I'm asking you to be the responsible one and remind me to be prudent. Can you do that?"

"This means there will be a next time?" she asked in a suggestive tone, sliding closer and letting her hand drift down over the taut muscles of his abdomen to the coarse hair at his genitals.

He grinned with tempting allure and spoke in a husky, deep voice that sent a rushing fever into her senses. "Undoubtedly, darling. Sooner rather than later, I should think."

Then he moved over her with a smile. He imprisoned her mouth in his, planted his hips firmly between her eager, parting thighs, and Evelyn feared she might very well die of happiness—for the rest of Cowes week was surely going to be the most remarkable week of her life.

Chapter 15

The next day brought sunshine and a swift breeze from the west, which lured many of the competitors out onto the water to test their skills. Evelyn had eaten lunch with Lord and Lady Radley and was now strolling along the Esplanade with them, while they speculated about who would improve their times over last year and who would fare worse.

They reached the pavilion at the far end of the Green and encountered Lord Breckinridge with his first mate, Mr. Sheldon Hatfield.

"Good afternoon," Lord Radley said, greeting Breckinridge with a pat on the back. "I'm surprised you're not out there with the rest of them, practicing your maneuvers for race day."

Breckinridge bowed to Evelyn and Lady Radley. "One needn't practice with a boat like the *Endeavor*, at least not in front of the opponents. We wouldn't want to give away our secrets, now would we?"

Lord Radley nodded. "Smart man. Overtake them when they least expect it."

"We're going to overtake them whether they expect it or not," Mr. Hatfield interjected. "No one stands a chance against the *Endeavor*, least of all the Cowes champion and his obsolete boat."

He spoke with such contempt, Evelyn found it immensely unsettling. "Perhaps you would be wise not to underestimate the competition," she said. "From what I hear, Lord Martin is a very gifted sailor."

And gifted in other areas, too, she thought to herself with a pleasant recollection of what had occurred in her bed the night before.

Everyone's gaze shot to her face, and a noteworthy silence ensued until Lady Radley came to her rescue. "Yes, indeed, you are quite right, Evelyn. I once heard that Lord Martin can recall the exact details of every race he's ever been in and all the mistakes the other skippers made, and he doesn't require a chart or tide table when he's at the wheel. He keeps everything stored in his head like a scientific tactician."

Hatfield's lips twisted into a most unattractive scowl. "That is all idle gossip, madam, blown out of proportion. He was a classmate of mine at Eton, you see, so I know him better than anyone here. I assure you, when it came to practical applications like science and arithmetic, he was the worst student in the school. He never did a stitch of work, and he constantly misbehaved in class."

"Perhaps he was simply bored," Evelyn said in Martin's defense.

Mr. Hatfield and Lord Breckinridge both stared fixedly at her, their eyes narrowing.

"Well!" Hatfield said, slapping his hands together. "I think we should go out there and show everyone how it's done."

But Breckinridge wasn't listening. He was still staring at Evelyn. She shaded her eyes with a gloved hand and looked out at the boats.

At last he turned to Mr. Hatfield. "I believe we *will* go out. It's a good day for a pleasure cruise. Anyone care to join us?" He directed the question specifically at Evelyn.

"That's very tempting, my lord," she replied, "but I don't think I have the fortitude to endure these rough waters today. Perhaps another time when the wind is not so swift?" And when she did not have plans to meet Martin in her room for tea and sweets at five o'clock.

He bowed politely. "Of course, but I will hold you to that promise." He raised an eyebrow at her—as if attempting to flirt—but after being on the receiving end of Martin's flirtations, Lord Breckinridge's attempt fell completely flat.

Nevertheless, she smiled in return.

"Come along, then," Mr. Hatfield said, already starting back to the yacht club. "It's time for the competition to begin."

"Look at you." Spence jumped from the foredeck into the cockpit of the *Orpheus* and approached Martin. "With your eyes on the sails and your hands on the wheel—you're the very picture of contentment."

Martin merely shrugged, though he was indeed content today, enjoying the sensation of the salty spray in his face. The hiss of the waves beneath the leeward bow was music to his ears, and he felt refreshed and optimistic. Ready to take on the world. He could not deny he had a certain not-so-virtuous widow to thank for that.

"I had a good night's sleep," he replied, careful not to reveal anything that might cause Spence to pry because he didn't want to discuss the intriguing particulars of his personal life at the moment, and certainly not with Spence, who would only make assumptions and state opinions, and Martin wasn't in the mood for it. He didn't want to overanalyze this unexpected affair he'd entered into, nor did he want to interrupt the pleasure of the sail.

"In about ninety seconds," he said, "I'm going to bring her around, and I'd like the spinnaker set to starboard."

"We're heading back then?" Spence asked.

"Yes, I think we've ironed out most of the wrinkles."

Besides, he had an appointment for tea at five o'clock and did not wish to be late.

Spence made his way forward and waited for Martin's command, while the rest of the crew knelt in a straight line near the weather rails.

"Ready to come about!" Martin shouted.

Spence raised a hand. "Prepare to release the jib!"

The scene on the deck suddenly erupted into activity as each crewman scrambled to his station. Martin turned the wheel hard over, hand over hand, every muscle in his body straining as he swung the *Orpheus* around.

"Boom coming across!" Spence shouted, and Martin ducked as it passed over his head.

Seconds later, the spinnaker pole was run out, and the colorful sail filled with wind, snapping taut at the bow. The apparent wind became still, and all was quiet again on deck.

Martin nodded at Spence. They'd managed the maneuver well.

For the next half hour, they sailed on until they spotted another yacht in the distance, also turning and heading back to Cowes.

"Isn't that the *Endeavor*?" Spence said, joining Martin at the helm.

"I believe it is," he replied, his eyes fixed on the black sloop.

They continued on their starboard tack, gaining upon the other vessel, which was traveling on a slower port tack.

"She's not setting any records, is she?" Spence said.

"Certainly not." That fact gave Martin pause. "We have the right of way," he added a moment later. "Mark our direction in the log if you will, Spence."

Spence understood and quickly obeyed, and was back at Martin's side a minute later, looking anxiously at the *Endeavor*, then at Martin, as the yachts sailed toward the same point on the horizon.

"Do they *want* us to overtake them?" Spence asked, then he stepped up on the bench and grabbed hold of a line. "What the blazes are they up to? They must know they have to give way."

Martin kept the wheel steady and glanced up at the sails, then down at the whitecaps on the water. He raised a hand into the air to feel the wind. "We're doing eighteen knots. Mark it in the log."

"How fast are *they* going?" Spence asked as he scribbled. "They seem to be picking up speed."

"I'd say sixteen. Maybe seventeen."

"Bloody hell, Martin, if they don't give way, we're going to collide."

Martin continued to hold the wheel steady, aware of his crew staring at him in silence with mouths agape, waiting for a command to trim a sail, drop the spinnaker, anything to slow them down or alter their direction.

"They must give way," he firmly repeated, noting the distance between them, closing and closing . . .

Spence shot an enraged glare at him. "We have to turn, Martin."

"No. *They* must turn."

"Do you have a death wish?"

That question—for some reason he did not wish to contemplate too deeply at the moment—captured his attention. For a long moment, he and Spence stared at each other as the yachts continued on a certain collision course, until Martin finally shouted, "Drop the spinnaker! We're turning starboard to windward! Release the jib and main, and *hold on!*"

At the very last second before they rammed the *Endeavor*, Martin turned the wheel and the *Orpheus* heeled impossibly, tossing one crewman into the rigging, while foaming white water poured across the deck. The tip of their mast came only inches from tearing apart the *Endeavor*'s mainsail.

"Bloody bastards!" Spence called out to Hatfield, who was standing on deck, saluting extravagantly with a crooked smile as he and Breckinridge took the lead back to Cowes.

"You did the right thing," Spence assured Martin as they marched up the landing stage toward the club. "Otherwise, we'd all be at the bottom of the sea right now."

Martin shook his head, still furious over what had occurred. Breckinridge had broken one of the critical rules of the water, endangered all their lives, and he'd mocked him after the fact.

"I'm not so sure about that," he said. "Breckinridge was playing a game, testing me to see what I would do, and I should have called his bluff. I should have forced him to give way."

"That would have been an awfully big risk with your boat and the lives of your crew," Spence replied. "I will not change my opinion on this, Martin. You made the right choice. Breckinridge is at fault, not you."

They walked at a swift pace up the drive and pushed through the Squadron gate to find Breckinridge and Hatfield standing on the back lawn with drinks already in their hands.

"Looks like we arrived first," Breckinridge proudly announced.

Everyone on the lawn fell silent and stared uneasily at Martin. There were a few quiet whispers.

I should not have given way, he thought, stopping just inside the gate and looking around at everyone.

But there was no way to change what had already occurred, so he strode forward with Spence at his side and met Breckinridge in the middle of the garden.

"I should have you disqualified," Martin said.

Breckinridge's eyebrows flew up in surprise. "I beg your pardon? You want to disqualify *me*?" He shook his head. "That is low, Lord Martin, even for you."

Martin darted a glance at Hatfield, who was eyeing him with disdain.

"You know as well as I do," Martin said, "that a boat on a starboard tack has right-of-way over a boat on a port tack."

"Yes, and we were on a starboard tack."

Spence stepped forward and pointed a finger. "Liar! We were on the starboard tack, not you!"

Head drawing back elegantly, Breckinridge paused for a few seconds. "I had always heard you were reckless, Lord Martin, but this is beyond reproach."

Martin felt the muscles in his jaw clench. "What exactly are you suggesting?"

But he already knew what Breckinridge was trying to do. He just wanted to hear him say it.

"I am suggesting that you are trying to have me removed from the race," the earl said, "because you know you cannot win."

Martin glared at him while Spence scoffed and took a step backward in disbelief. Everyone on the lawn was watching in silence.

"Or perhaps it is *you* trying to remove *me*," Martin replied. But from an entirely different race, he suspected.

Breckinridge glanced around at the others and raised his voice for all to hear. "I am a gentleman, Lord Martin, and I would never risk a boat or the lives on it. You, however, have a different history in that regard, do you not?"

Martin bristled and clenched a fist, while Spence stepped forward, almost nose to nose with Hatfield.

Just then, Sir Lyndon came trotting over, pushing the men apart and glancing uneasily from one to another. "Now, now, surely we can resolve this. It's a misunderstanding, that's all."

Martin never took his eyes off Breckinridge. "If a man can misunderstand what tack he's on, he has no business at the helm of a sailing vessel."

Hatfield's lip twitched. "I'm telling you this as a friend, Martin—you really ought to leave now before you find yourself disqualified from the race."

Martin glared at Hatfield. *As a friend?*

Spence took another menacing step forward, but Martin raised a hand to stop him. "No, Spence. Let's go."

They both backed away and headed for the gate.

"I would have liked to knock Hatfield on his fat arse," Spence said as they strode down the hill. "If it weren't for the ladies looking on . . ."

"I wanted to do the same thing to Breckinridge, that pompous ass."

Spence stopped on the road. "So what are we going to do about it?"

Martin stopped, too, and considered it for a moment. "Part of me would like to somehow retaliate, but I would never disregard the laws of the sea. My feeling is that we must sail this race as gentlemen and let Breckinridge and Hatfield hang themselves. If there is any justice in the world—and pray God there is—they will. The truth will come out, and people will see them both for what they are. We must have faith in that."

Spence raised an eyebrow at Martin, as if he weren't quite sure he agreed.

What had become of him? Evelyn wondered irritably, touching the teapot in her room and finally resigning herself to the fact that she would have to send it back because it was cold. It was now five minutes past six. He did not appear to be coming.

She sat down on the bed and chastised herself for assuming he would keep their appointment for a teatime rendezvous. He had made it clear on more than one occasion that he did not wish to become involved in any meaningful or lasting relationships. Their encounter the night before had been wonderful, but certainly no promises had been made and today he had probably changed his mind about . . .

Just then, a knock sounded at her door. She froze and did not get up right away. Her pride would not let her go leaping across furniture to answer it.

Taking her time to breathe, she rose from the bed and crossed the room. She opened the door and there he was, standing in the corridor looking windswept and weary, raking a hand through his hair.

"I'm sorry," he said with impatience, not looking at all like the seductive charmer she had expected an hour ago. "I'm late."

She did not step back and invite him in because she was not even sure she wanted him to come in. She certainly did not wish to be an inconvenient obligation.

"I didn't mean to keep you waiting," he added with a dispirited nod of his head.

With half her body still shielded behind the door, she recognized stress lines in his expression, and began to wonder if his tardy appearance might not be what she thought. "Apology accepted," she cautiously replied. "But why are you late? Did something happen?"

He turned to look down the corridor as if he didn't quite know what to do with himself, then faced her again. "Can I come in?"

"Of course." Curious, she stepped aside to let him pass, and closed the door. "I'm sorry the tea is cold."

He walked all the way in and waved a hand as if to say it didn't matter, then he sat down on the bed.

"What happened?" she asked.

He raked a hand through his hair again. "I have been accused of foul sailing tactics by your friend, Lord Breckinridge." He looked up at her with fire in his eyes.

"I wouldn't call him my *friend*," she decisively informed him. "But what happened? What did he say?"

"It's worse than what he simply said," Martin replied. "It's what he did. The man is a liar and a cheat, Evelyn, and I hope to God you never consent to become his wife."

Taken aback, she probed for more information. "What in the world did he do?"

"He broke one of the laws of the sea by refusing to give way on a port tack, and we almost collided."

"Good heavens. Was anyone hurt?"

"No, we're all fine, but only because I made a last minute turn to avoid him, and then he had the gall to tell everyone at the Squadron that it was *me*—that I was the one on the port tack. He lied—he and Hatfield both—so it was our word against theirs. And we all know the world considers him a perfect gentleman with a flawless reputation. He even had the audacity to bring up the boats I wrecked three years ago." Martin's fingers flexed over the edge of the mattress. "Not a day goes by that I don't regret being so bloody foolish back then."

Evelyn sat down beside him. "But you were devastated over the loss of your wife and child."

"You're very forgiving," he said flatly, almost resentfully. "Not everyone is. There are many people here who think me a reckless sportsman and would like to see me fail." He paused. "But do *you* believe me about today?"

"That you were not in the wrong? Of course."

She knew beyond a shadow of a doubt that despite his scandalous reputation, he was an honorable sailor and a gentleman on the water. Hatfield, on the other hand, she was not so sure about.

"And here I've kept you waiting for over an hour," he said, his irritation beginning to diminish. "How very rude of me."

She managed a smile. "You had a legitimate excuse."

He shook his head. "I was fit to be tied an hour ago," he said, "which is why I did not come. Spence tried to convince me to go back out on the water because he thought it was the only thing that would calm me down."

She rubbed her hand over the top of his thigh. "If it calms you, why don't you go?"

"Because I promised you more pleasures in bed, my dear, and I never break a promise to a lady."

Her heart turned over in her chest. "Why don't we go sailing together, then? And I will promise to release you of any obligation for sexual favors."

Her magnanimous offer amused him. The lines of stress around his eyes disappeared. "All right," he said. "Let's go, but I want you beside me at the wheel. No one but you."

"Why just me?" she asked shamelessly.

He hesitated—as if he had to think about how to answer that—then he spoke with affection and humor. "Because you distract me, of course, from the dastardly deeds of that cheat who calls himself a sailor. The same cheat who thinks himself worthy enough to be your husband—which he is not."

Evelyn smiled, for she liked that answer. She liked it very much.

Martin stood. "Shall I go ready the *Orpheus*, then?

"Yes, Captain, if you please."

Chapter 16

Shortly after sunset, Martin steered the *Orpheus* into a quiet cove and dropped anchor. The moon had already appeared low in the sky, and the wind had become a faint whisper through the creaking rigging.

As soon as the boat was secure, he approached Evelyn, who sat on deck near the wheel, smiling up at him. "Would you like some wine?" he asked.

"Please."

He nodded and went below, lit a lamp and opened a bottle of his finest, then climbed back up the companionway with the wine and two glasses.

"You mean to tell me we're not drinking out of the bottle tonight?" she said.

"We can do anything you wish," he said with a knowing glint in his eye.

She laughed and waved a hand. "No, I think I would like at least *some* propriety this evening."

Holding both glasses in one hand, he tipped the bottle up and poured. "Should I be disappointed to hear that?"

Because he'd been very hopeful they would engage in a great deal of *im*propriety now that the anchor was over the side.

He set the bottle down. Evelyn accepted the glass he held out.

"I was referring to our consumption of fine wine," she replied.

"Well, that's a relief, I must say." He sat down beside her and held up his glass. "To your beauty."

She raised her glass as well. "And to your great success in the race."

They both sipped the wine, then Evelyn slid closer to him. "Are you feeling better about what happened today? You were very agitated when you knocked on my door. I hope our sailing together had the desired effect."

"I was indeed agitated, and I apologize. I should not have burdened you with that."

"Of course you should have," she argued, sounding stunned that he would suggest otherwise.

"What is a lover for if not to ease the hardships of life?"

He grinned. "I don't think those are the hardships most people wish to ease with their lovers."

She brushed the tip of her nose across his cheek. "You can ease any hardships you like with me, Martin."

His body heated instantly with a rush of desire, which he felt almost painfully in his loins. "You are a temptress, Evelyn, but I want you to know, you are a great deal more than that as well. You were my safe harbor today. You reminded me that the race is not everything, nor is this boat, which is something I often forget. I want to thank you for that."

She smiled, and he pressed his lips tenderly to hers, holding her in the moonlight while the boat rocked beneath them. Her lips tasted of sweet wine, her skin smelled of roses. She sighed with pleasure, and he needed no further bidding as his pulse began to pound with insistence.

He set down his glass and brushed his lips across her soft neck, then whispered in her ear, "Let me make love to you."

"I thought you would never ask."

He stood and led her down the companionway, below to the cozy, private forward berth. Shadows from the lamp on the bulkhead danced across the walls as the boat dipped on the gentle nighttime swells. Evelyn removed her spectacles and set them on a shelf, then pulled the pins from her hair and shook it loose down her back. God, but she was an exquisite woman. He couldn't take his eyes off her.

They crawled into the master's quarters and sank down on the soft mattress, entwined in each other's arms. Martin captured her lips in his own and wondered how long it had been since he'd felt such fiery depths of yearning for more than just the promise of one night with a woman. He didn't wish this to be everything. He wanted more from her, and he wanted to *give* her more. He felt the strangest compulsion to reveal things to her and confess things he'd never confessed to anyone, which rather unnerved him.

But it was not something he wished to contemplate too carefully when she was here in his bed, eager for the pleasure he intended to give her.

Kneeling back, he undressed her slowly, beginning with the buttons on her bodice, then moving down to her skirts. Next he removed her undergarments—her corset and drawers and chemise. She lay patiently looking up at him, and when she was naked at last, he let his eyes feast leisurely upon her lovely face, her beautiful breasts and firm belly, and down to the narrow triangle of bushy brown hair between her legs, to which he would soon give his full care and attention.

Just the thought of it made him swell and

stiffen. He began his own disrobing, and seconds later, he, too, was nude in the berth, sliding his arm around her narrow waist and passing his lips across hers. She quivered with delight and strained upward, and he slid his hand down, feeling for the soft warm paradise between her thighs. She moistened at his touch.

Their tongues meshed wildly together, and she slipped her own hand down and wrapped it around his heated erection. Her body was warm and tender beside him, her thighs spreading wide, her sweet mouth open beneath his own.

He rolled over on top of her and licked eagerly over her nipples, which were hard as dark cherries and every bit as sweet. He was convinced no woman's breasts were as beautiful, or so thoroughly licked and pleasured as hers were in those frenzied moments while he tasted them.

She wiggled and worked her bottom, rubbing her pubic hair against his stomach until he could delay no longer. He'd been wanting to make love to her all day, and it was all he could do to keep from exploding before he'd done all he could to give her the full measure of his abilities.

"We have all night," he whispered, needing to apologize in advance for his eagerness, and vowing to give her everything he was capable of before dawn, "but I must have you now, Evelyn. I must."

"I want you, too. I thought of nothing else all day. I can't wait any longer."

Their eyes locked on each other as he rose on one arm and reached down with the other hand to guide his way to her damp, primed opening. With a groan he slid some two inches into her, then withdrew and returned for the full onslaught of his passions. She implored him to drive deeper by cupping his buttocks in her hands and gyrating her hips as he drew in and out with unstoppable lust.

"Open wider," he growled, and she readily obeyed, throwing her head back on the pillows and gasping with hungry desire.

He rose on one arm again and dipped his face to suck furiously on one of her breasts, while the friction below sent an excruciating fire through his body. He made love to her with everything he possessed as a man, watching her face, studying her responses and wanting only to pleasure her in every possible way. She was a pure angel. She deserved everything wonderful he could give her.

Soon, her fingers dug into the flesh at the small of his back and she bucked wildly beneath him and cried out into the night, arching her back, throbbing and flexing around his burning, blissful erection. He plunged down hard, crushing her soft form beneath him as she continued to climax;

then, when he was sure she was fully satisfied, he pulled out and exploded and poured onto her belly with a tremendous gushing of breathless pleasure.

"Oh, Captain Martin," she sighed, her arms falling limp on either side of her as he rolled off her onto his back. "Did you say we had all night?"

He wasn't sure he had the strength to speak. "I did."

"Then I think I died and went to heaven."

"I must have died and gone with you."

They lay together in the quiet cabin, the boat bobbing up and down on the swells beneath their bodies, and Martin thought perhaps he *had* gone to heaven. He had not felt such contentment in a long time and didn't want to let it go.

What would it be like to come home to Evelyn and share his bed like this with her every night? he wondered curiously. To keep her forever as the only woman in his life, and never say good-bye?

The very fact that he was asking himself that question sent a jolt of apprehension straight to his core for all that it implied. He did not want to be a husband or father again. That's not why he'd entered into this affair. He'd entered into it for pleasure's sake because he could not resist her, and she'd assured him that was all she wanted as well. It was not a courtship for the purpose of marriage. That much he knew, as did she. He could not let himself forget that.

* * *

Over the next four days, Evelyn and Martin went sailing together whenever they could sneak away unnoticed. They spent countless hours braving the wind and waves around the western tip of the island, and when they weren't relaxing on board the *Orpheus* in calm waters, they were sailing her to her limits, reaching tremendous speeds and testing themselves with complicated maneuvers. At night, if they weren't on the boat, they were making love in his hotel room or hers, and talking about anything and everything.

Though they never discussed the future beyond the week's end.

Of course Martin had to prepare for the race as well, so on the fifth day, he and his crew took the *Orpheus* out, while Evelyn spent time with Lady Radley, browsing in the shops and socializing on the back lawn of the yacht club. They talked and gossiped, but she avoided questions about her whereabouts on various occasions when she was otherwise "occupied," as she did not wish to share the details of her intimacies with Martin. She was hiding the particulars in the very deepest places in her heart. Not even Lady Radley would be privy to them, even though the sweet woman would undoubtedly applaud Evelyn for her choice to enjoy herself this week.

Although to imply that she was merely "enjoying" herself was not entirely accurate, for her feelings went far deeper than that. These days with Martin had been the most exciting, passionate of her life, and she was quite sure she had fallen hopelessly, irreversibly in love with him. She had come to know his heart and soul and understood his joys and desires as well as his sorrows, and she longed for him to be happy.

And that night, when she saw him at the ball on board the steamship *Dartmouth*, after being away from him all day, it was the best she could do to remain on the other side of the room, sipping champagne while anticipating the moment he would ask her to dance. At last it came. He approached, looking devastatingly handsome in his black-and-white formal attire, his dark hair thick and wavy about his shoulders. He had attracted the gaze of every woman in the room and had charmed everyone he spoke to. She felt fire in her blood when he requested a spot on her card, along with a spot on Lady Radley's and also on Mrs. Studebaker's, who was a distant cousin of the host. The two ladies giggled and fanned themselves after he left, while Evelyn merely sipped her drink, masking her true feelings with cool composure.

Meanwhile, Lord Breckinridge and Mr. Hatfield remained on the opposite side of the room. They did not speak to Martin, nor did he speak to them, and if anyone was still chattering about the near collision, they did not speak of it openly, at least not in front of Evelyn. Perhaps all was forgotten. She hoped it was. She hoped it had truly been a misunderstanding.

Later, after a number of lively dances, the moment arrived. Martin found her and led her onto the floor to claim his dance.

They behaved as if they were nothing more than polite acquaintances, even though Evelyn became feverish from the mere touch of his hand upon her back. They danced the entire piece with gazes locked, never speaking a word, until the very end when he escorted her back to the Radleys.

"I will knock on your door later," he said, leaning so close, she felt the heat of his breath in her ear and shivered with anticipation.

"I'll be waiting," she replied, before she thanked him at the edge of the dance floor. He bowed respectfully and left her with her companions.

Strangely, at that moment, something prompted her to look toward Lord Breckinridge. He was watching her with a frown. As soon as their eyes met, however, he smiled and raised his glass to her, and she nodded in return. Later, she danced with him as well, and he behaved as he always did. He was meticulously polite.

That night in bed, Martin made love to Evelyn in the balmy heat of summer, losing himself completely in the sweet lushness between her thighs and the delectable flavor of her lips. He simply could not get enough of her, and there were moments—moments like these, when he was deep inside the soft warmth of her flesh—when he actually forgot why he had come to Cowes in the first place. He had to remind himself that he was here to defend his title as champion of the race. He was not here to have sex every hour of the day and become sleep-deprived, which was exactly what was happening. His speech had been slurred that afternoon when they'd rounded the northeastern point of the island because he'd been up all night with fire in his blood and an angel in his bed.

God help him, if he had to skipper a boat right now, he'd run it aground, because his brain was throbbing with nothing but the need to drive himself home, to grind himself up onto Evelyn's shore with the thrust of a fierce, foaming rogue wave. It was madness, complete and utter madness, and it had commandeered his brain—for on top of his negligence as a competitor in the race, he was in danger of taking another chance tonight, for he did not want to withdraw.

Just then, the headboard began to bang against the wall. He stopped what he was doing and shoved a pillow down between it and the wall to stop the racket, and immediately resumed his pace.

Beneath him, Evelyn's tiny moans brought him

closer to the brink, until he felt the first squeezing pulsations of her orgasm. She arched her back and cried out, and he tried to hold off just a few seconds more, but couldn't. All at once, his own climax loomed. His body hummed and quaked, but before he spilled into her, he heard the ever-present voice of caution in his head. He pulled out at the last second and climaxed so explosively, the product of his pleasure hit the headboard.

"God in heaven!" he ground out, his body convulsing.

"God in heaven is right! The driving force of that would have put a child in my womb for sure."

She was joking, he knew, but he could not laugh. Her words sobered him, made him realize how many chances they had taken this week, even though it was supposed to be a safe time. He had been careless too often and feared he was losing control.

Thank God he had withdrawn tonight—though it had not been easy.

Entirely spent, he toppled to the side, tipping over like a felled tree and coming down hard upon the bed. He covered his forehead with a hand and tried to keep his tone light, despite the fact that he was shaken by the force of that climax. "I feel like I disintegrated."

She reached for his hand and held it. "But you didn't. You're still here, thank goodness, because it's only midnight, and I'm not the least bit tired."

He turned his head to the side, looked at her enchanting profile in the darkness, and felt very confused all of a sudden. He'd enjoyed himself more than he ever thought possible this week, and he did not want it to end. He wanted to keep making love to her. He did not want to give up this bliss or lose her to another man.

But neither did he want the things that would come with a promise of forever, and the clash of those two desires was tearing him apart inside.

He only hoped she would not be hurt by it.

Chapter 17

T he next day, Evelyn was invited to an afternoon garden party. Struggling to keep
from yawning and trying not to walk oddly after a full week of lovemaking at every opportunity, she arrived at the stone villa on the Green.
She was welcomed by Mrs. Cunningham, the
amiable hostess who was famous for her cook's
moist and delicious crab cakes.

"It is a pleasure to finally meet you," the woman
said, shaking Evelyn's hand. "Especially after listening to Lord Breckinridge sing your praises
during dinner last night. He speaks very highly
of you, my dear, and now I see why. What a lovely
creature you are."

Evelyn made an effort to hide her surprise, for she was not accustomed to being told she was the subject of dinner conversation or that she was a lovely creature for that matter, though with Martin, she was certainly getting used to it. "Thank you, Mrs. Cunningham," she replied.

She mingled about and sipped tea and tried the crab cakes, which were indeed the best she'd ever tasted. Though she had earlier considered catching up on some sleep instead of attending, she was now glad she had not, for the sunny afternoon in Mrs. Cunningham's garden was proving to be highly enjoyable.

"I see you've tried the famous cakes," a masculine voice said from behind her, and she turned to find herself gazing up at Lord Breckinridge.

She quickly dabbed the side of her mouth with a napkin and swallowed. "Yes, they are certainly delicious."

He immediately raised a hand to signal a footman, who approached with a tray. Breckinridge picked up one of the little cakes and sampled it. "Ah, yes. Pure perfection."

She was thankful that Lord and Lady Radley joined them at that moment, and they all began a discussion about the food and weather and the many enjoyable parties they had each attended since they'd arrived in Cowes.

"But alas, the week is coming to an end," Breckinridge said. "The race takes place the day after tomorrow, which means I am going to have to collect on a promise now, Mrs. Wheaton, and secure a commitment from you before it is too late."

"What promise is that?" Lady Radley asked, biting into a blueberry tart and glancing anxiously at Evelyn, who raised her teacup to her lips and took a composed sip.

"The promise Mrs. Wheaton made to me a few days ago," he explained. "I am to take you sailing, remember?"

Unease seeped into her bones as she recalled making that promise. "Yes, but surely you'll be preparing for the race between now and then. I couldn't possibly impose."

"It would be no imposition," he argued, "as I have no intention of exhausting my crew the day before a race. We will simply enjoy a pleasure cruise." He directed his gaze toward the Radleys. "You are both invited, of course, and the weather promises to be fine."

Caught off guard, Evelyn wondered if she could come up with an excuse, but Lord Radley spoke for her before she had the chance. "We would be delighted to join you on the *Endeavor*," he said. "And you must come, Evelyn. You've spent far too much time cooped up in your hotel room this week. You should get out on the water and experience the thrill of the sea."

Lady Radley was notably silent on the matter.

"Yes, Mrs. Wheaton," Lord Breckinridge implored. "I would relish the opportunity to show you the island from the water. There is a magnificent rock formation called The Needles, and you cannot visit the Isle of Wight without seeing it in all its glorious splendor."

She took a breath to speak, but he interrupted. "Surely you don't have any *other* commitments, do you?"

He looked at her with accusation, as if he knew everything she'd been up to the past week, including the thought-provoking gymnastics on the tabletop in Martin's room that very morning.

"No, of course not," she said with a forced smile, and Lord Radley nodded at her with approval.

"Excellent," Breckinridge replied. "I will go and inform my first mate of our plans. If you will meet us on the landing stage at noon?"

"We'll be there," Lord Radley said, and as soon as his nephew was gone, his face lit up with cheer. "It's going to be a marvelous afternoon, Evelyn. Breckinridge is an expert sailor and a charming host to be sure. I don't doubt that most of the other women here will be very envious to know he has chosen *you* to join him tomorrow."

"I'm sure it will be a wonderful day," she replied, her only consolation the fact that Martin—unlike Lord Breckinridge—*would* be out with his crew at that time, practicing his maneuvers for the race.

* * *

Later that evening while dressing for dinner with Lord and Lady Radley, Evelyn began her monthly, and was completely astonished when she burst into tears.

Good God, she should have been relieved! She should have wept tears of joy and imagined the irreparable damage to her reputation if she had become pregnant with Martin's child, for she and Martin had risked out-and-out scandal over the past week.

He would most certainly be relieved to know he would not be a father. Relieved also to know that he would not be obligated to propose when he wanted no such thing. He had made that very clear from the beginning, and she had accepted that when she entered into this affair.

She would tell him tonight, she decided, as she finished dressing and fastened a necklace around her neck. And she would tell him how relieved *she* was, too. She would not tell him she had cried. She still didn't quite understand it, because she had not made love to Martin for the purpose of conceiving a child. She had simply wanted him with inescapable passion. He bewitched her—he always had—and this week she had finally given up the fight. She'd surrendered to her desires and seized the opportunity to love him—both physically and otherwise. She had no business being disappointed that she had not conceived, despite the fact that she had always wanted a child of her own.

She sat down in a chair and slipped her feet into her shoes, then stared absently at the window. She sighed despondently.

Oh, damn her foolish heart! Damn her mind for those dreamy moments when she'd imagined what would happen if she *had* found herself in the family way. She'd imagined him wanting to marry her. She'd pictured him pleading with her to say yes and getting down on one knee, and promising her that this bliss would never end.

She shook her head at herself. She had been such a fool to think she could be intimate with him and make love with him and escape all of it unscathed. The fact was, she had fallen desperately in love with him, and now she had to prepare herself for the inevitable. By the beginning of next week, she would be back in London, and this incredible week with Martin would be nothing more than a memory.

And she was going to be devastated.

It was almost midnight when a knock sounded at Evelyn's door. Dressed in her nightgown with the buttons fastened tightly at her neck, she went to answer it.

It was Martin, as she'd expected. He was leaning at his ease against the doorjamb, wearing his black-and-white dinner attire, looking devilishly handsome and smiling at her with that seductive glimmer that, despite her courses, aroused a passionate fluttering deep within her womanly core.

He continued to stand there, pulling his white bow tie from around his neck and tossing it over his shoulder. "Sorry I'm late," he said, "but the dessert took forever. When it finally came, I swallowed it whole because I couldn't wait to get out of there."

"You needn't have rushed," she said, her hand still on the doorknob. "There's no reason for you to stay tonight anyway."

She realized suddenly that she had spoken with some hostility, which was not fair because he had done nothing wrong, and he had just apologized for being late, and he really wasn't so very late in the first place. She was simply irritable because her monthly had begun and their affair had been cut short, when it had already been far too brief to begin with.

"What's wrong, Evelyn?" he asked, pushing away from the doorjamb.

She hesitated, realizing she couldn't very well explain the circumstances while he was standing out in the hall. Someone might hear. So she stepped aside and waved him in. He entered and faced her.

"It's good news," she said, burying her disappointment and the heartache that had already begun. She walked around him to close the book she'd been reading, then faced him again. "My courses came tonight."

He stared at her for a moment, then let out a breath, his mouth forming a perfect O. His eyebrows lifted, and he went and sat down on the edge of the bed. Evelyn waited for him to say something—anything—but for the longest time he just stared down at his hands in his lap. At last he looked up.

"That is good news."

Evelyn swallowed uneasily. "Yes," she replied. "I'm very relieved." She carried the book to her dressing table and set it down, then moved a perfume bottle to the opposite side of the silver tray that held her creams and fragrances. She forced herself to face Martin again and leaned back against the dressing table. "Don't feel you have to stay."

He seemed to be studying her eyes. "I'll stay if you want me to."

"What would be the point?"

He frowned. "To enjoy each other's company?" he replied. When still she did not speak, he rose and crossed to her. "Evelyn, you told me you would not be hurt by a temporary affair. We discussed it, remember?"

Every nerve in her body tightened, for he had seen straight through to her traitorous feelings. "I'm not hurt," she assured him, her pride willing it to be true.

"But you're angry with me."

She stood motionless. Yes, she was, even though she had no right to be. She had known the rules when she entered into this affair, and she could not blame him for the fact that her feelings had changed. He had never lied to her or misled her, and she had promised herself she could weather it.

She could and she would. Her pride demanded it.

"I'm not angry," she firmly said.

"I don't believe you."

She looked down, then went and sat on a chair. "All right then, if you must know I was . . . a little disappointed."

He was quiet for a minute. "Because we can't make love tonight? Or because there is no child."

"Both."

His shoulders rose and fell. "But I don't want to get married again, Evelyn. You know that."

She was not surprised to hear this, but it frustrated her just the same. "How can you feel that way after the week we just spent together? It was wonderful, and you know it was, Martin. I don't understand how you can let it all end."

He stepped toward her. "Yes, it was wonderful, and I *don't* want it to end, which is why I am here. I want to be with you. I just don't want to get married again. Nor do I want to have a child."

She sat back and shot him a steady look. "So

you're telling me you want to make love to me, but you cannot offer me a commitment, or any kind of future?"

His Adam's apple bobbed.

"I am sorry, but that is not enough for me, Martin. I admit I entered into this affair without expectations. I only wanted to know what passion felt like, and I know I told you that I would not be hurt by any of it. I believed it was true at the time. But the truth is, I am already hurt by the fact that this cannot last forever. I have discovered that I am not so superficial, you see. I cannot love you with just my body and overlook the fact that it will one day come to an end. My heart has become involved, and I must now wrestle with the fact that I want more than just a casual, temporary affair. A great deal more. I need to know you are mine and I am yours and that you return my feelings."

He dropped his gaze. "I don't want to lose you, Evelyn."

"Then *don't*!"

He stood silently for a few seconds before he turned and strode to the window, where he looked out at the darkness over the water. Evelyn wondered what he was thinking about. His wife and child? The week they'd just spent together? Or perhaps his future alone?

He bowed his head, then turned and faced her. "Maybe I should go."

Her stomach knotted with despair. So this was

it? And to think, all she had wanted was to be like those other women he flirted with and made love to. Now she was. She was another name on his long list of conquests.

He reached the door and put his hand on the knob, but paused before he left. "Maybe we can talk about this tomorrow," he said. "I'm taking the *Orpheus* out in the morning for one last test run, but I'll be back in the afternoon."

Evelyn lifted her chin. "I won't be here. I'll be out sailing."

"With whom?"

"Lord Breckinridge."

She should not have taken such pleasure in announcing it, but there it was. Breckinridge had made no secret of the fact that he wished to marry her. He wanted to give her what Martin could not.

A muscle flicked at his jaw. "Are you sure that's wise? You're not going alone with him, I hope."

"No, Lord and Lady Radley are coming, but even if they weren't, it would be my decision to make."

She was lashing out at him, and she knew it.

Martin's brow furrowed with frustration or concern, she wasn't quite sure which. "Don't go, Evelyn."

"Why not?"

"Because he's a cheat, and he only wants you for your money."

She knew he did not mean to insult her, but it was a direct hit to her pride. "You don't think it's possible that he might find me moderately interesting?"

"Evelyn, don't."

"Don't what? Don't consider a future for myself? He might not be perfect, and maybe he's an incompetent sailor who doesn't know the difference between port and starboard, but he is at least offering me something—a commitment, a life, children. And why should you care? You don't want any of those things."

"I just don't want to see you settle for less than you deserve."

"And what do I deserve, exactly?" she asked with bitterness and bite.

"A husband who loves you."

The air sailed out of her lungs. It was what she wanted, too, more than anything in the world, but she wanted that husband to be him—the only man she had ever loved. And *would* ever love.

"Well, that's what I want, too," she said. "I realize that now." It was true. All of it. Every last word.

He stood before her saying nothing, doing nothing. He just stared at her, his eyes dark, his brow furrowed with tension.

All the muscles in her body squeezed tight with a yearning she wished she did not feel. All she wanted to do was dash into his arms and hear him say he was sorry—that he was wrong and loved her and wanted to be with her. She wanted him to forbid her to go sailing with Breckinridge tomorrow, because she belonged to him and no other.

But he said none of those things. His gaze dropped to the floor. He shut his eyes and pinched the bridge of his nose. "I can't do this, Evelyn. I have a race to win, a crew who is depending on me. I've been neglecting them all week, and—"

"You don't have to explain," she said, locating her dignity even though her heart was breaking. "We had an agreement that it would be temporary, and it was wonderful while it lasted, but now is a good time to end it before we spoil it. If we haven't already."

His eyes flashed upward. "Nothing could ever spoil it."

He continued to stand at her door with an unspoken apology in his eyes, and though she knew he did care for her in his own way, it still crushed her to know that he did not want more. That he could not love her the way she loved him.

"Good night, Evelyn," he said, and walked out.

Chapter 18

⁓⁓◯◯⁓⁓

"**W**hat a glorious day for a sail!" Lord Breckinridge shouted as he stood at the helm of the *Endeavor* wearing his black captain's hat and crested, navy blue blazer.

"Indeed it is," Lady Radley replied. "Thank you so much for inviting us out today—the very day before the race. It will make everything so much more exciting tomorrow, to think that we sailed on this famous yacht."

Evelyn noted that Lady Radley did not say the "winning boat." She wondered what the others thought about how well Martin would fare against this obvious racing machine. Not that she should care, of course, for it was over between them.

"Would anyone like some champagne?" Breckinridge asked.

"That would be delightful," Lord Radley said.

"Go below and get our best bottle, will you, Hatfield?"

Mr. Hatfield headed toward the companionway. "Aye, aye, Captain."

As soon as Mr. Hatfield disappeared below, Breckinridge leaned closer to Lord Radley, and said, "What's the use of a first mate, I ask you, if he can't serve you drinks?"

Evelyn recognized immediately what Breckinridge loved most about sailing—and it was not the thrill of the wind through the sails or the sense of "heaven" certain other captains experienced, as she herself did. For Lord Breckinridge and Mr. Hatfield, it was all about the champagne and the power and fame.

She let out a sigh and turned in the opposite direction. Glancing up at the mainsail, she wondered when they planned to raise the jib.

Mr. Hatfield reappeared, looking more than delighted to be getting into the bubbly so early in the day. He handed each of them a glass and poured, then poured his own and made a toast. "To winning the trophy tomorrow and becoming the new Cowes champions!"

"Here's to that!" Breckinridge said, holding the wheel with one hand while he tipped his glass up with the other.

*   *   *

Martin stood at the helm of the *Orpheus*, steering her toward the crowded waters in front of the Royal Yacht Squadron. They hadn't had much luck with the winds that morning, for it was almost a dead calm. They eventually gave up waiting for any great rush of speed and decided to call it a day. The best thing they could do was rest up for the race.

Spence, who was standing at the bow holding on to the halyard, turned and called out to Martin. "The *Endeavor*'s approaching." He raised a hand to shade his eyes from the sun and continued to watch.

Martin stretched to see, too, because he knew Evelyn was on board. They would pass each other—the *Endeavor* heading out to sea, the *Orpheus* on her way back in to her mooring . . .

Spence made his way aft and came to stand beside Martin at the wheel. "No danger of any collisions today," he said. "He's got a crowd with him."

Then the *Endeavor* passed them by.

Martin's heart seemed to go still for a second while he stood on the deck, staring at Evelyn, who was standing next to Breckingridge at the wheel of the *Endeavor* with a glass of champagne in her hand. The others on board were waving.

"Ahoy there!" Lady Radley called out across the water.

"Ahoy!" Spence replied with reserve.

Martin said nothing. He couldn't. He felt numb.

There she goes, he thought, wondering how it was possible that over the past week, there had been moments when she'd made him forget everything that plagued him—his obsession to win the Cowes trophy, his enduring grief from what he'd lost. He had felt joy—real joy—and all that seemed to matter now was his regret over their argument the night before, and his need to have her at his side, and know that she would never marry Breckinridge or any other.

He swallowed with difficulty and turned around to watch the *Endeavor* grow distant. Evelyn, too, was standing at the stern, watching the *Orpheus*.

Martin realized suddenly that he wasn't holding the wheel. He swung back around, but Spence had already taken over. "Don't worry, I've got it," he said.

Martin continued to stand there speechless, staring astern.

"You look pale," Spence said. "Maybe you should sit down, or better yet, turn this boat around and go after her."

Martin shot him a glance. "Are you referring to the *Endeavor,* or the widow on board?"

Spence merely cocked a brow.

"Bloody hell," Martin said, taking at least some of his friend's advice by sitting down on the bench. He felt like a lead weight. "How much do you know?"

"Mostly everything. I'm not stupid."

Martin leaned forward. "When did you figure it out?"

Hands on the wheel, his eyes darting up at the trim of the sails, Spence spoke lightly. "About ten years ago. She was the only girl in Windsor you complained about on a daily basis, and the only one who made you wear that face."

"What face?"

"The one you're wearing now. The *I-wish-I-could-have-her* face."

Martin directed his frustrated gaze to his first mate. "And yet you discouraged me. You told me to leave her alone."

"No," Spence firmly retorted. "I told you not to toy with her. There's a difference."

"But why didn't you say anything this week? You let me go ahead and do just that. You said nothing while I carried on a casual affair with her."

Spence adjusted the wheel slightly. "I didn't want to make you think about it too much, you harebrain, because you spend far too much time thinking about how guilty you feel about the things that could make you happy and debating with yourself over what you should and shouldn't want instead of just going ahead and taking it."

Martin rested his elbows on his knees and

clasped his hands together. "Well, I certainly took it this time."

"Finally," Spence replied.

"I can't lose her."

"No, you can't. So what are you going to do now? Go back to the club or turn this lady around?"

Martin paused a moment, then stood and reclaimed his position at the wheel. He gripped the spokes tightly in both hands. "We're going to take her back to the club."

Spence frowned. "Coward."

"You didn't let me finish," Martin replied. "I'm taking you and these sloppy crew members back, then I'm turning around on my own—because as soon as I get that widow back on this boat, I'll have no need of you people."

Spence laughed out loud and slapped Martin on the back. "Aye, aye, Captain." He strode to the front of the cockpit and called out to the crew. "Prepare to bring in the jib, gentlemen, because if we don't slow this boat down and get the hell off, our skipper will toss us overboard!"

She was indeed a phenomenally fast boat, Evelyn realized as they sailed past The Needles and headed out to open water. Martin would have his work cut out for him in the morning when the starting cannons fired at the Squadron.

"What a splendid sight!" Lady Radley said,

holding on to her hat as they sailed past the light-house on the point. "What do you think, Evelyn? Isn't it the most remarkable thing you've ever seen?"

She held on to her hat, too, as the wind gusted harder. "It's magnificent!" she called out.

But the truth was, it was not nearly as magnificent as it had been a week ago, when she'd sailed here with Martin and seen all of this and so many other things for the first time.

She looked back at Breckinridge, who was speaking to Lord Radley, while Mr. Hatfield stood at the wheel, still drinking champagne.

She could never marry the earl. She knew that now. Nor could she marry for security or respectability, nor wed a man who only wanted her money. She was worth more than that. She wanted and deserved devotion and commitment and passion and love. She had learned that from Martin.

And heaven help her, it was killing her to think that he could never be hers. She wondered wretchedly if she had made a mistake telling him she needed more. Perhaps if she had agreed to continue the affair on a casual basis, he would have fallen in love with her in time. Perhaps she had demanded too much too soon.

Just then, the wind shifted, and her hat blew off her head. It spun through the air and floated lightly down onto the whitecaps below.

"Evelyn, your hat!" Lady Radley cried, pointing as they sailed right past it.

But a silly hat was hardly important to her now, not when the only thing she truly wanted was back in Cowes doing God only knew what. Charming another widow perhaps? Or missing her, could she dare to hope?

Then all at once, her hair was whipping wildly around her head as her loose chignon pulled free. Mr. Hatfield and Lord Breckinridge stared at her in shock while she stood on the sloping deck, not really caring if she shocked them with her flying locks. She liked the way it felt, and, dammit, she was on a sailboat. She would do as she wanted. At least for a little while.

Martin tied off the wheel and moved across the deck to adjust the lines on the mainsail. Damn, but the *Endeavor* was fast. He couldn't bloody well catch her, which did not bode well for the race in the morning.

But that was the least of his worries. Breckinridge could have the title and trophy if he wanted them, just as long as he forfeited the other race— the one for Evelyn's heart.

Martin didn't care what it took, but he was going to win her back. He was going to catch them, sail up alongside the *Endeavor*, and tell Evelyn he was sorry. He was going to shout out loud that he couldn't live without her, and demand that

Breckinridge give her up. He didn't know if she would forgive him, or even what the future would hold for them, but he at least had to try— because he wanted to be a better man. For *her*. He had to get her back on this boat where she belonged.

Feeling the cold, salty spray sting his face, he braced a foot on a winch and pulled hard on a line, then wrapped it around a cleat. He hurried aft, swinging deftly around the shrouds. The wind was stronger now, which should help him gain some speed.

He hopped down into the cockpit and took hold of the wheel again, then reached for his binoculars. Peering through them, he could see the *Endeavor* in the distance, miles ahead. They'd already sailed past The Needles and were heading out to open water.

God almighty, but she was fast.

The waves roared past the hull, the spray continued to sting his face, but he held tight to the wheel.

Chapter 19

Eventually, Evelyn went below to pin up her hair again. She was just sticking the last few pins into a sounder knot when a shadow moved into the companionway. She turned to discover Lord Breckinridge coming down to join her.

"I am so sorry about your hat," he said, stepping into the cabin. "You must allow me to replace it."

"Thank you, Lord Breckinridge," she replied, "but that's not necessary. It was an accident—my own fault entirely. I should have kept a better hold on it."

He stood looking at her for a moment—creating that awkward silence that had become so predictable between them and for which she had lost all patience. It was another way in which she had changed, she supposed, for there was a time she would have considered this normal. That was no longer the case. She now knew that she and Lord Breckinridge had nothing in common, nor did they have that essential ease that existed between two people who understood each other. It was yet another lesson she had learned from Martin.

The earl strode toward her, reached into his pocket and handed her a crisply folded handkerchief. "Permit me to inform you that your spectacles need attending."

She stared at him for a moment. Ah yes, they were indeed coated in a salty film, so she accepted the handkerchief he offered and removed them. But while she was wiping them clean, the boat dipped below their feet and tossed them both to the side. Evelyn knocked her elbow against the table and a sharp pain shot to her shoulder. Lord Breckinridge quickly reached to help her regain her balance.

"Are you all right, Mrs. Wheaton?"

"Yes, thank you," she replied, putting her spectacles back on and steadying herself. "That was quite a swell."

But as soon as she managed to focus through her newly polished lenses, the man's mouth came down hard upon hers, and his hands gripped her shoulders.

Her eyes flew open in shock. Another swell tossed the boat, and together they went falling against the bulkhead. The force of the impact squeezed the air from her lungs, and she shoved Lord Breckinridge away. *"My lord!"*

Breathing hard, he took a few lumbering steps back into the galley.

She was breathing hard herself. It had all happened so quickly. What did he think he was doing? Had he no shame? She wiped the distasteful kiss from her lips.

"Mrs. Wheaton, surely the time has come for us to discuss what has been weighing upon both our minds this week."

"And what, may I ask, is that?"

He grabbed hold of the table to steady himself. "A marital union between us, of course. You must acknowledge that we have much to offer each other. You have a great fortune. I have a title and respectability."

Her mouth dropped opened in dismay. "I beg your pardon, my lord, but I don't require either of those things. I want only love." There it was, spoken most daringly.

His expression darkened with intolerance. "That is very romantic, Mrs. Wheaton, but I feel it is my duty to inform you that you are quite wrong in one respect at least. You *do* require something from me—and that is respectability. You're an intelligent woman. Surely you know what I am referring to."

She narrowed her gaze at him as anger flared hotly in her veins. "No, sir, I do not know. Speak plainly, if you will."

The boat dipped beneath them again.

"I wish to protect your reputation, Mrs. Wheaton, and I mean to rescue you from a very lonely, desolate future."

She glared at him with reproach. "My future will not be desolate."

"I am of the opinion that it will be," he replied, "once the gossip begins. Society is already chattering, you see, about your very decadent activities over the past week here in Cowes."

She was thrust off-balance by another swell and had to grab hold of the bulkhead. "Are you threatening me?" she demanded to know. "Are you trying to blackmail me into marrying you? Because I assure you I will not have it."

"I am not trying to blackmail you," he said, sounding surprised at the suggestion. "I am trying to save you. And I advise you to think carefully about my offer before you refuse, Mrs. Wheaton, as it would give me great pleasure to be your champion." He studied her face for a moment. "Promise me you will at least think about it during our return."

Think about it? Indeed she would. She would think about all the different ways she could tell him how to chew and swallow that pompous captain's hat he wore on his head.

He stood up straighter and adjusted the hat. "There's foul weather upon us," he said in a commanding voice. "We'll be turning around now and heading back to Cowes. Perhaps tomorrow, when I accept the trophy after the race, you will do me the honor of allowing me to announce some happy news?"

Stunned, Evelyn stared at him. The boat rose high on the crest of another wave and dropped into a cavernous trough, and she held tight to the bulkhead. "I will not change my mind, Lord Breckinridge, nor will I be forced into a future which I—"

Just then, there was a loud crack on the deck like a gunshot.

Breckinridge turned. "What the blazes . . ."

He scrambled up the ladder. Evelyn followed and popped her head out of the cabin hatch. She looked up and saw the tall mast above her bending like a snake. Cleats were being torn from the deck, and lines were snapping in all directions. Then the mast broke, and the boat began to tip as the great post went over the side in a tangled mass of ropes and canvas.

"Hatfield, you bloody fool!" Breckinridge shouted as he ran to the wheel and shoved his first mate up against the transom. "You wrecked my boat!"

He punched Hatfield twice in the face, while Lord and Lady Radley clung to each other near the cabin hatch.

Evelyn ran to the side and looked over at the mast and sails floating in the water, the lines still pulling while no one was at the wheel. The wind had picked up considerably, and ahead, black clouds whirled across the sky. She felt the sting of rain on her face.

"Lady Radley!" she shouted. "Go below!"

By this time, Breckinridge was leaning over the rail, looking down at the mast and sails floating in the angry sea, while Mr. Hatfield was doubled over, nursing a bloody nose, crouched in the corner behind the wheel, which was turning on its own, back and forth. Evelyn ran to it and took hold.

"What should I do?" she called out to Breckinridge, waiting for instructions.

"How the hell should I know!" he yelled, whipping around to face her with water dripping from his nose and chin. "Dammit, we're out of the race now!"

"Forget about that!" she shouted. "We're still connected to the wreckage!"

A savage gust of wind tossed them to the side, and more cleats snapped from the deck. "We need to cut the lines before we're pulled over!"

A flash of understanding reached his eyes, and

he stopped to think. He turned and looked at the ropes still attached to the sinking mast.

"Yes, we need to cut the lines!"

Mr. Hatfield hurried to his feet and held out a knife. "Use this!"

Enraged, Breckinridge slapped it out of his hands. It skittered across the slippery deck. "I'll take no help from you! And I need an axe!"

Hatfield went looking for one while Breckinridge nevertheless dug into his own pocket for a knife, wasting precious seconds while Evelyn squinted into the driving rain.

"Hurry!" she shouted, hearing the creaking and moaning of the boat as it swiveled on the foaming waves. The wheel trembled and shook in her hands. She could barely hold it steady.

Finally, Breckinridge leaned over the side and frantically cut at the ropes, while Hatfield returned swinging an axe.

Just then a rogue wave came surging up from the sea, pouring across the deck and sweeping Breckinridge overboard. The boat began to tip and roll.

Evelyn held tight to the wheel, struggling to keep her footing on the slippery deck. Before she could comprehend what was happening, the *Endeavor* was tipping over onto her side and Evelyn was plummeting into the sea. She hit the frigid water and went under, her whole head engulfed by the muffled sound of the ocean in her ears. Her skirts wrapped around her legs and weighed her down as she sank into the cold, dark depths. Dizziness overwhelmed her as she struggled, but she seemed only to be going down.

But she could not die here. She could not! *Kick! She had to kick!*

Suddenly, she was pushing to the surface, fighting against panic as she rose through a tangled web of sheets and lines. A wave struck her in the face, stinging her skin, and she gasped for air, choking on salt water, her arms flailing in all directions. Everything was a blur as she tried to focus on the overturned boat, searching the water for the others—Lord and Lady Radley, Mr. Hatfield, Breckinridge . . . She could see none of them, only the foamy, churning waters and the *Endeavor*'s shiny black hull sinking downward into the sea.

Chapter 20

Squinting through the driving wind and rain, Martin approached the foundering *Endeavor* and acted quickly. He tied a rope around his waist and tethered himself to a jack line, then continued on a close-hauled course, pushing *Orpheus* to her limits.

"Evelyn!" he called out, circling around the wreckage. He hurried along the weather rails with the life ring in his hands and desperately searched the stormy waters. Where was she? She couldn't have gone under. She had to be holding on to something.

God help him, it was too familiar, all of this. It was making him sick. He couldn't bear it . . .

"Martin!"

He heard her frantic cry over the roar of the waves and spotted her, then flung the ring with all his might. It landed a few feet from her, and she swam to reach it.

Bracing both feet against the rails, he pulled the rope, hand over hand, using every muscle he possessed to drag her through the swells until he could reach down and grab hold of her. He didn't think. He didn't feel. All he did was pull her forcefully onto the deck. She crouched on hands and knees, sputtering and coughing up water.

Martin shouted over the storm. "You have to go below!"

"What about the others?"

"I'll find them!"

With the rain and waves driving across the deck, Evelyn crawled to the companionway and slid down. Martin shut the hatch behind her, then went to the wheel to turn the boat around and circle again.

He spotted the Radleys treading water together. Working hard not to lose sight of them, he called out, "Don't try to swim! I'll come to you!" But he wasn't sure they could hear him over the noise of the sea.

When he was close enough, he threw the life ring out again, then dropped the jib halyard and eased the main to stop the boat. He pulled them aboard, one at a time, until his body was shaking with exhaustion.

Lord Radley crawled to his wife and hugged her desperately. "Are you all right? My darling, oh my darling. If I ever lost you!"

By this time, the *Endeavor* was completely gone, swallowed up by the sea, and all that remained as evidence of her existence was some scattered debris—a captain's hat, some cans and bottles.

"Have you seen the others?" Martin shouted, kneeling on one knee beside Lord Radley, wiping the stinging water from his eyes.

"We saw Hatfield!" the baron replied. "I don't know about Breckinridge."

Martin simply nodded. "Go below."

"I can help," Radley said.

Martin glanced quickly at the man' wife, who was barely able to get to her feet. "Take her below, then come back up."

Radley nodded and obeyed, while Martin looked over the side, searching the water for the others. *"Hatfield! Breckinridge!"*

He walked up and down along the weather rails, then heard a voice. He went to the wheel and steered the boat around again, then spotted Hatfield and tossed the life ring out. Radley appeared beside him at that moment, still soaking wet, and Martin was never so relieved to have assistance. "Help me pull him in!"

They worked together tugging the rope, but when they brought Hatfield up alongside, he slipped through the ring and disappeared.

"He went under!" Radley shouted, dropping to his hands and knees at the rail.

In the flash of a second, Martin untied the rope around his waist and handed it to Radley. "Tie this around yourself and steer the boat in a circle, and don't let us out of your sight!"

He turned and dove over the side.

In the cabin below, Evelyn finally managed to stop shivering. She took off her wet skirts and made sure Lady Radley was calm, then climbed back up the companionway wearing her bodice and drawers. She left the cabin and slammed the hatch door shut behind her, and saw Lord Radley at the wheel.

"Where's Martin?"

"He dove in to get Hatfield!"

Stark terror lit through her veins, and she dashed to the side to look for him. *Where? Where are they?*

She couldn't see them. She looked everywhere. The swells were enormous. Then she pointed. *"There! Over there!"*

Martin was swimming, holding Hatfield's head out of the water, and it looked as if he were trying to make it to the life ring.

"We're coming!" she shouted.

Martin reached the ring and placed it over Hatfield's head.

Evelyn began to pull on the rope, but it took all her might. "Help me!" she cried to Lord Radley, who quickly came to pull, too. Soon, Martin and Hatfield were at the side of the boat. Hatfield appeared to be unconscious.

"Pull him up!" Martin shouted. "Then throw me another line!"

Lord Radley leaned over the side and grabbed hold of Hatfield under the arms, while Evelyn threw another rope to Martin. He seized it in his hands and held on.

"Hurry!" Evelyn screamed. It took both of them to pull Hatfield up on deck. If the boat hadn't been heeled so far over to their advantage, they never would have succeeded.

Lord Radley reached for Martin, and they locked arms. The baron groaned as he pulled Martin up onto the deck. They collapsed on their backs, sucking in air.

"Are you all right?" Evelyn asked, while she held Mr. Hatfield's head on her lap.

"Yes." He rolled over onto his hands and knees. "What about him?"

"He's alive," she said. "But we have to get him warm."

Just then, the mainsail began to flap wildly as the boat bobbed up and down like a toy on the waves.

Martin rose to his feet. "Take care of him!"

"What about Lord Breckinridge?" Lord Radley asked.

"Keep looking and calling his name!"

Radley did just that, while Martin leaned into the driving spray to release the mainsheet. He ran back to the wheel and turned it hard over, then pushed on the boom. The boat began to move backward, then he quickly trimmed the sails and steered them straight, bringing the *Orpheus* around again to continue searching for Breckinridge.

No one said much of anything on the rough journey back to Cowes. The women remained below with Mr. Hatfield, who had regained consciousness but was still too weak to do anything but lie still, while Martin and Lord Radley remained at the helm, sailing them back to safety.

Breckinridge was not with them.

Wrapped in a wool blanket, Evelyn rose from her seat at the table and went to look in on Mr. Hatfield, who was resting in the forward berth. She was relieved to see he was no longer shivering, but wished his color would return.

"Can I get you anything?" she asked, holding on to the bulkhead to keep her balance as the boat pitched and rolled over the rough seas.

He was lying on his side and did not turn to look at her. "No."

She understood he was weak and did not wish

to talk, so she simply said, "If you change your mind, let me know."

He made no reply. Evelyn returned to the table and sat down again.

"It's a miracle we're alive," Lady Radley said.

Evelyn shivered and pulled the blanket tight around her shoulders. "Yes, there was a moment I thought we were all done for."

The boat heaved over a monstrous wave, and they both grabbed hold of the table. Lady Radley's eyes widened.

"Don't worry," Evelyn assured her. "Lord Martin knows what he's doing."

"That's very clear." They both sat in prolonged silence, contemplating what they had just been through, then Lady Radley said, "We were lucky he came along when he did, but what was he doing there? When we passed them earlier, they were on their way back in, and he was alone when he reached us. He must have turned around and followed."

Evelyn felt so strangely cold and numb inside, she couldn't make sense of any of it. "Perhaps he knew we were heading into bad weather and had come to warn us."

"But why wouldn't he have brought his crew?"

Evelyn pondered that. "Maybe he wanted to test himself against the *Endeavor* for the race."

"Do you really think so? Or do you think perhaps he was coming after you?"

Evelyn stared into Lady Radley's eyes. She could not bring herself to think of it, not after everything that had just happened. They had all nearly perished on the sea. Breckinridge was gone, Mr. Hatfield was ill, and they still had to make their way back through this storm to Cowes. She could not think of her affair with Martin or her broken heart over the loss of him. Life could be so very cruel sometimes. She was too afraid to hope.

"I'm sure that's not the case," she said, and held on tight as the boat heaved to and fro over the wild, angry sea.

It was dusk and still raining when Martin sailed the *Orpheus* right up to the Squadron steps and secured her. Lord Radley began to assist everyone off the boat, and Spence came running down from the clubhouse. "Thank God you're back! I've been watching for you for hours."

He tried to assist Evelyn, who was still wrapped in the blanket, but she held up a hand. "I'm fine, Lord Spencer, thank you. But Lady Radley is very weak, and Mr. Hatfield will need help, too. He was in the water the longest of any of us."

Spence moved to take Lady Radley's arm. "Thank you so much," she said. "You're a very helpful young man."

"It's no trouble, madam." He glanced over his shoulder at Martin. "The *Endeavor*?"

"Gone," he flatly replied.

Spence stared as the rain struck his face. "And Breckinridge?"

Martin shook his head.

Spence digested the news in grave silence, then they all headed up to the club, except for Evelyn. She remained on the dock, waiting for Martin.

"Can you untie that line and toss it aboard?" he asked without looking at her. He was moving around the boat, busying himself, coiling ropes and testing knots.

"Why?" she asked. "Where are you going?"

"I have to take the *Orpheus* back to her mooring."

She recognized the detachment in his voice, devoid of warmth or feeling, and any hopes she had begun to entertain that he might have changed his mind about ending their affair were dashed instantly by his obvious need to be away from her. "Is that really necessary right now?"

He stopped what he was doing. The rain was coming down hard and fast at an angle, but he hardly seemed to notice it drizzling down his face. "Could you just throw the line please?"

Evelyn's heart squeezed with anguish. He did not want to deal with her. He was withdrawing in every sense of the word from the intimacy they had shared. He wanted only to be alone. But why? Because of what had happened? Was he merely exhausted, or was it something more? Was he angry with her for going sailing with Breckinridge in the first place?

Reminding herself that they had just been through a terrible ordeal, she did not let herself question too much or argue. Instead, she bent to pick up the line and tossed it onto the deck, and said simply, "You know where to find me if you want to talk."

He barely looked at her as he nodded. The boat eased away.

She continued to stand on the dock in the pelting rain, clutching the blanket around her shoulders—her heart aching with confusion and despair as she watched him sail away.

Chapter 21

***

Three hours later, Martin woke in the dark, forward berth of the cabin and sat up. Something had knocked against the side of his boat. He heard footsteps tapping along the deck, and the light from a lantern swung past one of the skylights. He didn't move, however. All he could do was lie there and wait, because he felt like he'd been hit by a train.

The cabin hatch swung open, and Martin squinted at the sudden light in his eyes. Two shiny boots stepped into view in the companionway and descended. Martin flopped back down onto the mattress.

"You're not dead, are you?" Spence asked, crossing the cabin, holding the lantern up to shine in on Martin's face.

He lifted a hand to shade his eyes. "Regrettably no."

Leaning a shoulder against the bulkhead, Spence studied him for a moment. "I brought you a sandwich."

"Did you bring whiskey?"

"Yes," he replied, "but by the look of things, I probably shouldn't have. I have half a mind to toss it over the side."

Martin sat up again to lean on one elbow. "Why? Are you afraid I might drown myself in it?"

Spence took a seat at the table. "I know you're at least going to try."

The boat rocked gently on the water, which had calmed substantially in the past hour. Spence set the lamp on the table and turned the key to lift the wick and brighten the cabin. He looked around at Martin's jacket strewn on the bench, his boots on their sides in the middle of the floor.

"I'll take that sandwich now," Martin said. "If you don't mind tossing it into my dark pit of despair." He shut his eyes and listened to Spence digging into a bag, then a sandwich wrapped in cheesecloth hit him in the face and dropped. Without flinching, he felt around the berth, found it, and took a bite.

Spence stretched his long legs out and crossed them at the ankles. "They've canceled the race, obviously."

"I assumed they would. How are the Radleys and Hatfield?"

"They're all fine. But aren't you going to ask about the widow?" Martin merely shrugged, causing Spence to lean back with frustration and throw his hands up in the air. "You're unbelievable."

"Bugger off, Spence. I didn't ask because I already know she's all right."

"And how do you know that?"

He ran a hand through his hair. "I just do, all right?"

Spence sat forward again. "So what happened? You got there, and the boat was going down, and you saved the day. But did you tell her why you were there in the first place?"

"Of course not," Martin replied. "Not after everything that happened."

"But did you talk to her at all?" Spence persisted. "Did you at least tell her you were glad she was alive?"

Martin took another bite of the sandwich. He really didn't want to do this now.

Spence's tone took on a hint of resignation. "I didn't think so."

"It wasn't the right time," Martin explained.

"And I have a feeling it is never going to be the

right time after what happened today. You're going to bow out, aren't you? You're just going to pack up and go home."

Martin suddenly wasn't in the mood to eat. He set the sandwich down and waved a hand through the air at his friend. "*Jesus*, Spence! I've just been through hell. Someone died, and for a few unspeakable moments, I thought they had all been lost, Evelyn included, and you know my history in that regard. Can't you understand that and ease off a bit for once?"

Spence lowered his head and shook it. For a long time he just sat there, then he leaned an elbow on the table and cupped his forehead in a hand. "You're right. I'm sorry. I apologize."

They sat in silence until Spence dug into the bag again. Martin had been lying with his eyes closed, but when he heard the sound of a cork popping and liquid gushing into a glass, he sat up.

Spence stood and handed him some whiskey, then poured a glass for himself.

"I thought you said you were going to toss it over the side," Martin said.

"I changed my mind." Spence raised his glass. "What else is there to do after a boat goes down but open a bottle?"

Martin raised his glass, too, and sighed. "It's been a wretched day, Spence. Thank you for the whiskey and thank you for understanding. Bottoms up."

* * *

The next morning, the starting cannons fired, but not for the race. They went off in memory of Lord Breckinridge and to acknowledge the tragic end of the ill-fated *Endeavor*.

There was a gathering at the Royal Yacht Squadron, and for this day alone the ladies were permitted inside. Evelyn arrived with Lady Radley and accepted a glass of sherry, then made her way around the crowded room.

She thanked those who offered sympathies and condolences, and she and the Radleys repeated the details of the accident more than once—about how the squall had come upon them very suddenly and snapped the mast.

There were also a few questions about how the boat had been handled, and Evelyn explained that she did not know, for she had been belowdecks when the mast broke, and everything had happened very quickly after that.

"Of course, of course," was always the sympathetic reply. All the while, she waited for Martin, wishing he would come. She was worried about him, for he had not returned to his room since the accident. He'd spent the night on board the *Orpheus*.

A short time later, she approached Mr. Hatfield, who was feeling better, though he was still pale and weak.

"It never should have happened," he said.

"You're very right," she replied. "It was a terrible tragedy, and I doubt any of us will ever get over it completely."

"Lord Breckinridge should not have been lost."

Recognizing the regret in Mr. Hatfield's voice, she touched his arm and worded her response with great care. "We did everything we could to save him."

His eyes narrowed critically. "Do you really think so? I confess I'm not so sure."

Evelyn blinked and stared wordlessly at him. "Of course we did."

He scoffed.

Her brows drew together with anger and dismay. "I would like to know what you are insinuating, sir."

"I think you are already quite aware."

She faced him squarely. Her voice hardened. "I do *not* know. You are going to have to say it, and I warn you, sir, be very careful what accusations you make."

Eyeing her somewhat warily, he leaned closer. "Don't you think it's a strange coincidence that out of all of us, Martin left Breckinridge for last? The very day before the race? The same day the earl proposed marriage to you?"

She could barely contemplate what she was hearing. Mr. Hatfield was suggesting that Martin had let Breckinridge drown on purpose? "He did everything he possibly could, and I am shocked you could even suggest such a thing."

He shrugged a shoulder.

She became filled with sickening revulsion for this man. "Might I remind you that he risked his life to save yours?"

"Only because he didn't want to dive in after the earl. And aren't you curious what happened to the mast? Don't you find it suspicious that it could snap like that? Perhaps it was tampered with."

Whatever remained of Evelyn's previous compassion for Hatfield's grief and weakened state vanished instantly and turned to blistering rage. "That is the most ludicrous thing I have ever heard, and I swear, if you speak a word of this idiocy to others, I will tell everyone that when the mast broke, you were at the wheel, filling your belly with champagne. If anyone is to blame for the earl's death, sir, it is *you.*"

He drew back in surprise, then his gaze went stone cold. "You're just trying to protect Lord Martin because he is your lover."

She felt bile rise in her throat. "And you are trying to ruin him because you are jealous of his success and are afraid the accusations of incompetence are going to be directed at *you.* I have nothing else to say to you, sir. Good day."

Disturbed and shaken, she turned and shouldered her way through the crowd to find Sir

Lyndon Wadsworth, commodore of the club, who was on the other side of the room. "Sir Lyndon, may I speak with you?"

He recognized her obvious distress and excused himself from the others. They went to a quiet corner. "Mr. Hatfield has just made an appalling accusation. He has suggested that Lord Martin might have tampered with the mast on the *Endeavor,* and that he let Breckinridge drown intentionally, and I am here to assure you that that was absolutely not the case. Lord Radley was there, too. He will attest to the fact that the storm broke the mast, and Lord Martin did everything he could to save all of us. He made no mistakes."

Sir Lyndon was leaning forward, listening to every word until she finished, then he straightened and cleared his throat uncomfortably. "I am aware of the situation, Mrs. Wheaton. There have been a few others who have voiced their uncertainties about what happened. There will have to be an investigation."

"An investigation!" Her mouth fell open in shock. "Have you lost your mind? The man deserves a medal!"

He glanced across the room at Hatfield. "I promise it will be a fair investigation. You know I admire Lord Martin and believe him to be a great sailor and a gentleman as well, but questions must be asked, because the two men were rivals."

Evelyn's gut wrenched with sickening disbelief.

Just then, Martin and Spence arrived, and a hush fell over the room. She knew at that moment that Hatfield had already planted seeds of doubt in the minds of some people.

The vile snake walked past them without a word and left the club, slamming the door behind him.

Sir Lyndon was quick to go and greet them. "Thank you for coming, gentlemen. I apologize for that."

He took them aside, and Evelyn watched as he explained the situation and quietly described what was afoot. The three of them discussed it at length.

She watched Martin turn and shake hands with some of the other gentlemen, and was relieved to see that they did not all shun him. Some seemed to believe the truth—perhaps those who knew what kind of man Hatfield was.

But oh, her heart ached for Martin. He looked so very weary.

For the next half hour, he was thanked by many club members, but not everyone. Some people turned their backs on him or walked out the door in a huff. Eventually, he met her gaze across the room and held it for a moment. He nodded at her, then returned to his conversation.

It was as if they had never known intimacy

together, she thought, feeling a pain beneath her breastbone at the loss of it. But she could not concern herself with such selfish thoughts, not after everything that had occurred.

Soon, he made his way around the room to where she was standing with a group of women. "Mrs. Wheaton," he politely said, taking her hand and clasping it in both of his. "You're feeling better today, I hope."

"I am," she replied, "thanks to you."

It was all very proper and somber, and the others soon engaged him with their own gratitude and appreciation. She was pleased these women seemed to believe the truth.

"I did what any man would have done in the same circumstances," he said with enormous modesty. "I was lucky to have come upon them when I did."

"Indeed," one of the ladies said. "And rest assured, Lord Martin, none of us are listening to a word from that detestable Mr. Hatfield. He has no right to spread such rubbish around, and Sir Lyndon will make sure everyone knows it, I'm sure."

Evelyn had to fight hard against tears as she watched Martin bow his head with dutiful gratitude, when she sensed he didn't even care what anyone thought. It was as if he had given up the fight, which was not at all like him.

Her temper flared anew. He did not deserve

this. He was a hero. She and the others would be lying at the bottom of the sea right now if he had not come to their rescue.

Bowing slightly, he excused himself from their group and turned away. Evelyn knew at that moment that she loved him with every inch of her soul and always would. He meant everything to her, and she owed him for her life in more ways than one.

She would not let him go down for this.

Chapter 22

Later that afternoon, sitting in her room at the Royal Marine Hotel, Evelyn finally heard the sound of a key in the lock across the hall. The door creaked open and clicked shut, so she closed the book she'd been trying to read.

She'd been waiting hours to talk to Martin. She could not leave Cowes without speaking to him about the accident and assuring him that he had her utmost support, no matter what occurred between them on a personal level.

Quietly, she opened her door and peered out into the hall, then tiptoed across and knocked.

"I need to talk to you," she said when he answered.

He stood motionless for a moment, looking not only exhausted, but lukewarm to the idea of her presence. He stepped back nevertheless and invited her in.

She noticed his trunk lying open in the middle of the room. "When are you leaving?"

"Soon, along with most everyone else. Cowes week is definitely finished."

Martin moved to the chair and sat down. He set his elbow on the armrest and rubbed his jaw. Evelyn sat down on the bed.

"Are you recovered from yesterday?" she asked.

He made a shrugging gesture, as if to say no one could ever recover from an experience such as that.

"It was the second time you saved my life," she mentioned.

It was actually the third, if she considered what the rest of her life might have been like if she'd not spent this week with him. She might have ended up married to a man who did not truly care for her, a man who only wanted her for her fortune.

He dropped both hands to his knees and just looked at her for a drawn-out moment.

"I wish you would say something, Martin."

He inhaled sharply. "I don't know what to say. It was an ordeal, and it ended tragically. I wish it hadn't happened, but it did."

"But it could have been so much worse," she

argued. "You were a hero yesterday. I hope you know that. I hope you're not punishing yourself because of what Hatfield said. He is a spiteful worm, and most people know it—at least the people who matter."

"Believe me, I know he's a worm. I stopped putting any stock in what he said years ago."

"But what about his accusation that you tampered with the mast? Does that concern you? It's a very serious charge."

He shook his head at the outrageousness of it all. "The *Endeavor* was built for speed and nothing else, certainly not for weather like that. The mast was hollow and made of fine steel, so it was light. Every yachtsman in Cowes knows it, so it should be obvious that I didn't tamper with it, and I certainly didn't call up the storm. Hatfield is turning this into a bloody circus." He paused a moment, tapping his fingers irritably on his leg. "At any rate, even if the mast had been made of solid English oak, he wouldn't have known how to handle the *Endeavor* in those winds. He lacked experience and didn't know he should have released the tension in the sails."

She let out a breath. "Have you told Sir Lyndon all this?"

"Of course."

"Then everything should be all right." She noted with a sinking feeling in her stomach, however, that he would not look at her. He would only look at the clock on the wall. "But there is still something else bothering you," she said, because she knew his heart. "What is it?"

She had to wait a long time for him to speak.

"What happened to the mast was not my fault," he said. "I know that and I take no responsibility for it, but the fact that we lost Breckinridge . . ." He closed his eyes and rubbed his temples. "I will always wonder if there was not something else I could have done."

"Of course there wasn't," she quickly said. "We did our best. His death is not your fault." She squeezed the edge of the mattress and felt her own disturbing twinge of guilt, however, when she recalled the events leading up to the catastrophe. Tipping her head back, she spoke in a low voice. "If it is anyone's fault, it is mine."

"What do you mean?"

She swallowed uncomfortably. "When the storm hit, I was below fixing my hair after I lost my hat, and that was why Breckinridge left Hatfield at the wheel—so that he could join me below. Perhaps if he had not done that . . ."

Martin regarded her with somber curiosity, and his eyes narrowed with concern. "What did he want, Evelyn?"

"He came down to apologize for the loss of my hat. Or so he claimed."

An angry frown flashed across his features. "Tell me what happened."

She drew a deep breath. "He surprised me when he appeared, as I had not invited him to join me, then, quite without warning, he kissed me."

Martin's hand flexed open and closed upon the armrest. "Did he do anything else? Did he hurt you?"

"No," she replied, dropping her gaze. "I pushed him away."

"I'm glad."

"But there's more," she said hesitantly. "He insinuated all kinds of things about you and me and what we'd done together this week, then said he would be willing to salvage what was left of my reputation by making me his wife."

Martin smacked a fist on the arm of the chair and pushed himself to stand. "He said all this to you and tried to pressure you to accept him, while a storm was brewing outside, and he'd left a drunken fool at the wheel to be responsible for his boat and all the lives upon it?"

She nodded.

His voice deepened as he ground out words. "Damn him to hell and beyond, Evelyn. You could have died out there. We all could have."

"I know."

"It was not your fault," he said firmly. "Do not for one minute of your life think otherwise."

Evelyn sighed drearily. "It's pointless, you know, the two of us asking these questions, confessing things, trying to accept or assign blame.

We will both simply have to accept that it happened, someone died, and nothing will ever change that. We cannot go through life questioning our roles in it. There would only be grief and torment if we did that."

His voice simmered. "Sometimes grief and torment cannot be avoided."

"What are you saying, Martin?" But she had a feeling she already knew where his thoughts had gone.

He exhaled harshly—as if frustrated by her questions—stood up, and walked to the window. "I am no stranger to guilt and blame," he quietly said. "It has taken over my life, and after yesterday, I am beginning to wonder if I am destined to be tested with it until the day I die."

"In what way?" she asked.

He kept his back to her. "There's something I did not tell you, Evelyn, about the death of my wife and child, and I think it's time you knew. Maybe then you would understand why I can't give you what you want."

Evelyn's blood cooled in her veins. "You told me they died in a fire."

"They did. But it was not so simple as that." He paused briefly, and she feared he was going to change his mind about telling her.

"What happened, Martin?"

He turned to face her and leaned back against the windowsill. "The night that it happened, we had sent the servants out because it was my birthday and we wished to be alone as a family. Unfortunately, we ate too much cake and Owen developed a bellyache, so Charlotte took him upstairs early to tend to him. I went out to the stables to pass the time, but I was careless . . . I did something I will never forgive myself for."

"What? What did you do?"

"I left a candle burning in the parlor. It was too close to the curtains, and the window was open so the breeze was blowing in . . ."

She steepled her fingers together in front of her nose. "Oh, Martin."

He looked around the room at the pictures on the wall, the carpet on the floor, the empty trunk at his feet. "What makes it worse is that I smelled smoke from the stables very early on but dismissed it. I assumed it was coming from the chimney over the stove in the kitchen or the fireplace in the bedchamber. But then, when I thought of the candle, it was too late. I ran back, but the house was already in flames. I tried to get in, but couldn't get to the stairs. I tried everything, Evelyn, *everything*, but eventually all I could do was watch from the road as the house burned and collapsed to the ground in front of my eyes, with the bodies of my wife and child trapped inside."

She was assailed by a grief so horrendous, she could barely speak. "I am so sorry, Martin."

He met her gaze directly. "Sometimes I dream about my son in that fire, and I wake up sobbing."

Evelyn rose and went to him. "But you can't blame yourself forever," she gently said. "It was an accident."

"I know it was," he replied, "and every day I try to convince myself of that. Spence tries to convince me, too, but it doesn't make it any easier. I will always wish I could have gotten in to save them, or that I had done something differently, just as I will always wonder if I could have done something differently yesterday."

Evelyn rested her chin on his shoulder. "We did everything anyone could possibly do yesterday. And if you had gone into that burning house, you would be dead, too."

"Maybe that's how it should have been."

She laid a hand on his chest. "No, do not say that. You saved four people yesterday. We'd all be dead now if it weren't for you."

He nodded, but she knew it was a polite response, meant only to appease her, to make her feel as if she were helping, when it was clear that nothing could ever take away his pain. He would carry it with him to his grave.

He said nothing more, and she sensed he wanted to be alone and pack his things. But how could she bring herself to walk away from him now and say good-bye to him? To leave him when he felt so low?

"Don't go yet, Martin. Stay another day. Stay with *me*."

"No," he said. "I can't do that."

"Why not?"

He hesitated. The cloudy light shone through the glass, while he gazed for a long time out over the water. "Because the truth is Evelyn—yesterday when I watched you sail away on the *Endeavor* with Breckinridge, something happened to me, and I didn't care about the race or the trophy or the wretched life I had been living for the past four years. All I wanted to do was catch up to you and force Breckinridge to give you up, because I wanted you for my own."

Shock poured through her as she absorbed his reply. He *had* been coming after her. He had not wanted her to marry Breckinridge.

"But what about today?" she asked, glancing down at his open trunk. "Do you still feel that way?"

He glanced down at the trunk, too. "No. I feel very differently."

She felt as if she'd been slapped. "Why?" But she already knew the answer to the question. It was why he had told her about his wife and child.

"Because when you fell off that boat I feared you were going to drown," he explained, "it made me remember why I have been alone all these years, and why I wish to continue to be alone."

"But yesterday you—"

"I was feeling impulsive and romantic and Spence was encouraging me. But I had forgotten some things about my life and what I want and do not want. Fate, however, saw fit to remind me."

God help her. He would never love her now, because he had relived a tragedy, which confirmed his greatest fear.

She had promised herself she would let him go when the time came. She had intended to hold on to her dignity. But oh, how it stung to think she had come so close to winning his heart only to lose everything the moment that wretched mast had snapped.

He closed his eyes. "I'm sorry, Evelyn. I don't want another family."

She sank into the chair. "I almost wish you hadn't told me the truth. I wish you had told me you were just trying to race with the *Endeavor*, and that's why you were there. But now I have to accept that you did care for me, but you love your pain more, and you *want* to be unhappy, and there is nothing anyone can do about it."

"Please understand, Evelyn," he replied.

But she did *not* understand. How could she? She loved him.

She stood and went to him and laid her hands

on his chest and tried one more time to make him see. "I just had the best week of my life with you, Martin, and I know you enjoyed it, too. I love you, and I want a chance to try and make you happy, to help you let go of that pain."

The color drained from his face. "I'll never be able to let go of it, Evelyn. I had a son who died in front of me."

She shook inwardly at the words. "But maybe someday you could learn to live with the loss, but find new joy at the same time—and not the kind of joy that just distracts you and makes you forget. You could start again, Martin. You could have another child."

His eyes flashed with shock, then he shook his head and backed away. "No."

An aching defeat centered in her chest. "So that's it? All I can do is watch you leave?"

She held him in her gaze one final moment, then realized miserably what she was doing. She was pleading with him for his love. She was begging in the face of rejection.

Having decided years ago that she would never beg or plead with any man who did not want her, she steeled her heart and her emotions and finally just nodded at him.

"I'm sorry, too," she said. Then she turned around and walked out.

Chapter 23

W hen Evelyn returned to her London residence on St. James's Square, she was
more than grateful for the familiarity of her regular routine, for it distracted her from her heartache. She kept very busy, filling each day with
activities and projects at home—such as chang-
ing the layout of the furniture in her drawing
room and tending to the mountains of correspon-
dence, which had piled to overflowing on her
desk while she'd been away. There were invitations to accept or decline and a number of personal letters from various acquaintances, which
took a significant amount of time to answer.

She did her best not to hope for a letter from

Martin—even if it was only to make contact and tell her again that he was sorry. It was a challenge, however, each time a footman approached her with a letter. She would freeze for a brief instant and stare at the envelope upon the silver salver, held by a white-gloved hand, and her heart would race.

There were never any letters from him, of course. Everything was as it had been that last day in Cowes. He had cut her loose without the slightest wavering—swiftly and decisively, the same way he sailed his yacht—and she was not surprised.

So she did the only thing she could do. She resolved to cut him loose from her heart and mind as well and set her gaze upon the future. She accepted invitations to balls and assemblies. She purchased new hats and gowns and dug out her mother's jewels, which she'd never had the courage to wear before. She was determined not to retreat into her widow's weeds and don her famous mask of cool detachment. She would embrace the woman she had discovered within herself in Cowes and join society eagerly and with a smile, while fighting relentlessly against the pain she felt inside.

The following week she let it be known she would be at home for callers every afternoon and received a number of visitors she'd never met before—the majority of them her social superiors who had sons seeking to marry money. She received them all with great warmth and graciousness, poured tea for them, and learned about their homes and families. By the time their fifteen-minute calls were up, most of them left with smiles and adulation. The Countess of Aldersleigh even went so far as to say to Evelyn on her way out: "Mrs. Wheaton, you were not at all what I had expected."

"I hope that is a compliment," Evelyn replied with a flash of humor in her voice, which she struggled hard to portray.

The countess handed over her card. "Oh yes, my dear. Have no doubt. The gentlemen of London will be quite pleasantly surprised to meet you in the coming weeks, and I predict you'll be the topic of many intriguing conversations."

Evelyn accepted the card and said good-bye. As soon as the countess was gone, however, she returned to the sofa and studied the fine print, wishing she could feel more triumphant. She would soon have a ready supply of potential husbands to choose from, all waiting to make her acquaintance. She should be ecstatic and eager to meet them, but all she felt was a sinking dread.

Just then, the butler appeared at the drawing-room door and said, "Another visitor to see you, Mrs. Wheaton. The Duchess of Wentworth."

Evelyn blinked with surprise and laid an open

hand upon her breast. "Good heavens. Please show her up."

As soon as the butler turned, she set the countess's card on a table with the others, then glanced around, hoping the room looked its best. She was hardly prepared for the famous American duchess. More importantly, Martin's sister-in-law. What was she doing here? Did he know she was paying this call?

Smoothing her skirts and taking a deep breath to compose herself, she sat down and waited. At last, the door opened, and a woman entered. She wore a crimson gown of soft China silk piped with velvet, and a matching hat with a wide brim, turned up at the sides.

"Good afternoon, Mrs. Wheaton," she said.

Evelyn was immediately spellbound by her shimmering blue eyes and charismatic smile. She was astonishingly beautiful, surely the most stunning woman Evelyn had ever met.

She rose and curtsied. "Your Grace, it is a pleasure."

"The pleasure is all mine," the duchess replied, still standing in the open doorway.

"Please." Evelyn gestured to the chair opposite hers. "May I offer you some tea?"

"That would be very nice, thank you." She crossed the room and took a seat. "You have a lovely home."

Evelyn reached for the teapot. "You're very kind

to say so. It was my father's final purchase before he passed away."

For the next few minutes they engaged in lighter chitchat, discussing the weather, the current opera at Her Majesty's Theatre. Then the duchess set her teacup on the table in front of her.

"I confess, Mrs. Wheaton, I can only manage light conversation for so long, then I must speak what is on my mind. It's one of those American traits I cannot seem to shed. I hope you do not mind."

"Of course not," Evelyn replied, setting her own cup down as well.

The duchess closed one black-gloved hand over the other. "I came to see you today because I wanted to speak to you about what happened at Cowes. I am concerned, you see, about my husband's brother, Lord Martin."

Evelyn maintained her straight posture. "In what regard?"

"We have heard there has been some talk."

Not certain whether the duchess was referring to the tragedy on the *Endeavor* or Evelyn's torrid affair with him, she sat forward slightly and pressed for clarification. "What kind of talk, Your Grace?"

"I understand that there are some who believe Martin had intended to eliminate Lord Breckinridge from the race because he feared he would lose against him. More specifically, they say he tried to have Breckinridge disqualified in a near collision, and some are even suggesting that he tampered with the *Endeavor*'s mast and intentionally left the earl to drown. I am assuming, since you were on board the *Endeavor* when she went down, that you know about all this?"

"Yes," Evelyn replied. "I am aware there has been talk, but I can assure you, Your Grace, that your brother-in-law acted honorably in every way. He came to our rescue when the boat overturned and risked his own life to save all of ours. He did not tamper with the *Endeavor*'s mast. It was flimsy to begin with, and any sailor who has seen her can attest to that. The *Endeavor*'s designer certainly could. His name is Joshua Benjamin, and he is here in London. And regarding the near collison, Martin was not at fault. It was Mr. Hatfield and Lord Breckinridge who disgraced themselves by breaking the laws of the sea and lying about it afterward. They were the ones who wished to eliminate their opponent—your brother-in-law, Lord Martin."

The duchess sat very still, her expression serious. "Were you there when the near collision occurred?"

"No," Evelyn replied.

"Then how do you know Martin was not at fault?"

"Because he told me, and I believe him."

For a long moment, the duchess gazed thoughtfully at Evelyn, then she reached for her tea and held it on her lap again. "I'm relieved to hear you say that, Mrs. Wheaton. I was sure he would never do such a thing, of course, but I wanted to know what *you* thought." She raised her cup to her lips and took a sip, then spoke with fervor. "Martin is a good man. He has already had far too much tragedy in his life. He does not deserve any of this."

"Believe me, I know that," Evelyn said.

They looked at each other contemplatively for a moment, then sipped their tea.

The duchess finished hers, then set her cup and saucer down on the table again. "May I impose upon you with one more question, Mrs Wheaton?"

"It is no imposition, Your Grace."

The duchess lowered her voice. "Some are also saying that you had become secretly engaged to Lord Breckinridge while Martin, too, was vying for your hand. I would like very much to know— is there any truth to this?"

Evelyn carefully considered how she should reply, for she was not sure Martin would want his family to know all the details of his personal life. "I was not engaged to Lord Breckinridge, although he did propose just before the accident. I refused him. And your brother-in-law was never vying for my hand."

"But you and he were . . . *acquainted* with one another?" she said, tilting her head to the side.

What exactly did she know? Evelyn wondered. "Yes. I admired him very much, and we were . . ." She paused. "We shared some special moments together during the week, Your Grace."

"I see."

But did she see? Was she presuming their affair had been sordid or superficial? Or did she know how deeply Evelyn cared for him?

The duchess rose from her chair to leave. "Well, I suppose I must leave you to your afternoon."

"But wait . . . *Please*," Evelyn quickly said, holding up a hand. "I must know, Your Grace . . . How is he?"

The duchess slowly sat back down and clasped her hands together on her lap again. "I'm afraid he has not been himself since Cowes."

Evelyn heeded this news with both sorrow and concern. "It ended tragically, there is no doubt. I hope this additional, unfortunate hearsay has not caused him an undue amount of stress."

"It has caused him a great deal, I regret to say. But he is not one to show his temper or complain. Instead, he has kept his solitude since his return to London, which is why my husband and I have become concerned. He has not been so reticent in a very long time."

Evelyn's chest rose and fell heavily as her breathing quickened. "Your Grace, I know of the guilt your brother carries with him regarding his wife and child, which is why this terrible injustice *must* be resolved. I have made my opinions on the matter known to Sir Lyndon Wadsworth, the commodore of the Royal Yacht Squadron, and your husband should speak also to Lord Radley, who is Breckinridge's uncle. He will defend Martin, I know he will, and I, too, will speak publicly if it will help. He has many supporters, and I believe all of this was started by Mr. Sheldon Hatfield, a spiteful, deceitful man. He is jealous of Martin and always has been. If your husband could perhaps also speak to Mr. Hatfield and inform him that no one believes his ridiculous accusations, then it might help to—"

"My husband is paying a call to Mr. Hatfield at this very moment," the duchess explained. "So do not worry, Mrs. Wheaton. We are behind our brother in every possible way. His happiness means everything to us. I just wish it meant something to him. Sometimes I fear he is determined to punish himself for the rest of his life by depriving himself of joy."

Evelyn sat back. She certainly understood what the duchess was saying. "Does he know you are here?" she asked.

"No," Her Grace replied. Then she sat back, too, and smiled. "I must confess, this visit was more for me than anyone else—to satisfy my curiosity about you. Now, having met you, I can feel good about the time he spent with you in Cowes. That despite all of this, the week wasn't a complete waste of time, that he did allow himself some happiness."

Recognizing the teasing humor in the duchess's eyes, Evelyn relaxed slightly. "We enjoyed each other's company very much."

"I'm sure you did. And I thank you for defending him."

They both rose, and on the way out, the duchess handed Evelyn her card. "I hope you will call on me sometime, Mrs. Wheaton. I am at home at Wentworth House on Tuesday and Thursday afternoons, and it would be a great pleasure to receive you. I would enjoy getting to know you better."

"Thank you, Your Grace."

After the duchess was gone, Evelyn gazed down at the card and tried to imagine herself calling upon her. Would Martin be there? Would he receive her, too?

With a disturbing tremor of anxiety, she slipped the card into her pocket and watched out the window as the duchess climbed into her shiny, black, crested coach and it slowly pulled away.

"What the devil did you think you were doing?" Martin demanded to know, bursting into his brother's study later that evening. "You had no right to speak to Hatfield on my behalf."

James Langdon, ninth Duke of Wentworth, was comfortably seated behind his large mahogany desk with an electric lamp shining brightly on his papers. He looked up, grinned wickedly, then set down his pen and leaned back in his chair. He stretched and put his hands behind his head. "I thought that might get a rise out of you."

"I can bloody well take care of my own business," Martin said. "I don't need you going behind my back as if I am guilty and require your mighty intervention."

His brother eyed him shrewdly. "So you're *not* guilty, then."

"Of course I am not, and you damn well know it."

His brother stood up and walked to the cabinet. He poured two glasses of brandy and offered one to Martin. "I never doubted it for a second. I only wondered why you were letting this nonsense go on for so long. It's not like you."

Martin accepted the glass and swirled the amber liquid around. "Hatfield's an ass. Most people know that."

"Perhaps they do, but it's never wise to let the ass think he is in charge of the cart. He needed to be dealt with."

Martin raised the glass to point at James. "By me. Not you."

"Then why have you not done it?"

Martin stared at him for a moment, then strode

across the room to the fireplace. He watched the flames dance and listened to the snap of the sparks in the grate. "I don't care what people are thinking or saying about me. I'm no stranger to gossip."

"Idle chitchat about your bedroom antics is one thing," James said. "Lies and false accusations about a man's death are quite another."

Martin sat down in front of the fire. "So what, dare I ask, did you say to him?"

"I asked him for proof that you tampered with the *Endeavor*'s mast, and he cowered like a baby and said he had none."

Martin glanced up at his brother sardonically. "I doubt it was as polite as all that, James. Will he have a blackened eye the next time I see him? Or did you harmlessly aim a pistol at him from across the room?"

James chuckled and sat down. "I did none of that. I just asked the man some questions, and he denied ever saying anything ugly about you— which was complete rubbish of course—and claimed he had nothing to do with the gossip. Like I said, he cowered like a baby." James raised his glass and took a drink.

Martin gazed into the fire. "You didn't need to do that, James. He's a cheat and will hang himself with his own rope eventually."

"That might happen sooner than you think," James said.

"What do you mean?"

His brother crossed one leg over the other. "Hatfield still wants to beat you. He is claiming that the *Endeavor* would have triumphed over the *Orpheus* if she'd only had the chance, and he wants to prove it."

"How the hell does he plan to do that?"

"He has just purchased another yacht—the *Endeavor II*, an exact replica of the first. He asked me to deliver the challenge to you personally. He is suggesting another race in six weeks to end all speculation about who would have taken the trophy if the accident had not occurred."

Martin tipped his head back and sighed wearily. "Bloody Christ. His friend has been dead little more than a week, and that's all he can think about?"

He felt his brother's speculative gaze boring into him. "I'm surprised," James said. "This is just the sort of thing that would have invigorated you a month ago. What has changed? You have not been yourself since Cowes, and it's not just the accident. There's something else. Care to tell me about it?"

Martin lifted his head off the back of the chair and gazed intently at his brother. "How much do you know?"

"Not a lot. Only that she is very rich and impossibly lovely."

"Who said that?" Martin asked.

"My impossibly lovely wife."

Martin said nothing for a moment, then set his glass down on the side table and leaned forward. He rested his elbows on his knees and clasped his hands together. "She is lovely indeed, but she has ruined it for me."

"Ruined what?"

"My superficial life. The temporary excitement of meaningless affairs and the fleeting triumph of crossing a finish line. All of that used to be my salvation, but now it has lost its appeal. I'm spending far too much time fighting against the pathetic urge to go soul-searching and settle myself down with a woman who understands me and everything that torments me—as well as everything that exhilarates me."

"Maybe it's time you stopped fighting it," James said in a low voice.

Martin glanced up irritably. "You think I should go and propose to her? That if I stick a ring on her finger and make myself a husband again, all will be well after the wedding night?"

"No, I don't think anything of the sort. I think if you married her or anyone else tomorrow, it would be a mistake and a dismal failure."

"Thank you for the vote of confidence."

James stood up and walked around the back of his chair. "Let me ask you this. What did you do four years ago after you buried your wife and son?"

"I came home," he replied. "There was certainly nothing to keep me in America. I had no home, no belongings. Everything was gone."

"So you boarded a train the very next day and were steaming across the Atlantic before a week had passed."

"That's right." He paused. "Then you bought me my first yacht."

"Which you promptly wrecked," James said. "I remember it all very clearly. Now, however, I fear that gift from me might have been a mistake."

"Why? It took my mind off what happened."

"Precisely, which is why you need to do what you should have done four years ago, Martin."

"Which is what?"

"You need to grieve for your wife and son."

Chapter 24

A few days later, on a sunny afternoon while strolling in Hyde Park, Evelyn encountered the Duchess of Wentworth, who was also out walking with a friend.

"Mrs. Wheaton," the duchess said cheerfully as she approached. "What a pleasant surprise."

"Your Grace," Evelyn replied, lowering her parasol and pulling it closed. "How lovely to see you."

She had not called on the duchess since her visit, though she had every intention of doing so before ten days were up, as she admired her very much.

The duchess gestured toward the woman at her side, who was tall and strikingly beautiful with brown eyes and hair the color of mahogany. "Clara, this is Mrs. Wheaton, whom I mentioned to you last week? Mrs. Wheaton, this is my sister Clara Wolfe, the Marchioness of Rawdon."

Ah yes, one of the duchess's American sisters. If she remembered correctly, the marchioness had married Seger Wolfe, one of the most notorious rakes in London, though he was now a respectable husband and father who took his seat in the House of Lords very seriously. "It's an honor to make your acquaintance, Lady Rawdon."

"Would you care to join us?" the duchess asked. "We are walking to the lake."

"I would be delighted."

The three of them lifted their parasols and started off along the path and spoke about the weather, light politics, the social events of the upcoming week—the usual light fare that was considered polite and acceptable conversation for a stroll in the park.

Then they entered a shady section of the path with trees and bushes on either side. Evelyn recalled what the duchess had said to her the other day—that she could only bear light conversation for so long before she had to speak her mind—and suspected they had a great deal in common.

"Your Grace," she said. "May I inquire after your brother-in-law, Lord Martin?"

The duchess lowered her parasol as well and

turned her eyes to Evelyn. "Have you not heard what has transpired recently?" she asked.

"No, I've heard nothing," Evelyn replied.

The marchioness, who walked at her sister's side, was notably silent, and Evelyn wondered how much she knew.

"If you may recall," the duchess carefully said, "the day I called upon you, my husband was paying a call at the same time to someone else."

"Mr. Sheldon Hatfield," Evelyn said. "Yes, I remember."

She remembered everything.

"The good news is," the duchess continued, "Mr. Hatfield retracted his accusations about Martin's alleged role in the *Endeavor*'s tragic end. Or rather, he denied saying anything untoward in the first place."

"That is indeed good news," Evelyn said. "But I assume there is bad news to go along with the good—as there usually is when one opens with the good news?"

"Yes," the duchess replied, smiling at Evelyn. "The fact is, I'm not sure I would call it bad news, exactly, but there is certainly new fodder for the gossips and their insufferable grapevine. Mr. Hatfield has purchased an exact replica of the *Endeavor* and has challenged Martin to a race as soon as it can be arranged."

"Good Lord." Evelyn squeezed the handle of her parasol. "Has he accepted this challenge?"

"Yes. The race is to take place at the Squadron six weeks from now."

Evelyn looked down at the path and pondered this for a moment. He was going to return to Cowes to race against a man for whom he held no respect. Did he fear his honor was at stake, and that to refuse was to admit Hatfield had been speaking the truth—that he *was* afraid of losing when he had never been?

"That is most underhanded of Mr. Hatfield," Evelyn said. "He is a wretched man. I hope Martin wins. I hope he leaves Hatfield bobbing up and down in circles in his wake. Then Hatfield will then be forced to admit Martin is a better sailor and that he himself has been jealous and ungentlemanly all along."

There was fire in her voice, she realized suddenly, and both her companions were staring at her with great surprise and scrutiny.

"I do beg your pardon," she said, softening her tone and clearing her throat. "That was most ill-mannered of me."

The marchioness spoke matter-of-factly. "You needn't apologize to us, Mrs. Wheaton. We're American."

All the tension drained from Evelyn's body, and she laughed. "Thank goodness for that."

They all shared a smile and continued walking until they reached the lake, then left the path and strolled to the water's edge. The marchioness knelt, removed a glove, and dipped her fingers into the water, then flicked the drops away and pulled her glove back on.

"Mrs. Wheaton," she said, rising again and facing Evelyn. "May I share something with you, and perhaps offer some wisdom? I assure you, I only want to help."

Caught off guard by the woman's forthright request when they'd only just met, Evelyn nevertheless said, "Of course."

Lady Rawdon hesitated a moment, as if she weren't entirely sure how to say what she wished to say, then she gazed out across the lake. "When I first met my husband, he, too, was grieving for a woman he'd lost years before, and for a long time it seemed impossible that he would ever let himself love again. But I did not give up, nor did Sophia under similar circumstances when her husband wished to preserve an emotional distance after they were married."

"You are referring to my relationship with Lord Martin," Evelyn said, just to be clear.

"Yes. We have put the pieces together regarding your acquaintance with him, which is why we wish to tell you that you, too, must not give up, at least not without a fight."

Evelyn scoffed. "But what can I do? I cannot get down on my knees and beg and plead for his affections. My pride will not allow that. I have been hurt too may times by a father who pushed

me away and a husband who never really wanted
me, and now Martin. I'm afraid I am not adept at
this kind of thing. I am too careful with my emotions. I do not openly hand over my heart."

"There is a very fine line," the duchess said,
"between pleading for what one wants and fighting intelligently for it. There are ways."

"But I don't know what to do other than to go
and knock on his door and tell him I love him.
That is the truth, and I cannot pretend otherwise.
And I told him as much that final day in Cowes,
but it didn't make any difference. He left anyway,
confirming what I have known all my life."

The two women glanced uneasily at one another. "The fact is," the duchess said, "you wouldn't
be able to speak to him now even if you wanted to,
because he is not here."

A heavy sense of dread settled over her.
"Where is he?"

"He left London two days ago and has returned
to America."

Evelyn digested this news with a painful still-
ness of heart, as if all her hopes had just drained
out of her. She felt the distance between her and
Martin stretch even wider. "Is he coming back?
But of course he must be, for the race."

"Yes. He'll be back for that."

"Was he so very miserable here?" she asked,
trying not to feel hurt that he had not been missing her or hoping they might see each other again,

as she had been hoping. He had left the country entirely, and had not even said good-bye.

"Contrary to what the world thinks," the duchess said, "that he is a lighthearted, cavalier charmer without a care in the world, he is in fact the opposite. He is a deeply passionate man. He cannot love halfway, nor can he easily let go once he has allowed someone into his heart. So yes, he has often been unhappy over the past four years."

But Evelyn knew that, didn't she? She had experienced his fiery passions and recognized the depths of his grief for the loss of his loved ones.

Inhaling deeply, she wandered away from the duchess and marchioness and watched a blackbird fly from one of the treetops out over the water. She recalled the night she and Martin had sailed together by moonlight back to Cowes. He had not seemed so unhappy then, nor during the days and nights that followed when they stole every opportunity to be together. He had seemed genuinely content, and she was certain it had not been an act.

"Why did he go?" she asked as she turned to face the ladies. "What does he hope to accomplish?"

"He intends to visit the place where he lived with his wife and child, and see the friends they had made there. My husband encouraged him to do it, Mrs. Wheaton. He felt it was necessary."

She sighed. "There was a brief time in Cowes

when I thought I could make him forget about all that. I thought I alone could make him happy, that I could be the cure to what ailed him."

"But you *were* the cure," the duchess said, striding forward. "You pulled him out of that false life he was living. He has gone back to America to face the past and lay it to rest. He would not be doing that if it weren't for you. So we are all very grateful to you, Mrs. Wheaton. Whatever it is you did, *thank you*."

Evelyn felt a strange inner satisfaction spread through her. "I don't know what I did—except to love him."

Both her companions looked at each other and smiled brightly, then the duchess approached and took her by the arm. She led her back onto the path while Lady Rawdon followed.

"First of all," she said, "from this moment on, you must call me Sophia."

"And me, Clara," her sister added.

"But before we talk about anything else," Sophia continued, "we must return to our earlier conversation about not giving up and not being afraid to risk your emotions. My brother-in-law is worth it, Mrs. Wheaton, and I hope you will return to Cowes for the race and see him again. Not on your knees, but on your feet, looking very beautiful in just the right gown and shoes, and charging forward, swinging your sword in all your feminine glory."

Evelyn felt an indefinable lightness lift her spirits suddenly. Sophia was right. Evelyn was not the same woman she had been before that magical week in Cowes, and she could not go back to being afraid. She had already learned to take risks. She'd entered into an affair with Martin, the man she'd always loved from afar, and she'd survived the loss of him, hadn't she? She'd also survived a sinking yacht on stormy seas. If she could do all that, she could do this, too. She'd come too far to give up now. And she loved him.

"*Yes*, Sophia," she said with a smile. "I believe you are right, and thank you for saying it. Perhaps it's time I took charge of the situation and finally got behind the wheel of my life. He is worth it. I have no doubt of that."

"That's what we were hoping to hear," Clara cheerfully said.

Evelyn turned back and linked her arm through Clara's as well. "But I might need your help. Both of you."

"Of course," Sophia said. "Anything. What can we do?"

"You can come shopping with me for my arsenal of weapons," Evelyn replied. "And I think we should definitely begin with the shoes."

Chapter 25

Six weeks later

"**O**h, *please*, Evelyn. Just this once. I need you. You must come with me."

Evelyn stood in the lobby of the Royal Marine Hotel on the Isle of Wight only a few hours after she'd checked in, and could not help but smile. It was not the first time in her life she had been asked to do something like this—something horrendously and unspeakably naughty. This was in fact very familiar.

Yet it was different, too, because she was not the same person she had once been. It wasn't just the way she looked or was dressed—which was very fashionable, she had to confess, in her fine emerald green *godet* skirt and matching jacket with pleated, puff sleeves. She felt different on the inside, too, knowing at last what she truly wanted and deserved, and knowing also that she was strong enough to go after it, without fear of the consequences.

"No, Penelope. I won't go with you." She pulled on her gloves and started walking to the door.

Penelope followed. "Why not?"

"Because we're not children anymore, and you're just going to get yourself into trouble."

Penelope trotted quickly behind Evelyn, who had exited the hotel and was now crossing the street to walk along the waterfront toward the Royal Yacht Squadron.

"It's easy for you to say such things when you're so happy with your life. You have every bachelor in England either proposing to you or planning on it the next time he sees you. But don't you remember what it was like before, when you were only just recently out of mourning and came here in search of a husband? That is *me* now, Evelyn. I've been alone for almost thirteen months, and I need excitement. I must have love. I cannot go on like this. I die a little more each day. I can't be alone."

Evelyn stopped and faced her friend. "First of all, you have three beautiful children who love you, so you are not alone, and secondly—there is nothing *wrong* with being alone. It might even be good for you."

"But this will be fun," she pleaded.

Evelyn started walking again. "Not for me. And surely you can think of better ways to meet nice gentlemen than what you are proposing."

"It wouldn't take long," Penelope said. "All we'd have to do is row out a little ways and drop the oar. The earl would have no choice but to come to our rescue."

They reached the gate. "No, I am not doing that. Just be yourself, Penelope. You don't need plots and schemes."

Evelyn entered the back lawn of the yacht club and stopped just inside. All at once, her belly filled with excitement. So much had happened here not so long ago, but it seemed like ages, for she no longer believed her only attractive quality was her fortune. She now knew she had much more to offer.

To the right man, of course.

Taking a deep breath, she looked around at the guests on the lawn—the same faces from last time, sitting in the same wicker chairs, spinning parasols. Then she spotted Lord and Lady Radley, who waved at her from the other side of the garden. They immediately came to greet her.

"Evelyn, my dear," Lady Radley said. "It is so good to see you. And this must be your friend we've heard so much about."

"Yes. Please allow me to present Mrs. Penelope Richardson."

They all shook hands, then discussed the upcoming race.

"It will be very interesting," Lord Radley said. "What do you think Evelyn? Will you bet on the *Orpheus*?"

She felt those exhilarating butterflies return. "Lord Martin is indeed a master on the water," she replied. "We've all been witness to that."

"Indeed we have," Lady Radley agreed, and her husband smiled affectionately at her.

He led them to the other side of the lawn for a better view of the boats in the Solent, and raised his old-fashioned quizzing glass. "Have you seen her yet? She just came in a few minutes ago, sailing at a fast clip. Do you remember last time, Evelyn? Remember how we thought Lord Martin was going to collide with the *Britannia*?"

She smiled at the memory. "Yes, but he was in complete control the entire time, wasn't he?"

"Most definitely."

Penelope clicked open her ivory fan and fluttered it in front of her face. "They just came in, you say?"

"Yes," Lord Radley replied. "They should be landing at the Squadron steps in a matter of minutes."

Penelope's eyes flashed with mischief. "Then we

should go down and greet them, don't you think?"

"I believe I'll remain here," Evelyn replied, opening her parasol and lifting it over her head to block the sun.

Lady Radley raised an eyebrow and leaned close to whisper in her ear. "You still prefer to be the challenging one, I see?"

Evelyn felt her cheeks flush with color and gave Lady Radley a confident smile. "I have the advantage of knowing what lifts his sails," she whispered.

"Well," Penelope said, "I think I'll go down and greet the champions. They've not lost their title *yet*, and deserve a warm welcome."

"Indeed they do," Lord Radley said. "Shall we go down, dearest?"

His wife grinned flirtatiously at him and linked her arm through his. Evelyn felt a warm glow move through her, for since the accident, they had embraced this second chance at life and rediscovered their love for each other.

The others left the garden, and Evelyn, now alone, turned around and saw Sophia and James standing over by the fence. They spotted her and waved, so she crossed the lawn to go and speak to them.

Martin stepped onto the landing stage at the Squadron and looked up at the crowd gathered on the Parade, most of them women.

"Look who I see there," Spence said, pointing. "Ahoy there, Lord Radley!"

"Ahoy to you, too, son!" Radley replied.

Martin patted Spence on the shoulder, and together they strode up the steps to a great round of applause. He stopped at the top and gave them what they wanted—a great, sweeping bow—and wondered with a resigned sigh if Cowes would ever change.

"We have our bets on the *Orpheus*," Lord Radley said, shaking Martin's hand when he reached them. "It's so good to see you."

"It's good to see you, too, sir. You look well."

"You were abroad, I hear," the baron said. "Did you do any racing, or go looking for new design innovations?"

"No," Martin casually replied. "I didn't really have a chance."

Lord Radley directed his gaze to Spence. "And what about you, my boy? What have you been doing with yourself since we saw you last?"

"I've done nothing but wait for this day to come, so I could get out on the water again and claim that trophy for another year. Can't stand to be on dry land."

Martin nudged him in the ribs. "Sometimes I think you were born a duck."

At that moment, a tall, fair-haired woman stepped forward.

"Gracious," Lord Radley said. "Pardon our manners. Lord Martin and Lord Spencer, may we present Mrs. Penelope Richardson? I believe you may have met before, years ago when you both attended Eton? Mrs. Richardson's parents reside in the Windsor countryside."

Martin's gaze fell upon the attractive woman before him, her smooth flaxen hair pulled into a loose knot on top of her head, her gown and hat the color of a wild pink rose, her lips moist and full. She smiled alluringly and offered him her gloved hand.

Ah yes, he remembered . . .

"Lord Martin, is it really you?" she asked. "I had no idea we would meet again under these circumstances. You are the reigning champion of Cowes, I understand. I will look forward to seeing you race tomorrow."

She had not changed a bit. She still spoke in the same melodious way. He remembered also how she used to follow him around and was always pretending to bump into him unexpectedly. And of course he could not forget how she had snuck into his dormitory with Evelyn that unfortunate night.

All at once, his heart turned over in his chest. He glanced over her head, searching the faces in the crowd. He had not known what to expect when he had set sail for Cowes the day before. He didn't know whether she would be here or not.

He did not see her.

He took a deep breath and forced himself to smile. "It's a pleasure to see you again, Mrs. Richardson."

She gave him a coy smile.

"Can I interest you both in some fresh chowder?" Lord Radley asked. "The aroma was most enticing out on the back lawn. Would you ladies mind?"

"Not at all, darling," his wife replied. "Penelope and I will join Evelyn out back."

His gaze shot to Lady Radley. "Mrs. Wheaton is here?"

"Yes, she arrived this morning."

But she had not come down with the others to greet him just now. He wondered if she would even wish to speak to him at all. He could not blame her if she didn't, not after the way he'd treated her all those weeks ago, then left the country without a word. He owed her an apology at the very least. That was certain.

"She didn't want to miss the race tomorrow," Lord Radley added.

"She'll be cheering for the *Orpheus,* I presume?" Spence asked.

"Of course," Lady Radley replied with a cheerful countenance. "She has a deep affection for the vessel that came to our rescue. And none of us could possibly cheer for that ungrateful Mr. Hatfield after the things he said about you, Lord Martin."

Lord Radley acknowledged the comment with a nod, then laid a hand on Martin's shoulder. "Come, come. We mustn't think of that. You boys must tell me some stories, and I'll tell you everything I've heard about your competition."

"That sounds like a perfect plan," Spence said.

They made their way to the club and found a table in the dining room. Their coffee had just been poured when Sir Lyndon appeared in the doorway and spotted them. He waved and immediately came over to their table. "Gentlemen, I'm glad to see you've finally arrived. May I join you?"

Martin gestured toward a chair. "Certainly. How the devil have you been?"

"I've been keeping busy as always, and I hear you've been hard at it as well. You just returned from America?"

"I stepped off the ship only four days ago."

"Well, I hope you are well rested after such a lengthy voyage. You'll need your wits about you tomorrow, I dare say."

Spence sipped his coffee. "To race against the *Endeavor II*? I hardly think so. Not with Hatfield at the wheel. The bumbling idiot couldn't navigate his way out of a bathtub, not even sober, which is a rare occurrence."

Sir Lyndon glanced uneasily at them. "But you *have* heard . . ."

"Heard what?" Martin asked.

Lord Radley's eyebrows lifted.

Sir Lyndon hesitated a moment, then spoke quietly. "Hatfield knows he doesn't have the brains or skills to beat you in a race, Martin, so he has recruited a very proficient first mate. Some say he is pure genius on the water."

They all went silent, except for Martin, who was the first to speak up. "Who is it? Have I raced him before?"

"His name is William Leopold, and he is George's younger brother, now the sixth Earl Breckinridge. He's out on the back lawn right now, boasting about this new boat being faster and better than the original, and he just made a very sentimental speech about how he's racing in honor of his late brother."

Spence leaned back in his chair. "Oh, Jesus. And here I thought we were a sure thing."

Martin shook his head. "Don't be too quick to think otherwise, Spence. How long has he been sailing?"

"A few years I'm told. He was residing on the Mediterranean until recently, when he returned home to bury his brother and inherit the title. There was some competition between them, I'm told, which is why George had built the *Endeavor* in the first place. To show him up."

Martin sat back, astounded. He had had no idea young Breckinridge was a sailor, much less a brilliant one, and the news knocked him completely off kilter. "They certainly kept their secret well guarded. You didn't know, Spence?"

"Of course not. I would have told you if I did."

Martin sat in silence for a long moment, staring down at the tablecloth while he digested this news. "You know," he said, "I'm sure there are still those here in Cowes who believe I let Breckinridge drown simply to hold on to the title. They'll be rooting for the *Endeavor II*, no doubt. And the young earl might even be out for revenge."

"No, surely not," Spence said.

"You did everything you could to save the earl," Lord Radley said, "and we have all attested to that. I was there. I witnessed your heroism."

Spence raised his coffee cup. "Here, here. We will win this race tomorrow to prove you would never need to resort to such ungentlemanly tactics in the first place. You're a champion, Martin, and that's all there is to it."

Martin thanked them for their support and joined them in a toast, but found himself gazing toward the back lawn again and thinking of something else entirely.

The pre-race ball that night aboard the *Ulysses* was a glittering affair, with enough food and champagne to sink the ship. The ladies flaunted their finest gowns, while the gentlemen stood around in their formalwear, paying tribute to the

late Lord Breckinridge through stories and re-
membrances. The evening was solemn at times,
lively at others, and the music was second to none
while many guests made their predictions for the
race the next day.

Evelyn had danced with a number of handsome gentlemen throughout the evening, but had
not yet seen Martin. She could not deny she had
been watching the door. It had been quite a while
since she'd spoken to him, and tonight, all she
wanted to do was look into his eyes and tell him
she was happy for him—happy he had finally
done what he needed to do for his own peace of
mind and heart.

She would tell him also that *she* was happy.
That because of him, she had found joy in life
and learned not to take herself so seriously. She
had made two wonderful new friends and no
longer felt she was alone in the world. She had
great hope for the future.

She had other hopes, too, concerning him, but
she would reveal those in due course.

As the night wore on, however, she did not
have any such opportunities because he hadn't
even come. She worried that he didn't wish to see
her again. He had confided nothing to Sophia
and James after all. He had been very circum-
spect about his trip abroad, his desires for the
future, his feelings about her.

Sighing with a frustration she did not wish to

feel, she excused herself from the others and decided to go up on deck and look at the stars. Gathering her skirts in her hands, she slowly climbed to the upper deck and was thankful for the fresh, cool air once she got there. The orchestra below began to play one of her favorite pieces, and she strolled to the rail—the place she and Martin had stood once before. She leaned out and looked down at the dark water below. A fish jumped and caused a little splash, so she watched the shiny surface for another.

Then a presence loomed in the silence behind her. *"Evelyn."*

She recognized the voice immediately, and her body began to hum. Closing her eyes for a brief second to search for calm, she wet her lips and slowly turned.

There he was, her hero, looking as handsome as ever in his black-and-white formal attire, his dark, wavy hair curling around his collar in the most appealing way. He was a striking and beautiful man, that had not changed, and she still loved him with every breath of passion in her body. "Hello," she said with a warm smile.

"Hello," he replied, making his way closer, hands in pockets while his eyes took in her evening gown of white satin, embroidered in peach lovers' knots, cut daringly low at the neckline. He even glanced down at her shoes of gilt leather with expensive jeweled toecaps.

"You look beautiful," he said, and she smiled when she recognized the wonder in his eyes. She had definitely picked the right gown for tonight.

He gazed at her appreciatively for another few seconds, then raised his eyebrows and let out a whistle, as if he couldn't quite recover from the sight of her in this dress. It was just the response she had hoped for, and it sent shivers of delight down her spine.

"I heard you were here," he said. "I was glad you decided to come."

"I wouldn't miss it for the world."

Sauntering closer, he took another moment to gaze at her in the moonlight. "How are you?" he asked.

"I'm very well. And you?"

He shrugged a shoulder. "Fine, I suppose. As you know, I have a race to win tomorrow."

"Which I'm sure you *will* win," she said, working hard to sound casual and blithe when in reality, her emotions were overwhelming her senses. "You'll take the prize without any problem at all."

He settled at the rail, only a few inches away, and her heart began to beat even faster still.

"You don't think the *Endeavor II* will end my reign?" he asked.

Evelyn tried not to lose herself in the blue of his eyes, the sheer mightiness of his presence. He was a champion in every sense of the word, and nothing would ever change that.

"She doesn't stand a chance. I know what kind of skill a race requires, and with Sheldon Hatfield at the wheel . . ." She puckered her lips. "Well, you know . . ."

"Yes, unfortunately I do."

She turned and set her hands on the rail, and Martin did the same.

"But you must have heard," he said, "that Hatfield's first mate is an expert sailor, and he has everyone's sympathies, having just lost his brother."

She sighed. "I confess I did hear that, but my faith still lies with you."

In more ways than one, she thought.

They both turned to look down at the water below.

"It's a long way down," Martin said in a relaxed, but mischievous voice. She remembered he had spoken the same words on this very spot the last time.

"Yes," she replied with a grin, "and I'll have you know, we are standing on twenty-four-hundred tons of pure luxury."

He chuckled with recollection, and she was glad he remembered everything, too.

"I'm relieved you are speaking to me, Evelyn," he said. "I wasn't sure you would."

"Why wouldn't I?"

He pondered it for a moment. "Because of the way we parted that last day. I was very selfish the whole time, and I treated you appallingly."

She was taken aback, for she had not expected him to bring up their trying past, at least not this early in the evening. "It wasn't so bad," she said.

"Yes, it was. I should never have entered into an affair with you when I knew I would only disappoint you in the end, which I did, quite brilliantly, I might add. I am sorry for that."

She sucked in a breath. Was he telling her he regretted all of it? That if he could go back, he would never have made love to her in the first place?

"I'm not sorry," she firmly said. "I had the best time of my life, and I learned that I am worth more than the amount of my fortune. I intend to find true happiness now, Martin, and I have you to thank for that. I would not change a thing."

He looked at her in the moonlight. "Well, I suppose I must thank you for something, too. I assume you heard I was abroad?"

"Yes, I know you went to America, and that you only stepped off the ship four days ago."

"That's right, but do you know why I went?"

She had heard most of it from Sophia, but wanted very much to hear it from him. "Tell me."

"I went because I had to revisit my old life."

She placed her hand on top of his on the rail, then realized with the skip of a heartbeat that she was touching him, connecting with him. Not wanting to push for too much all at once, she withdrew her hand.

"I had to do it, Evelyn, because after we spent that week together, and I almost lost you to the sea, I just couldn't *feel* anything anymore, and nothing had meaning for me or even the slightest pleasure, not even the things that used to amuse and distract me. So I left England and went back to visit their graves . . . Charlotte's and Owen's. I also went to see Charlotte's family, and it was good for me. I learned that I can't just ignore the past anymore. I am living with it now, and life feels more real. But it would not be this way if I hadn't gone back there, and I certainly wouldn't have gone if I hadn't spent that week with you and felt real joy for the first time in years."

He faced the water again, but continued to explain. "I think the catalyst was something you said to me that final day, about learning to live with the loss but finding new joy. Those words stayed with me the whole time I was gone."

Evelyn became aware of an easy contentment flooding through her. She had repaid him for his heroism and saved him, too, in her own way.

"I am glad you were able to do that," she said, her voice almost a whisper.

Just then, heels came clicking noisily up the stairs. "There you are!" her friend Penelope said, reaching the top and huffing with frustration. "I've been looking for you, Evelyn. And Lord Martin, you are next on my dance card."

Evelyn and Martin shared a brief, amused glance.

Oh, Penelope, she thought. Her old friend needed a few lessons in subtlety.

He bowed slightly at the waist and spoke with his renowned charm. "Mrs. Wheaton, if you will excuse me?"

"Of course," she said with a smile, feeling wonderfully invigorated after their conversation and confidently hopeful for more special moments just like this. For her fight had really only just begun.

He strode to Penelope and offered his arm. "Shall we dance, Mrs. Richardson?"

"Oh, yes!" she replied, allowing him to escort her down the companionway.

Evelyn remained on the upper deck a few more minutes, then retrieved her dance card. She supposed it was time to go below and fulfill her own obligations—and interestingly enough, the final dance of the evening belonged to Martin's rival, the sixth Earl Breckinridge. She wondered with great curiosity what kind of man he was and if he was anything like his late brother. It appeared she was about to find out. Perhaps it would give her some insight about what to expect once the race began at noon tomorrow.

Chapter 26

Martin and Spence entered the hotel dining room for breakfast the next morning to meet James. They perused the room and spotted him by a window, having already secured a table. He was sitting with a cup of steaming coffee in front of him, reading the newspaper. They approached the table and sat down, and a server arrived to pour their coffee.

James folded the paper and set it aside. "You both had a good night's sleep I presume? I certainly don't want to hear later today that you were both yawning during the race before you even reached the halfway mark."

"No worries there," Spence said, laughing softly.

"I dragged your brother back to the hotel last night before our opponents even began waltzing."

"And yet you still look exhausted," James said, eyeing Martin, who picked up the steaming cup of black coffee and touched it carefully to his lips.

"The truth is, I didn't sleep well at all," he said. "I tossed and turned all night."

"Why?" James asked. "You weren't thinking of the tempting little flower in the white satin gown, were you?"

Martin sighed. "You know me too well, James."

"Then why don't you do something about it?" Spence suggested.

"I can't. At least not now. I have this race to worry about."

"You know, we really don't need that trophy," Spence said in a quieter voice. "We could tell Hatfield to go shove his precious *Endeavor* right up his fat—"

James chuckled and held up a hand. "Now, now."

"It has nothing to do with the trophy," Martin said, leaning closer. "It is my honor I must defend. Whether I win or lose doesn't matter so much, but I certainly can't bow out. I must prove I was never afraid to face the *Endeavor*."

Who should enter the dining room just then, but Lord Breckinridge and Mr. Hatfield, who paused at the door waiting to be seated. Breckinridge met Martin's gaze and immediately crossed the room to their table. "Good luck to you today, Lord Martin."

"Good luck to you as well," Martin replied, then they shook hands, and the earl bowed to James. "Your Grace."

"Breckinridge," he coolly replied.

The earl headed for a table on the other side of the room, and Martin glanced over his shoulder to see Hatfield on his way to the same table. The man raised a bushy eyebrow and smiled arrogantly.

As soon as they were seated, Spence leaned forward and whispered, "What the blazes was that? Are they trying to intimidate us? Damned ungentlemanly behavior if you ask me."

Martin shook his head. "Don't let it get to you, Spence."

"I suppose I should tell you," James said, leaning forward slightly as well, "that the earl danced with your lovely widow last night at the ball after you were gone."

Martin set down his cup with a *thunk*. "I beg your pardon?"

"He danced with her," James repeated.

"I heard you the first time." He turned around to glance over at their table. "He hasn't set his cap for her, has he?"

"Who knows?" James replied. "But I wouldn't be surprised if he has. She's a catch to be sure with all that money—and a delightful smile and intelligence on top of it. She even knows how to sail, thanks to you." James glanced at the earl and took in his overall appearance. "He's a young, active man in his prime, in need of an heir or two or three. Why wouldn't he be sniffing around her lovely skirts?"

"Dammit, James."

Spence was chewing his lip, looking on with apprehension.

"*What?*" James asked, as if he were being wrongly accused of something. "I will not apologize for pointing out the fact that all you're doing is tossing and turning in your bed when your perfect match is in danger of getting snapped up by some other man who is more than willing to enter the race without hesitation."

"I've only been back in the country four days," Martin replied. "Give me a bloody chance to get my bearings."

James picked up his coffee and took another sip. "Well, you better hurry up. The starting gun has already fired, and you appear to be trailing behind."

By noon, a magnificent crowd had gathered on the Green, and there was an almost tangible excitement in the air. Evelyn sat on a blanket on the grass with Penelope and the Radleys, while out on the water, fifteen or more yachts were sailing in circles in a mad state of chaos, waiting for the race committee to signal the countdown to start.

The goal for each boat—Sir Lyndon had explained to her that morning—was to cross the starting line at full speed just as the cannon fired. Consequently, they were all zigzagging around in an effort to secure the best position for precisely the right moment.

Then, *boom*! The cannon fired, and all the boats fell gracefully into line, heading westward toward the first mark, miles away.

Parasol in hand, Evelyn stood. Martin was out in front, skillfully moving ahead of all the rest, leading the fleet. She felt a wave of satisfaction and smiled, then said a silent prayer that he would remain in the lead position and that it would be an easy triumph.

An hour before the race began, Martin had studied the currents, he'd watched the shifts in the wind's direction and velocity, and practiced a few maneuvers with his crew. But by the time the gun fired, all he could think about was what James had said in the hotel dining room—that he was trailing behind where Evelyn was concerned.

He decided at that moment that he was not going to lose today. He was going to win—both the Cowes trophy and Evelyn's heart. And it wasn't just his competitive nature rising up for a new conquest because of the way James had taunted him at breakfast. After seeing her again last night, Martin knew what he wanted. He'd known it the minute he'd laid eyes on her. She was the only woman for him, there was no way around it, and he could not last another day without her. They'd been apart too long as it was, and he loved her. Yes. There it was. He loved her. And by God, he would have her.

Thankfully, everything was unfolding as it should today, at least in regard to *this* race. He was not trailing behind. His crew was relaxed and motivated, Spence was feeding him information about the wave conditions and the distances of the boats astern. On top of all that, the sun was shining brightly overhead, and there wasn't a cloud in the sky.

He closed his eyes, breathed in the fresh, salty sea air, felt the wind on his face and the tug of the wheel in his hands. Opening his eyes, he called out, *"Ready to tack!"*

His crew had been kneeling in a row on the port side, and as soon as they heard his command, they moved into position.

"Coming about!" He turned the *Orpheus* into the wind, putting the rudder hard over to the leeward side.

Martin ducked as the boom swung across. The crew released and trimmed the jib and main, then switched to the windward side, kneeling in a row again, awaiting his next command.

"Well done!"

He turned around and saw the other boats spreading out across the miles at a distance behind him, including the *Endeavor II,* with Hatfield at the helm. Facing forward again, he smiled at Spence, who was standing at the bow, nodding confidently at him.

An hour later, the *Orpheus* was approaching the halfway mark to turn. Martin looked back at the *Endeavor II* not far behind.

Presently—because he was on the inside of the turn—he had the right of way, and hoped that with Hatfield in charge, they would not disregard the rules of the race.

He glanced at Spence and saw that he, too, was watching the *Endeavor II* with concern.

"Thirty seconds!" Martin called out.

He continued on, approaching the mark, waiting for the right moment to swing the boat around.

The *Endeavor II* was directly behind them now. Would they overtake them before they reached the mark and seize the inside position?

"Ready, gentlemen!" he shouted. He checked over his shoulder. The other boat was approaching on the inside . . . "Ready . . ." he said, as their bowsprit reached the mark. *"Coming about!"*

He turned the wheel. His crew spread out across the boat.

At that precise instant, however, angry shouting erupted on the *Endeavor II* behind them. Martin and Spence looked back. Their opponent was turning short of the mark!

"Damn them!" Spence shouted, watching the *Endeavor II* cheat the rules. But as quickly as she turned, she swung around again, a full 360 degrees. Hatfield and his first mate were fighting for control of the wheel.

The *Orpheus* rounded the mark perfectly, the crew trimmed the sails for the new direction and let out the spinnaker, and as soon as that was done, they all stood on the deck staring back at the *Endeavor II*.

She was still turning in a circle and appeared to be getting caught in irons, stuck stationary in the no-sail zone, while Hatfield and Breckinridge fought over control. They were shouting heatedly at each other while the crew was scrambling about, struggling with their flapping sails.

Martin had the *Orpheus* on a straight starboard tack now, and the spinnaker was full of wind, driving them forward at a swift pace on the homeward run.

The other yachts were still on their initial reach toward the mark, gaining on the *Endeavor II*, which was stuck dead in the water. Young Breckinridge began calling out commands to the crew, who followed his instructions while Hatfield shouted profanities. The earl pushed hard upon the boom, doing everything he could to get them moving again before the other boats overtook them. Soon, they were turning and making their way slowly around the mark, and the last thing Martin saw was Breckinridge shoving Sheldon out of the way and taking hold of the wheel.

From that moment on, Martin kept his attention focused on the wind and the waves, his eyes fixed on the finish line.

When the *Orpheus* came into view again, Evelyn, Penelope, and the Radleys left their spot on the grass and ran down to the beach to watch the final minutes of the race.

Martin was in the lead, but the *Endeavor II* was not far behind. Their spinnakers were puffed out like balloons, and they were both sailing on a fast port tack.

"She's gaining," Lord Radley said, lifting his binoculars. "My word, they're moving fast."

Evelyn stepped forward all the way to the water's edge until her toes touched the waves. She was barely aware of it, however, for she couldn't take her eyes off the two yachts, both sailing at a swift clip toward the finish line. It was going to be close. They were almost side by side . . .

Chapter 27

Martin squeezed the wheel and looked to his left just as the cannon fired at the finish line. He couldn't believe it. It was over, and it had been so close.

Spence dropped to his knees on the foredeck and buried his face in his hands. The rest of the crew was silent.

Martin could hear the cheers and whistles from the crowd on the beach, but all of it seemed strangely muffled in his ears beneath the sound of the wind in the sails and the creaking of the ropes and rigging, the hiss of the water past the hull.

It was over. They had lost.

Meanwhile the crew on the *Endeavor II* was dancing around on deck, and Hatfield was popping the cork on a bottle of champagne.

"Bring in the spinnaker and lower the jib," Martin called out.

His crew quietly obeyed, and Spence made his way aft. "I can't bloody believe it," he said, hopping down into the cockpit. "How could they beat us after getting themselves stuck in irons?"

Martin shook his head. "She's a fast boat, Spence. That's all there is to it."

"But Hatfield is such an ass."

"He had little to do with it in the end. It was Breckinridge who made all the right decisions on the homeward run. He deserves the trophy for winning in *spite* of Hatfield. He raced as a gentleman."

Martin turned around and saw the young earl standing at the weather rail holding on to a line, watching the *Orpheus*. Martin removed his hat and waved it at his opponent, then bowed deeply to him.

Breckinridge waved his hat and bowed in return, and they smiled at each other over the distance, until the earl hopped back down into the cockpit to accept a glass of champagne.

Martin faced forward again, holding the wheel steady. "He beat us fair and square," he said to Spence, "and she's a miracle of a boat."

Spence squeezed Martin's shoulder. "I think

the biggest surprise of the day is that you're not banging your head on the deck. My God, do you even care?"

He looked at his crew, lowering the jib. "I'm disappointed for them. They worked hard for this."

"And you didn't?"

"I did, but I don't really need that trophy anymore, Spence, not like I used to." He slowed the boat down and turned her toward their mooring. "I've got my sights set on a different prize now."

Spence patted him on the back. "I'm glad to hear it. And I'm glad I won't have to be a nuisance anymore. I didn't enjoy being a nag. I'm sorry for that. I've not been a good friend."

"You were everything I needed. *Someone* had to keep kicking me in the right direction."

Spence smiled in return and strode forward to call out to the crew. "Prepare to drop the main!"

Feeling the wind in his face, Martin closed his eyes briefly and filled his lungs with fresh air. He felt a great sense of relief as he exhaled, for his reign as the famous Cowes champion was over.

Finally.

That evening, Martin and Spence walked down to the beach to watch the fireworks. By the time they arrived, a large crowd had already gathered on the Green—parents with their children, skippers with their crews, and the local residents of the island there to witness the excitement.

Martin spotted Sir Lyndon up on the grass, talking to some of the other yachtsmen. His gaze fell upon Martin, and he waved. He excused himself from the others and came down to meet them.

"You sailed masterfully today," he said. "I was pleased and proud to know you."

"Thank you, sir."

"And I am equally pleased to inform you that Mr. Sheldon Hatfield has been banned for life from the Royal Yacht Squadron, kicked out onto his flabby behind for illegal sailing tactics and false accusations regarding the facts surrounding Lord Breckinridge's death. All this was instigated this afternoon by his own first mate, young Lord Breckinridge, who has publicly denounced him as a cheat and a villain."

Spence glanced at Martin with pride. "You always said he would hang himself with his own rope."

Sir Lyndon continued. "Lord Breckinridge has also suggested that the *Endeavor II* be disqualified from the race today, and that the trophy be awarded to you."

Martin raised a hand. "That's not necessary, Lyndon. I will absolutely decline to accept it, as the earl overcame great obstacles to cross that finish line ahead of us. He deserves it more than anyone."

Sir Lyndon sighed. "I thought you might say that. But may I at least offer you this. A public, written apology has been made to you on behalf of the Squadron for any statements made by anyone regarding the former earl's death, and we will be presenting a medal to you for your courage and heroism."

Martin patted the commodore on the arm. "Thank you."

"I wish you the best," Sir Lyndon said.

"The same to you, sir."

They shook hands, then Lyndon bid them adieu and returned to his group.

"He's a good man," Spence said.

Martin watched him join the others. "Indeed he is."

They started off again, strolling along the Esplanade, continuing toward the pavilion at the far end of the Green, where they stopped on the walk, under a gas lamp. Just ahead, the new champion, young Lord Breckinridge, was surrounded by a crowd of pretty young ladies.

"I think we've been replaced," Spence said.

Martin watched the earl kiss a young woman's hand. She giggled and bounced up and down.

"Are you sorry?" Martin asked.

Spence considered it. "Maybe just a little."

Breckinridge spotted them on the walk, then turned to the ladies, bowed politely, and came to meet them. "Good evening, gentlemen," he said.

Martin nodded amiably.

The earl cleared his throat and held out a hand to him. "Let me just say, sir, that it was an honor sailing against you today, and I will never forget it as long as I live."

Martin accepted his proffered hand and shook it. "The honor was all mine, Breckinridge. She's a marvel of a boat, and you handled her like a true champion—and a gentleman as well. Congratulations."

The earl understood his meaning. "Thank you. And may I also express my gratitude for your great courage the day my brother was lost? My family is indebted to you for saving everyone on board his boat."

"Not quite everyone," Martin said with a somber tone. "I'm very sorry about your brother."

Breckinridge was quiet, then he raised his chin. "I know you are, sir. But you did more than anyone else could have done. You're a great hero." He bowed his head, and when he finally looked up, there was a playful glimmer in his eyes. "It has been a pleasure, but I'm afraid I must return to the ladies."

Martin chuckled. "It's a great responsibility, you know—being a champion. Are you sure you're up to it, Breckinridge?"

"I believe I am."

Martin smiled. "Then do the title proud."

The earl turned and sauntered over to the large

crowd of admirers. Penelope Richardson was waiting in front and was the first to welcome him back.

Martin watched them for a moment. Yes, he was more than happy to be handing over the various honors of championship to another, and he would be even happier if he knew the earl intended to enjoy bachelorhood for a little while longer . . .

"Lord Martin."

The voice came to him from behind. He felt a great jolt in his senses.

He turned and saw her—Evelyn—looking ravishing in a dark red silk gown and matching mantle. Her hair was swept up into a braided knot on top of her head, and she wore a fashionable black hat tilted forward at a daring angle.

He knew then that he really had made a difference in her life, for she was not the aloof young woman she had been in his younger days, nor was she the cool, dignified widow she used to be. She was proud and confident and dazzling in her beauty.

He suddenly wished he could sit down, because she was so lovely, he feared his legs might give out beneath him.

"Mrs. Wheaton," he replied in a polite, steady voice, nevertheless.

Spence greeted her as well, which startled

Martin, because he had all but forgotten his friend was still standing beside him.

"You both did very well in the race today," she said.

"Not quite well enough," Spence replied, "but we're surviving, aren't we, Captain?"

"Barely," Martin said.

They all smiled, but an awkward moment of silence ensued.

Spence turned around. "Oh, look at that. I see an old friend. If you will excuse me?"

"Of course," they replied in unison, gazing intently at one another, both fully aware there was no friend.

"Would you like to take a walk?" Martin asked, clasping his hands together behind his back.

Something flashed through her eyes—doubt, hesitation, a faint look of determination perhaps? He wasn't sure.

"That would be very nice," she said.

They started off past the pavilion and went up onto the road, where there were fewer people. They walked in silence for a moment or two, until Evelyn slipped her arm through his.

"You don't mind, do you?" she asked. "I'm feeling the chill of the night air."

He covered her gloved hands with his own, cupping them, trying to warm them. "Of course I don't mind."

They continued on.

"I was very proud of you today," she finally said, "even if you didn't win the trophy. You sailed like the honorable, principled champion you are and always will be."

Martin wet his lips, and all at once, his stomach was turning over with regret for everything he had not said and done when he had had the chance. And he was dreading the possibility that she might refuse him now when he was more than ready to give her everything she had wanted from him that last day in the hotel.

He hoped she still wanted it. From him and no one else.

"Are you very disappointed you didn't win?" she asked in that sweet voice that almost made him forget there was anything bad or unfair in the world.

He gazed down at her, still covering her tiny gloved hands with his own. "No. I'm glad Breckinridge won. He deserves the title, not only for his impressive sailing skills but for his integrity as a gentleman at the halfway mark. Did you hear what happened?"

"Yes, everyone did. Sheldon left earlier. Did you know that? He walked away in disgrace to a round of hissing on the back lawn after Lyndon expelled him from the yacht club permanently, but he has no one to blame but himself."

Martin nodded and breathed deeply. "So he

got what he deserved. I always knew he would one day, and while we're on that subject, I must thank you for standing up for me when he made those accusations. I will always be grateful to you."

"I was happy to, Martin. Truly."

He returned to more agreeable topics. "Young Breckinridge, on the other hand, is a man of high moral fiber. He'll be a worthy champion."

"Like you."

He smiled down at her. "I understand you danced with him last night. I suppose he has tossed his hat into the ring where you are concerned. You could certainly do worse, Evelyn. He's a good man."

"Are you making assumptions?" she asked. "Or trying to give me advice?"

He swallowed over the lump that was becoming quite a nuisance in his throat. None of this was coming out right. "Of course not. You are more than capable of making your own decisions."

The rhythmic sound of their footfalls on the gravel did nothing to ease the chaos in his mind, or relax the tension in his body. He had to fight to keep his voice steady.

He stopped suddenly. She did not expect it, and he almost pulled her off her feet. She stared back at him curiously. "What's wrong?"

He was breathing hard now. She tilted her head

to the side, watching him, waiting. Finally, he managed to speak.

"I must confess to you, Evelyn—I started off in that race this morning wanting very much to cross the finish line first," he said.

"Of course you did."

"No, Evelyn, you do not understand. I did not care so much about the trophy or the applause or the title that I would hold until next year. I only wanted to hurry back, so I could win *you*."

Her lips parted slightly, and she dropped her hands to her sides.

"I know I was a brick wall before, when we ended our affair," he quickly continued, "and that you are in a position to marry any man you choose. The very best of men. Breckinridge is certainly worthy of you in every way, and—"

"Will you stop referring to Lord Breckinridge?" she said. "We danced. That is all."

He paused to take a breath. "All right then. I will say what I have been wanting to say since I set foot back in this country—what I wanted to say ever since we parted, in fact. I *love* you, Evelyn. You saved my life. You made me want to breathe again and laugh again, and every minute I was away from you, all I wanted to do was come home. I thought of nothing the entire time but your smile and your eyes and your beautiful body in my bed, and I want you back. I want to marry you, Evelyn, if you will do me the honor."

She said nothing for a moment. She just stared up at him in the moonlight, then took a deep breath and wet her lips. "I've had more than a few proposals over the past six weeks," she said. "Did you know that?"

"I assumed you would have."

"Because of my fortune?"

"No, because of your beauty and your intelligent spirit."

She digested his reply. "Didn't you worry, while you were gone, that I might accept one of them?"

He bowed his head and looked at his boots. "Yes, I worried."

"You could have written to me."

"No, I couldn't. I wasn't ready. I had to take care of certain things first."

She laid a gloved hand on his chest, and he felt her touch like a flame. "I am worth fighting for, you know."

He met her gaze again. "I do know that."

Then she smiled and began to back away from him. "That's good to hear. But I'm afraid you are going to have to fight just a little bit harder."

A ripple of excitement danced up his spine as he watched her take a few more steps back.

"I'm not quite ready to accept a proposal," she

said. "I'm having too good a time. I'll need to think about it. I need to be sure."

Still backing away, she was like a colorful butterfly he was desperate to catch.

"What will make you sure?" he asked, following.

She smiled wickedly and tilted her head at him. "I don't know."

"Shall we return to the beach then," he asked, "while you think about it?"

She stopped decisively. "Yes. Your brother James is there waiting to see you, and your sister-in-law, Sophia. I met her in London recently."

"Yes, my brother mentioned it," he replied.

"She's lovely, Martin. You have a wonderful family. You're a lucky man.

Not as lucky as he would be if she accepted him and took a place in that family.

"We should return now," she said, "because the fireworks will be starting soon."

Just then, the heavens lit up with red and blue sparks, illuminating her face. A noisy *crack* cut through the night, and the crowd on the beach cheered and applauded.

But neither Evelyn nor Martin took their eyes off each other to look up at the weeping willow of fire in the sky over their heads, the sparks raining down like droplets onto the dark water. He simply waited while she returned and took his arm, then he escorted her back to the beach.

Chapter 28

The next morning, Martin woke early, but did not rise from his bed at the Royal Marine Hotel. He simply lay there with one arm bent under his head on the pillow, staring up at the ceiling.

He'd hardly slept a wink through the night—again—nor could he sleep now if he tried, for he was out of his mind with anticipation for the day. It had taken every ounce of will he possessed not to find out what room Evelyn was staying in last night and go knock on her door. He did not, however, because if he was going to fight for her, he would do it properly. He would court her like a gentleman and treat her with the respect she deserved. He would call on her today in fact, and take her walking to the Umbrella Tree.

Just then, he heard the sound of a note sliding under his door and skimming across the floor. He sat up, saw a white card at the foot of the bed, and quickly tossed the covers aside. Was it from Evelyn?

He strode barefoot and picked it up, then heard footsteps in the hall and hurried to the door. He peered out, but there was just a bellman disappearing around the corner.

Disappointed it was not her coming to pay him a call before a respectable hour, he shut the door and read the card.

Lord Martin,

I respectfully request your presence on the slip in front of the hotel at eleven o'clock this morning. Dress for the water and please do not be late.

Sir Lyndon Wadsworth

Martin glanced at the clock. It was twenty minutes past ten. He wondered what this was about.

Setting the note on the table, he washed and dressed, then strode out of his room at eleven. He passed through the crowded lobby and exited onto the street, dashing across to avoid being hit by a swift carriage. Sir Lyndon stood waiting for him at the top of the slip.

"Good morning," Martin said. "What's going on? It sounded important."

"I suppose it is," the baronet replied. "Someone has requested your expertise. Are you available for a test sail?"

"A test sail? Someone is purchasing a yacht? It's not the *Endeavor II*, is it?"

"No, it's a yacht with a new design. She arrived in Cowes just this morning, after being purchased out of Ireland."

Martin's keen interest in innovative boat designs was aroused, and he looked out over the water. "Where is she?"

Sir Lyndon gestured to the small launch waiting at the end of the slip. "The potential owner will take you to her."

Martin felt his blood rush to his head, for sitting in the boat, casually waving at him, was Evelyn.

"It's Mrs. Wheaton," he said, not moving from his spot, despite the fact that Sir Lyndon was trying to lead him down the slip.

"Yes, it is. She's very independent, you know. Purchased that vessel without saying a word to anyone about it. She informed me just this morning, and I assure you, I was just as surprised as you are now—judging by the look on your face."

Martin made every effort to regain his composure. "And what does she need me for?"

"She needs advice. She wants to be sure the yacht is well built before she signs on the dotted line, so to speak, and I thought since you have some experience with boat designs . . ."

Martin felt a slow smile spread across his face. "She wants to be sure, does she?" He started off down the slip. "Will you be coming, too?"

"No, I have far too much to do this morning. Besides, I know nothing about these things."

And thank God for that, he thought with a grin.

"Off you go," Sir Lyndon said, gesturing with a hand. "She's been sitting in that launch for over twenty minutes, and she's very eager."

Feeling rather eager himself, Martin started off down the slip.

"Good morning!" she said cheerfully. "Isn't this exciting? But before you step in, would you untie that first?"

He glanced at the rope she was pointing at, untied it, and a few seconds later, was stepping into the launch. It bobbed up and down beneath his weight, then Evelyn, God love her, began to row them out.

"You're buying a yacht?" he asked, with a mixture of admiration and amusement.

"I haven't quite decided yet," she proudly replied. "She's a beauty, though. Very hard to resist. Wait till you see her."

Concentrating on the gentle rocking of the boat on the waves, he struggled to unwind a little and leaned back on the transom. "Lead the way."

They rowed through the maze of sailboats moored in the Solent, and soon approached a yacht called *Phoenix*. She sported a shiny blue hull and a deck of polished maple. Martin sat forward, looking her over from top to bottom. "This is the one?"

Evelyn brought the launch up alongside. "Yes, what do you think?"

He squinted up at the tall mast against the bright blue sky, examined her smooth, graceful contours. He could tell she was not built for speed like the *Endeavor* or the *Orpheus*, but she looked impressively sturdy, built for a long haul in any kind of weather. "A forty-six-footer?" he estimated.

"Exactly."

As they rowed from stern to bow, he ran his hand along her side, and his seafaring senses began to hum. "She's definitely attractive."

Evelyn grinned. "I knew you would think so. Care to step aboard?"

He chuckled at the question. "Do you even need to ask?"

They shared a knowing smile, and Evelyn secured the launch next to the *Phoenix*. Martin assisted her aboard, then joined her a second later, looking around the large oval cockpit at the shiny brass fittings and brass wheel. His gaze traveled from the end of the boom across and up the mast, then he leaped up onto the foredeck. He walked to the bow and looked over the side, then turned to face Evelyn again. She was standing next to the wheel, watching him with interest.

"Can we take her out?" he asked.

"I was hoping you'd want to."

He raised an eyebrow, as if to say, *Was there ever any doubt?*

They both set to work in the sunshine, unfolding sails and freeing lines, and a short time later, they were hoisting the mainsail. Martin untied the mooring line, and they set off through the breezes with Evelyn at the wheel.

"How does she feel?" he asked, trimming the sails for a starboard tack.

"Wonderful. You have to come and try her out. She's very steady."

As soon as he could, he moved aft and hopped down into the cockpit. "May I?"

"Of course." She stepped aside and allowed him to take the wheel.

He wrapped his hands around the brass spokes and felt the tremendous power of the boat's wide hull and enormous sails. "She certainly is steady— solid as a rock, in fact."

Her eyes sparkled with excitement. "So you think she's a good boat?"

"She's perfect, Evelyn."

He smiled down at her, and she wrapped a

gloved hand around his on the wheel, as if to say *thank you*, before she strolled to the weather rail and looked over the side.

Martin watched her for a moment, then wet his lips and asked very carefully, "Have you given any thought to what we discussed last night?"

She turned to face him. "Which part? We discussed a lot of things." The minx was not going to make this easy on him, was she? With a teasing glint in her eyes, she sat down and faced the wind. "Let's just concentrate on the boat for a time, shall we?"

"Whatever you desire," he said, and they continued on their starboard tack.

A few minutes later, she asked him a question. "Did you know," she said, "that after the accident, when I returned to London, I thought I might not ever wish to sail again?"

He frowned slightly as he adjusted the wheel under a wind shift. "Were you afraid?"

"Yes," she replied, "but I've come to realize that fear is part of life. To feel apprehensive about certain things is normal, but in doing them, in conquering our fears—*that* is where the true rewards are. That is when we accomplish great things."

He gazed down at her lovely profile and wondered how it was possible that a woman could make him feel so content and inspired, yet so enormously randy at the same time.

"I agree," he said, struggling to focus on the

subject at hand. "Life has to be faced head-on with courage and fortitude." He had learned that very recently.

Suddenly he wished she would come closer and stand beside him, but before he had a chance to speak her name, she stood up and strode over. She wrapped her hand around his upon the wheel again.

"I am apprehensive right now," she said, her voice quiet and sultry.

An electrifying current coursed through him, and he searched her eyes with every instinct he possessed, wanting to know what she was thinking and feeling. "*Why?*"

"Because I invited you to come sailing with me, and I don't have the slightest clue what I'm doing."

"What do you mean, Evelyn?"

He wished she would not leave him in doubt. He needed to know.

But before she could answer, he let go of the wheel and dropped to his knees in front of her.

"Forget that," he said. "You don't need to tell me. All that matters is what I said to you last night—that I love you." He grabbed hold of her hips. "*I love you*, Evelyn, and I do not want to go one more day without you. Whatever it is I have to do to win you, I will do it. I will fight for you tirelessly until the day I die if I must, until you say yes and let me be your husband and the father of your children. And if you tell me not to fight, I believe I will disintegrate into dust right here on your shiny new deck."

Smiling, she stared down at him.

He realized suddenly that she must have let go of the wheel, too, because the sails were flapping uncontrollably over their heads. The boat was coasting to a halt.

She stared down at him with those beautiful green eyes behind those charming spectacles, and he thought that if she didn't soon say something, he would get up and throw himself over the side.

Finally, at long last, she spoke. "Please do not disintegrate, Martin, because I would die if I lost you again."

He gazed up at her with love in his eyes.

"And I *will* marry you," she said. "No more fighting shall be necessary. I am yours."

He shut his eyes tight and tried to calm his breathing, but he could not. All he could do was bow his head and sit back on his heels, his hands gripping her skirts while he thanked God in heaven for bringing her back into his life after so many years had passed since they'd known each other before.

The wheel was turning of its own volition now. The boat had pointed into the wind, and was blowing backward on the waves, but neither of them seemed to care. Evelyn dropped to her knees, too, and took his face in her hands. "I have loved you all my life, since that day you pulled me out of that frozen lake. And when you made love to me for the first time here in Cowes, I was so afraid to hope that it could last forever, but I couldn't stop myself. It was all I ever wanted and all I want now. And then when I believed I'd lost you—that's when I knew I couldn't go on being afraid. I had to be brave and try again, so while you were away, all I did was plan how I was going to win your devotion."

"You didn't have to do a thing to win it," he said, "because you already had it. And you never lost me, Evelyn. Not really. I always carried you in my heart, and I hoped you were carrying me in yours, too. Thank you for waiting."

He pulled her close and pressed his lips to hers, while the sails continued to flap wildly over their heads. But none of it mattered. He was aware only of the need to love her right now and every day for the rest his life. The feeling was so powerful and profound, he felt the force of it inside his chest.

Savoring the delicious sensation of her lips upon his, he laid more kisses across her cheek and down her neck.

"I'm so happy, I feel like I'm floating," she whispered breathlessly, tipping her head back.

"We *are* floating, darling, and God knows where the current is taking us."

Laughing, she looked him in the eye. "It doesn't matter where, just as long as we're together."

"So what's next then?" he asked, rising to his feet and pulling her up beside him. "When shall we marry, and what shall we do for a honeymoon? A trip around the world?"

She pondered that. "What if we hit rough weather?"

"We'll sail through it."

"What if we lose the wind?" she asked.

"We'll have tea."

She smiled again. "I will follow you anywhere, Captain."

"But this is to be *your* boat," he reminded her with a laugh. "So I will be the one who is following *you*."

She laughed, too. "It will be our boat, together. But what careless captains we are. I believe we are stuck head to wind."

They both looked up at the sails still flapping overhead. "Not to worry," he said. "I'll get us moving in no time."

"You always do."

"Take hold of the wheel." He turned and released the mainsail, then crossed to the forward deck and pulled the jib sheet taut. "Now turn it hard over to port."

While she did as he commanded, he moved aft and pushed hard on the boom, and soon they were moving again.

Martin trimmed the sails, then stood with the wind at his back, watching Evelyn steer the boat. There was a look of pure elation and anticipation in her eyes.

"Is this right?" she asked. "Do I need to turn her farther over?"

"You're fine," he replied.

And even though she didn't always know what she was doing, she was still the fearless captain of his heart, for she had taught him about life and what it is to sail through it. Everything was going to be fine, he realized, for there would be joy again.

"Where to now?" she asked, looking up at the sails and adjusting the wheel. "I await your command."

He sat down on the foredeck and clasped his hands together around his knees, relaxing comfortably in the wind while he watched his future bride, steady at the wheel.

"Take us out," he calmly said, and her smile was more dazzling than the sun.

Author's Note

By the late Victorian period, the town of Cowes on the Isle of Wight was well established as a fashionable seaside resort for high society, and is still popular today for its international sailing events and those interested in its colorful history. It's a picturesque town with narrow, winding streets and charming shops, and is home to residents who are more than happy to talk about its history with inquisitive visitors.

One of the significant points of Cowes's history involves the America's Cup, which is the oldest and most distinguished trophy in all sport. Its name comes from the yacht *America*, which won a prestigious international race hosted by the Royal

Yacht Squadron in Cowes 1851. The course went around the Isle of Wight, and the *America* crossed the finish line first, timed at eight hours and thirty-seven minutes, though there was some controversy over whether or not she properly rounded all the marks on the course. The committee officials deemed that the instructions were vague, however, and the cup was proudly taken back to the New York Yacht Club. It remained in the United States for 132 years until 1983, when an Australian boat won the race for the first time.

At the time this book is set, the Royal Yacht Squadron was enjoying its heyday during an era often referred to as the Golden Age of Cowes. In the late Victorian and Edwardian periods, the Cowes Regatta in August was attended by royals and aristocrats from England and abroad, and that week in particular inspired many of my ideas for the race week in this book.

In reality, the commodore of the Squadron was not my fictional character, Sir Lyndon Wadsworth, but rather Edward, the Prince of Wales, who was elected to the position in 1882. He was a passionate yachtsman with his own racing yacht, the *Britannia*, which he commissioned in 1892 and sailed triumphantly in many prestigious races. (I took some artistic license in mentioning the cutter throughout this book, which is set the year before.)

If you're interested in reading about Cowes and

its fascinating yachting history during the Edwardian period, I highly recommend the book *Sacred Cowes*, by Anthony Heckstall-Smith, who was born on the Isle of Wight and became a yachting journalist. I borrowed a few anecdotes from his book, such as the amusing reference to Queen Victoria watching her son's yacht through a telescope from her summer home on the hill. That summer home was Osborne House, a magnificent country estate that still stands today and is open to the public as a museum.

I hope you enjoyed Martin's story, and if you're interested in reading more about Sophia and James, you can read about their romance in one of my earlier novels, *To Marry the Duke*, which is set during the time Martin is suspended from Eton. It's the first book in my American Heiress series, and Sophia's sister Clara has a story as well. Hers is *An Affair Most Wicked*, the second book in the series.

For more information about my other books, visit my website at *www.juliannemaclean.com*, where you can enter my monthly contest or send me a letter via e-mail. I love to hear from readers.

Best wishes,
Julianne

Next month, don't miss these exciting new love stories only from Avon Books

Two Weeks With a Stranger by Debra Mullins

An Avon Romantic Treasure

Lucy, Lady Devingham, has been content to let her husband gallivant about London while she enjoys the pleasures of country life. But when she receives word that Simon's mysterious activities now involve another woman, Lucy throws caution to the wind to prove once and for all that she is a force to be reckoned with—and a woman to be loved.

Beware of Doug by Elaine Fox

An Avon Contemporary Romance

Meet Doug, the match-mauling canine. No matter what kind of man Lily Tyler brings home, casual friend or romantic contender, Doug is there with a nasty surprise. It'll take one very determined man to woo Lily . . . and sexy pilot Brady Cole thinks he's just the man for the job.

Night of the Huntress by Kathryn Smith

An Avon Romance

Bishop has spent centuries trying to heal the wounds between humans and vampires. All is put to the test when he is captured by a mysterious woman, the vampire slayer known as The Reaper. Bishop knows this is his last chance to prove to this woman that all is not as it seems.

Good Groom Hunting by Shana Galen

An Avon Romance

Josephine Hale is every bit the granddaughter of a pirate, and she is determined to track down her grandfather's lost treasure, no matter where the trail might take her. But when her search lands her in a partnership with the Earl of Westman, Josie finds herself suddenly in the middle of the adventure of a lifetime.

Avon Romantic Treasures

Unforgettable, enthralling love stories, sparkling with passion and adventure from Romance's bestselling authors

AVON TRADE *Paperbacks*

978-0-06-089022-3
$13.95 ($17.50 Can.)

0-06-081588-4
$12.95 ($16.95 Can.)

0-06-087340-X
$12.95 ($16.95 Can.)

0-06-113388-4
$12.95 ($16.95 Can.)

0-06-083691-1
$12.95 ($16.95 Can.)

Visit www.AuthorTracker.com for exclusive
information on your favorite HarperCollins authors.

Available wherever books are sold, or call 1-800-331-3761 to order.

ATP 0107